WELCOME HUGGE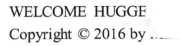
Copyright © 2016 by

All rights reserved. No part of this book shall be reproduced or transmitted in any form or by any means. No patent liability is assumed with respect to the use of the information contained herein. No liability is assumed for damages resulting from the use of the information contained herein.

Welcome Huggers # 2 – Verity is a work of fiction. Names, characters, and incidences are products of the author's imagination. Any resemblance to actual *persons living or dead, events, or locales, is entirely coincidental. *Except for one author.

Portions from this book may be used in the yet to come remaining book in the series: Welcome Huggers # 3 – Katie.

Printed in the United States of America
ISBN: 9781682738580

www.TheBookPatch.com

Photographs taken by Marilyn Stewart
The bridge and fall foliage were taken at Boyce Thompson Arboretum near Superior, Arizona.

i

Dedication:

My parents' lives of service, to any and all, which I witnessed growing up made a huge impact on my life. While being one of their children was often a challenge, it was also a gift. At a young age I began learning life lessons in acceptance, sharing, giving and loving. Kindness seemed to ooze from them. It was only after becoming an adult that I realized their dedication in serving their Lord and Savior Jesus Christ is what made them different. I'm grateful for their global journey of faith-filled, committed lives.

Thanks to:

Brother Dale – for the many hours of editing and ideas shared to ensure the accuracy of Verity.

Chris Carson – your dedication to excellence is unrelenting and so very much appreciated. Your suggestions, whether taken or not, have been insightful and extremely useful. Because of you, these books have been made available online – an amazing gift for which I am unceasingly thankful.

The men and women in our military – past, present and future. Immense gratitude to the families and friends who support them. Because of all of your commitments we live in peace.

Marilyn Stewart

Background

Over two years ago, Mercy and Katie started a group for single women from their three small neighboring towns of Welcome, Hope, and Unique. They'd come up with the logo 'WHUG' using the first letter of each town plus the letter G for girlfriends. Soon however, the townspeople began to refer to them as Welcome Huggers. The name stuck. The ladies ranged in age from nineteen to thirty-five and membership varied from twelve to a brief high of twenty-five.

Mercy, Katie, and Fairlyn were past presidents. Jasmine would soon join their ranks after the next election. There was a scheduled meeting – for everyone – once a month. Ladies with similar interests called each other during the month to hike, bike, play a sport, sew, or even go horseback riding. Jasmine looked at the latest request – anyone willing to double-date? She laughed while writing it down to be mentioned at their next get-together.

Welcome Hope Unique Girlfriends' Motto:

Let's listen without planning to speak
Let's laugh with, not about, each girlfriend
Let's love without sermonizing
Let's live with intention and joy

A song by John W. Peterson summed up their theme:
"Show a little bit of love and kindness..."

Verity's verse:
We live within the shadow of the Almighty, sheltered by God who is above all gods. This I declare, that He alone is my refuge, my place of safety; He is my God, and I am trusting in Him.
  – Psalm 91: 1, 2. Living Bible

Prologue

My name is Verity Tracker, but often, due to the way I learned to write an 'r,' it can appear to be 'Tacker.' Most of the 'Welcome Huggers' only know me as Verity or Ve.

I arrived in the town of Welcome due to friends of my deceased parents. They had requested I house-sit their cabin in the high country of Arizona for about a year and open a library in a vacant building on the main street of Welcome. The city would pay me for twenty-four hours' work per week. Knowing I had worked part time in a library, they asked if I would be willing to 'give it a go.'

The timing and surprise gift was an answer to prayer. I desperately needed a complete change, a time to heal and to rethink what I desired to do with my life. As I packed up my few belongings, I contemplated the facts. Growing up overseas and having missionary parents had been phase one of my life. The second segment had just ended. It had entailed a change in country, college life, death, and trauma. Now I was going to be moving to a new state and interacting with three small towns. I was more than ready to leave a huge impersonal metropolitan area, plus I would be living less than twenty miles from a half-brother and sister.

When I was told the name of the town, I have to admit I was not amused. I said to the couple, "Interesting name." They had agreed and shared a couple of stories of various types of welcomes they'd witnessed. All the time I was 'listening,' my mind was elsewhere, thinking – *so God, what are you planning for me to welcome into my life during my stay?* Quite frankly, I really did not want to know His answer. I was tired of being an outsider.

I breathed a sigh of relief when I crossed into Arizona. Pulling into a fuel station, I rechecked the map. Hope was about 60 miles from the interstate. Nine miles past Hope would be the biggest of the three small towns – that of Unique. As suggested, I stopped and bought some groceries before driving the final twelve miles to the tiniest town of the three – Welcome.

Marilyn Stewart

Within a day of arriving, I had visitors. Mercy and Katie were taking their turn on the Welcome Huggers Sunshine Committee. I'd arrived back from scouting out the library to find the two of them sitting on my porch, sporting huge smiles. They had with them a large basket of goodies and a small Pomeranian. This was my introduction to the open-hearted, caring ways of the Welcome Huggers and my new home.

I loved meeting with ladies my age and quickly signed up to join the Welcome Huggers.

As months passed, the only downside I found to living in a small town are the "sticky-beaks." These are incredibly nosy women (mostly) trying to pry their way into learning all about my background and private affairs. Having gone from living in an apartment complex where people next door did not even wish to know your name, to hundreds greeting me daily, has been an adjustment.

One

My folks had been missionaries in a country under British rule. Our family lived in close proximity to a primitive tribe for about eight years, where nuances in body language were the crucial dominant factors in communication. At ten, I was sent to live, for months at a time, far from home in a British-run boarding school. My cursive writing, spelling, and verbiage often continue to reflect my upbringing. Thinking of lollies, biscuits, and savories makes me wish for goodies not found here. I still think of the words "buss" or "snog" first instead of "kiss"; "dosh" rather than "cash"; "boot," not "trunk"; and "bumbag" instead of "fanny pack." Knowing a small town would not have vegemite – a treat on toast – I brought a large jar with me. Recently, it donned on me that I needed a better grasp of American culture, and in particular, their slang. In my schooling and while working in a library, I had been lectured not to use contractions. No "I've," "didn't," etc.— both words had to be used. So, I will apologize ahead of time for switching back and forth as I learn to adopt my birth country's speech patterns of running words together.

Soon after joining the Welcome Huggers, Mercy, an EMT, invited me to accompany her to the Ghost Town. It was about three miles past the town of Welcome. She said to begin with, there had been a large fire pit, two small abandoned buildings, and a lean-to – no cemetery. Boy Scouts used it for campouts and told ghost stories. Three years ago, after the first "Wounded Warrior Weekend" put on by the three towns, twelve to fifteen wounded warriors had set up camp. They usually left for the winter. Rumor had it that the ones living there right now were shooting a movie. Some were living in tents, others campers, and two had small trailers. The town had brought out a J-Jon, recycle and garbage dumpsters. There was no electricity or running water, but there was a creek about a quarter mile away.

Mercy had been there several times to treat their wounds and evaluate their needs. The first day I was with Mercy, I watched her work and supplied what she asked for. Her little therapy dog was cuddled, then passed along to be held by the next patient.

Members of "my tribe" would have been proud, for on that visit, I automatically checked and evaluated the area and the people and kept my thoughts to myself. As I scanned – absorbing the scene quickly while trying not to stare – my eyes, without intention, froze on a pair of vivid green orbs. My breathing sped up. In all my 24 years, I had never felt such an instant connection to anyone. It was as if I could see past his scowl and missing limbs to his inner soft core. I felt an irresistible pull towards this man with the amazingly expressive emerald eyes. I knew he had issues, but then, so did I – lots of them. He had quickly lowered his head and closed his eyes – blocking me out. One of the other men, Jake, had called him Lark.

Up until I arrived here, my dating record had been abysmal. Maybe it was because I was new in town that I had been invited out three times in my first three weeks. That was almost eight months ago. In accepting, I inadvertently ran afoul of three Welcome Huggers. How was I to know that, despite never having dated these hometown men, three girlfriends had their sights set on them? Now I check with Katie or Mercy before saying "yes."

You know how sometimes you meet a person and you just click? So it was with Mercy and me. Over these last months, I have gotten to know her – quite well – at first, due to overhearing others talking about her, and then, by listening intently whenever she spoke. I learned of her abduction, terrors, and reactions to touches and hugs. I watched as she tried to resist a hometown wounded warrior named Isaac (known to most as Uni or Unity), a guy who had had set his sights on her for ten years. Thanksgiving day last year, I was privileged to be one of her two bridesmaids.

When Mercy married, she had to give up her membership as a Welcome Hugger. Although she has become my best friend, I have yet to share much regarding my past. Of all the people in these three towns, Mercy alone has given me space and unquestioning acceptance. On the other hand, certain ladies seem bent on prying and teasing some of us in an effort to gain access to information we do not wish to share.

Welcome Huggers # 2 – Verity

I turned down two invitations to go out last month, but have decided to accept dates once again. My motive is crazy. I need to distract my heart from fixating on one certain guy – Lark.

Yesterday, Mercy called me, asking that I return with her to the Ghost Town. The number of wounded warriors living there had doubled. I want to go, but then again, I'd also like to avoid it entirely. My mind is dithering – I might have to talk with Lark. The two times I've been there helping Mercy, I haven't spoken, and I planned to do the same – if at all possible – on this visit.

I was quietly observing everything, when I was asked a direct question. The instant everyone heard my accent, the atmosphere changed. I could see certain men perk up – ready for some fun. A big guy named Tim pushed Lark's wheelchair closer to us girls. Out of the corner of my eye, I saw Mercy glance at Lark and back at me. I wondered if she was worried.

I saw Lark staring at me and heard him say, "Hi, Babe."

I frowned. "My name is Verity, *not* Babe!"

"Aw, Babe, don't be like that. You're British!"

"My birth certificate shows I was born in the USA."

Lark immediately responded, "But you weren't raised American, were you? I bet if I say a certain word, you will respond, whether you want to or not."

My eyes pleaded with him not to say the word, to no avail: he said it anyway: "napkin."

As he'd known I would, I blushed, but stayed silent and glared at him. He had known it would embarrass me and did it anyway. He sort of looked ashamed, then signaled Tim that he wished to leave.

Mercy whispered, "Wow, Verity. I've rarely heard him talk! Obviously he likes you. Clearly that word means something to you that it doesn't to me. Care to share?"

I grunted, "Funny way of showing it. Tell you later."

Jake moved closer. "Thanks, Miss Mercy and Miss Verity, for treating all of us with kindness and skill. Verity, please be patient with Lark – he is dealing with a lot of baggage. He rarely says anything unless it is related to the movie we're making. I'm shocked, but greatly encouraged to see his reaction to you. I agree with Mercy – he seems to be drawn to you. Come again – soon. This is going to be most interesting!"

We packed the supplies, and Mercy turned to leave. I can't say I planned to do anything. But as I took a fast glance over to where Lark was sitting, facing us with a scowl on his face, I felt great sorrow for him. I knew he would not appreciate my pity. I glanced briefly into his eyes and shot him a huge uncomplicated grin. I then twirled, heart pounding, as I ran to catch Mercy.

*****

In my first month, many of the Welcome Huggers came to dust, scrub, and paint the rooms for our library. The three towns tried to have a combined voluntary work day one Saturday each month. At the end of five weeks, one of the triple towns' projects was to lay the carpet and put up the bookshelves in the library. I was aiming to open it – at least part time – in two weeks.

My life was busy – rather hectic, actually.

One Saturday, Katie, Fe, Mercy, Annie and I went for a bike ride and took a picnic lunch. It was not for Welcome Huggers only, but a friends outing. As we were munching, Fe said, "Verity, did you know Annie and I are sisters? It was only last summer that we were reunited. It was such a "God thing" in which He used Katie and Jeff." She gave a nod to Katie to tell her side of this story.

"I know you've been interviewed by Jeff regarding the library."

I nodded.

"Well, his real name is Sir Jeffrick Dillon Daylight, and he is the owner of our local newspaper. He invited me on a date. I said I would go if we went horseback riding. He agreed, and I chose the place – the old abandoned (or so I thought) Ghost Town. To shorten the story – we raced in to save (or so we thought) a man hanging from a tree, but actually rode into the middle of a movie scene. That day I learned Jeff was a "Sir" and the person I thought was Fe turned out to be Annie. What a day that was! Jeff called my cousin Unity to bring Sam, while I called Mercy to fetch Fe and bring food for a huge picnic. The wounded warriors at camp that day were reunited with three military men they'd been told had died. And Fe was reunited with Annie and Lark."

I briefly glanced at Mercy, who was looking at me with a slight smile on her face. I had noticed Fe and Annie had green eyes, but to learn Lark was their brother was a shock. Mercy gave me a little nod. I realized they were waiting for me to say something. I would not mention Lark!

"Wow! One day I'd like to hear the entire story. Thank you so much for sharing this with me. What an outstanding party that must have been for all of you!"

Two

I was loath to return yet again to the Ghost Town. I had learned that while Lark visited his sisters in town, he preferred to live at the Ghost Town. I was on my own for this visit and planned to be in and out as quickly as possible. I took a deep breath and held it. The fragrance of the pine trees nourished my spirit. I really did not want to be here, but needed to check on Lark, or as his official name on this paperwork stated, Larkspur. A girlfriend who worked in human resources had a family emergency. She was supposed to have turned in this paperwork yesterday. Believe me, I had not volunteered for this assignment.

Spotting Lark, I resolutely walked over to where he was seated. I tightly grasped a pencil and began, "Hi, Larkspur. Your paperwork isn't complete. I was sent to fill in your answers to the following:

"Are you doing your exercises each day?

"Do you need a refresher course on how to do them?

"Are you using your crutches?

"How is your balance?

"Do you have or are you using a prosthetic hand or leg?

"Are you depressed?

"What are your dreams or ideas regarding your future?

"Lastly, do you plan to let Tim get a life or keep pushing you around?"

"Thank you, Verity, for coming to see me. Would you like a cup of coffee or tea? How about sharing a few niceties before hammering me with questions?"

I was taken aback by his many words. "Hey, Lark, I am just the messenger here."

"And what a messenger. Look at your lovely long legs. I'd love to get you in a movie. All I'd need is for you to walk away from the camera and into the trees."

I ignored his sidetracking comments. "Concentrate on answering the questions. Truthfully, please, Larkspur."

"Some days I exercise and don't need help remembering how to do them. Often I use crutches, am unsteady and depressed.

As you can see, at this time, I have no artificial attachments. I plan to continue making commercials, and hopefully, movies."

"Thank you, Lark. How about the last question? Do you realize Tim could help a lot of people in the hospital by pushing their wheelchairs? He wouldn't have to say anything if he didn't want to; however, I see he is very compassionate and skilled at what he does. I hope you both will talk honestly together. Change is never easy. It grows our character when we try to work with change rather than fight to stay static."

"You came here, Verity, to fill in paperwork, which you have completed. So what about you, Babe? What do you plan to do with the rest of your life? Do you work well with change? Have you found it to be difficult? Cat got your tongue? Whoa, look at the sparks shooting at me from your lovely eyes. I'll tell you something. You are no different from me. Some days we both hide from ourselves. I know Peter and Charity are related to you. I'm really sorry about your parents and sister being killed, and then...."

I shrieked at him, "Stop! Do not go there! Keep your mind and trap shut concerning me." I was upset by his knowledge and now felt humiliated by my loss of control.

Lark quietly remarked, "My wounds are obvious, but you, my dear, are suffering critical internal trauma. You are pretending all is well. Babe, you are wearing a mask. I am truly sorry for your pain. Why did you smile at me last time you...."

I turned and fled, totally blocking out the fact that he was still talking. Whatever he was saying, I did not want to hear it.

The tribe had taught me to ignore my pain and move forward – one foot in front of the other. This piercing pain, however, threatened to suck me back down into darkness. Too many reoccurring heartbreaks. I had tried to cope by living one day at a time after the death of my parents and sister by keeping focused and busy. My parents had been state-side on furlough for nine of their twelve-month stay. Three years before, they had left me in the USA to go to college. This time Ruby had planned to stay and begin college. On their way home from shopping, a drunk truck driver hit their vehicle head-on. Once again, good people had died and the oft-cited drunk barely had a scratch. His lawyer was still dragging it out – trying to fault the maker of the vehicle rather than her client! Some days I felt like calling and screaming at the lawyer about the unjustness of it all. Trust Larkspur to bring it all back. I sniffed twice, blew my nose, and kicked my car tire.

I hadn't heard Mercy arrive and visibly jumped when she said, "Verity, are you okay, my friend?"

Being startled and self-conscious at being caught crying, I ungraciously muttered, "What are you doing out here at the Ghost Town, Mercy? Were you sent to check up on me?"

"Ve, look at me, girlfriend. I didn't know you were going to be here. Do you need a listening ear, or a shoulder to cry on? Sheena sent me a text, then Bryce called to make sure I was coming. Since you're here, would you go with me to see them? I don't know what they want."

"I am sorry I spoke so sharply, Mercy, it was just..."

"Lark, I presume, has been pushing and prodding your hot buttons – again."

"Ah, Mercy, I should have known you of all people would pick up on his tactics. It seems as if to him, I am like a red flag is to a bull. His words kind of gored a tender spot."

"Verity, I see Lark as being very conflicted in regards to you. On the one hand he is drawn to you like a moth to a flame, while at the same time, he is trying to push you away so he won't or can't be hurt by being rejected by you."

I sniffed again, blew my nose, and slowly smiled. "Really, Mercy? I hadn't looked at it in that way. I see his beautiful emerald eyes, careful dignity, and then feel his oh, so sharp tongue. He seems to know far too much about me. Guess I'd better clean my face before going back with you and Gem."

"Verity, you listened to me for months and only rarely did you comment. You never criticized me, so now it is my turn, girlfriend. Any time you need to talk to someone, give me a call. Any time at all. I mean it, Ve. Okay?"

My heart warmed. "Mercy, you are the best friend I have. I trust you. We have more things in common than you know. I need to spill to someone safe. I will be getting in touch before too long."

Upon my return with Mercy and Gem, Lark gave a tiny grin and nodded his head. I caught his actions and silently glared at him before looking at Tim.

Lark piped up, "Hi, Mercy. Back so soon, Verity? Did you decide to return to accept my request for a date?"

Shocked by his words, I said the first thing that came to mind. "What? When did you ever ask me for a date?"

"A few minutes ago. Didn't I, Tim?"

"Well Boss, you did kind of whisper, and Verity was quite a distance from you."

"Thanks, Tim, for your honesty," I broke in. "Okay, Larkspur. After Mercy and I see Sheena, you and I will have a little chat."

As Mercy and I walked away, my brain finally kicked in – why had I said that? I barely heard Mercy's words: "Well done, Ve! I know he hasn't had a date since he lost his limbs. I've noticed he really comes alive every time you show up here."

My smart mouth had just put me in a bit of a pickle. I needed to confide in a "safe" friend. "Mercy, I know you and your husband Unity are working towards becoming certified chaplains. You both are great listeners. Later, would you check your calendars for a time we can get together?"

"Sure, Ve. I'll call Unity right after we visit Sheena."

I was almost sorry I'd requested a meeting – oh well. We approached Sheena and Bryce.

"Sheena, Bryce – how can Verity, Gem, and I assist you?" Mercy said with a smile.

"Mercy, Gem and Boo, the retired service dog Sam brought with him, have been such good therapy for us suffering from PTSD. We recently heard there are groups taking unclaimed dogs from shelters and pounds, training them, then giving the dogs to wounded warriors. You know both Sam and Unity trained or worked with dogs in the service. We were wondering if you would talk to them and see if they would be willing to start a program in one of the three towns. Sam brings Boo out a lot, but he still needs him as well. He also works with people in training their pets."

Marilyn Stewart

"Of course, I'll be happy to get the ball rolling, sign people up to be dog foster parents, and make a list of wounded warriors wishing to have a canine."

As Sheena held and petted Gem she said, "I needed Gem or Boo with me for a bit to calm me down. They're better than any pills, for they totally accept us. We never feel we are being judged. We'd like to be on the list for a dog. You live closer than Sam, so we text you instead of him."

Mercy queried, "Is there anything else we can do for you two while we are here? No? Glad we could help."

As soon as we left them, Mercy pulled out her cell phone and called her husband.

"Hi, Sweetheart. Verity needs to talk to us. What's on our calendar?" She turned to me. "Any nights that won't work for you, Ve?"

"Nothing I can't reschedule if necessary, Mercy."

Mercy turned back to the phone: "Do we have tonight or tomorrow night available? Thanks, Love. I'll see you soon."

She listened a bit longer and then, looking at me, inquired, "Ve, why don't you come to our place for supper tonight? I have a roast in the crock pot and we'll make a salad. We can chat either before or after – your choice."

"Thanks, girlfriend. I think sometimes I am going to drop the 'Mer' and call you 'Cy.' How about I come at six, and we'll talk first? Give my stomach time to settle so I can enjoy the meal."

"I've never had a nickname. I like it. I've always found talking before eating works best for me, too."

I hesitated briefly. "Mercy, I think it would be good for me to foster a dog for a wounded warrior."

Mercy smiled. "Way to go, Verity! You are expanding your comfort level. Now go talk to Lark. We'll see you later, Ve."

Ready or not, it was time for me to interact with Lark.

"Hi, Larkspur."

"Mercy's not staying?"

"No. She said we alone could sort ourselves out."

"Smart lady. Uni certainly got lucky, even if he had to wait a long time for her. They match each other – very special people.

13

Glad she chose love over fear. They still have a lot of issues. She listens and accepts wounded warriors like me."

"That's a lot of information. Are you chatting to distract me or renege on your invitation for a date?"

"Yes and no. I'd really like to go out with you, Verity."

I slowly said, "What are you thinking? Double date? Movie? Eating and dancing? Bowling? A walk? Horseback riding? County Fair? Fishing? I'm throwing out various ideas as I'm not sure what you'd be comfortable doing."

Just one of Lark's eyebrows flew up. "Wow, Babe. You don't pull your punches, do you? I do some of those things, but as you can guess, not always very well. Uni, Sam, Jeff, and I are playing racquetball as a type of mobility therapy."

"Racquetball? Really? That's great." I wondered how he could play when he was missing a hand and his right leg from just below the knee. Once again, my mouth took over without my brain in gear – not good.

"By the way, I'm going out with Ben to a gallery viewing on Thursday night. Just wanted you to know." I couldn't believe I had just told him of an upcoming date. Was I stupid, or what?

"I like that about you, Verity. You are the epitome of truth and honesty. I appreciate knowing. Maybe we need a trial run before a real date. How about I take you out for supper tonight?"

I shook my head. "Larkspur Lane – moving a bit fast there. Actually, tonight I will be at Unity and Mercy's home. Oh, rats, look at the time. I have to get to town for another follow up. 'Bye."

He raised his voice to call after me, "How about lunch today? You have to eat! I'll meet you at one o'clock at Welcome to Dine."

"Okay; see you later, Larkspur. Will Tim be with us?"

"No way, Verity. Just you and me!"

I grinned, then frowned as I retorted, "Yeah, right: just you, me, and a whole lot of people from a very nosy town."

Driving away, I went over our conversation and was appalled at how much information I had so easily shared with him.

*****

When I entered Welcome to Dine, a loud voice boomed, "Hey, Verity, I'm over here."

I am actually very shy and dislike being in the spotlight. When I arrived at his table, I couldn't resist whispering, "Sheesh, Larkspur. Nothing like making sure everyone now knows we are lunching together!"

"You are right. I wanted everyone to take note we were together before someone asked you to sit with them."

My intention had not been to make him happy, so the grin I received made me attack from another angle. "No wheelchair? Did you lie to me this morning, Mr. Lane?"

"No wheelchair and no lie this morning. My prosthetics were in getting retooled. I really didn't have them. They came by express delivery soon after you left. You're giving me an unbelieving look, but I'm telling you the truth, Babe."

"Borderline lie, Larkspur; not good. You know you permitted me to leave believing you had yet to be fitted for a prosthetic. You knew I had that impression, Larkspur, and you did nothing to clear the air. I thought you didn't like people who played those kinds of games."

"You're right, Verity. I apologize for misleading you. So what would you like to order? They know I usually order a salad, green beans, mashed potatoes, gravy, and meatloaf."

I knew his thinking was "case closed, moving on," so I followed his lead. "Water with lemon. Broccoli cheese soup and half a chicken salad sandwich for me, please."

Once we'd ordered, Lark said, "Verity, I have a question I've been pondering for some months now. In fact, ever since the kissing booth event at the fair – you know, the event last August before the Wounded Warrior Weekend in early September." He paused, so I guessed it was my turn to respond.

"I've only been to one fair here, and only one time ever in a kissing booth, so I do believe I remember the event. Both were quite memorable, but for different reasons. Sorry. You were sharing what it is you have been pondering upon."

"Verity, the day before the fair in August, Mercy came out to the Ghost Town to talk to us single fellows. She invited us to pay twenty dollars, and she would give each of us a list of single girls who wanted us to kiss them. This was before she was married. She requested we not tell Uni what she was doing. Sam was there and immediately handed over a twenty. Upon receiving his list of five, he grinned, kissed the list, folded it carefully, tucked it into his wallet, and walked away whistling.

"I was surprised to see Jake, Jenkins, Tim, and Ty each holding out a twenty for their own lists. After they moved away, Mercy came and sat on the ground in front of me. She'd no sooner sat down than Uni drove up and started towards her. She frowned shooed him away with her hand. Turning back to me, she'd said, 'Now, Larkspur, how about your list of five? I kid you not; each of these single ladies requested you specifically to be one of the five men with whom they'd like to share a kiss. The money goes towards the Wounded Warrior Weekend fund, so you know it is for a good cause. You don't have to kiss any or all five of them, or for that matter, stop at the five on the list. Wouldn't you love to know who wants you to kiss them? This paper could hold the key to future information or clues to whom you might like to ask out on a date. There are at least sixteen girls signed up to be in the kissing booth, and five of them are on your list.'

"Verity, why did you put my name at the top of your list? Maybe Mercy put my name first?"

I spooned up some hot soup to delay speaking.

"So Lark, you must have forked over twenty dollars. I thought maybe you hadn't since I didn't see you. Obviously you've been pondering this for several months. I did write you in as number one on my list. Maybe I wanted to see if your lips could compete with or even outshine your eyes."

"Well, that is a half answer. I was born with green eyes; so were my sisters. So it wasn't my alluring personality?"

I wanted to laugh. He'd scowled at me from day one. Alluring? No way! Suddenly he was 'making nice' with me. I did laugh. "You are fishing in waters that will, at this time, refuse to yield a catch."

"Ah, you are truthful to a point, then tricky like a wily old fish."

I was amused, but chose not to show it. "Nice, Larkspur, really nice, making me sound old, crafty, and slippery. But then again, maybe I am."

"So, will you go out with me if I ask you proper-like?"

"Are you asking or just checking to see if I might turn you down? Okay, Larkspur, let me tell you something. I am willing to go on one date with almost any fellow, as long as he is trustworthy, of good moral reputation, kind, and has a clean sense of humor. Any future dates would depend on what he believes regarding God, and a wrong answer would be my first deal-breaker. I am choosy, but open to invitations. I hope I have been clear as to my ground rules." I quickly learned my words had not discouraged him.

"I like your guidelines, Verity. Would you be willing to play miniature golf, or go to a movie and then out to eat with me this coming Saturday night?"

Obviously I'd not put him off. He wanted me to go out with him. "You tend to deliberately poke at my raw issues, Lark. I'm not sure if it is to push me away or get me to notice you. I would like to do those things with you, but not yet. I have a few things to deal with before going on a date with you."

He glanced down at his plate, then up at my face. I noticed his eyes had a watchful look. "Is my being a wounded warrior why you are going out with Ben, but putting me off?"

I glared at him. "No way. I can't believe you said such a stupid thing! Ben has a gallery where some of my pottery is going to be on display. We plan to eat as we talk over how best to exhibit my work. So it is sort of a working date – okay?"

He grimaced, then gave a slight grin. "Sorry, Verity, a bit of insecurity speaking. So how will I know when you have everything worked out?"

He looked startled when I laughed, then said, "Lark, just now you sounded like a sulky little boy. I honestly don't know. Sorry I can't be more specific. For some reason, I like you despite your gruff, sometimes moody ways and sharp words. You tend to tweak – fixate on my weaknesses. It is painful and makes me feel exposed. I don't like it. You don't like people pitying you."

Welcome Huggers # 2 – Verity

I watched his eyes as I shared these few home truths. I thought about reiterating the fact that I did not like to be called Babe, but decided to let it go for now. Maybe he would remember that I preferred to be called Verity or Ve.

We silently finished our meal. Lark suddenly said, "You're right, Verity. I don't like people pitying me. I'll try to be more sensitive to your issues. You can trust me with your secrets; I haven't shared my knowledge of your background with anyone. Just so you know, I definitely have you in my sights, Honey." With that he sat back, grinned, and winked at me.

I loved his grin, but was suddenly conscious of all the people watching us. I quickly rose and departed.

Three

It was early evening when I walked through the open door, reached down and picked up Mercy's small Pomeranian, Gem. "Thanks for welcoming me to your home and making time to meet with me on such short notice."

Mercy grinned. "It's lovely to have you in our home. Glad tonight worked for all of us."

I smiled as Mercy leaned comfortably back against Unity. He had his arms around her middle. She had come a long way in the last several months. While she still had many issues to overcome, right now she was obviously at ease. Unity, her husband, spoke over Mercy's head.

"Verity, do you wish to share with both of us, or only with Mercy? We want you to feel at ease – to share as much or as little as you choose."

"I thought about that on my way over and decided on both of you. I do not want you to have to keep a secret from each other because of me. I am not sure what you do or do not know, so I will begin with some of my background."

Mercy said, "Okay, Ve, but let's go sit in the living room."

*****

"Dad had been widowed with two children: Peter and Charity. Ruby and I were from his second marriage. For quite a while, my parents were missionaries in a remote area. Peter and Charity were accustomed to spending numerous months each year at boarding school a couple hundred miles from home. At six, I too was sent off, and finally, Ruby was there as well.

"One furlough, Peter and Charity, being quite a bit older, were left in the USA. The next time we returned to the States, I stayed behind to begin college. We knew Ruby would not be returning with our folks this time when they returned overseas. Ruby and I planned to room together. Knowing how hard it was to be separated from each other, Mum, Dad, Ruby, and I were making an effort to enjoy each day we had together. Peter and Charity came several times for brief visits. After so many years apart, we were treasuring our time, while relearning how to interact as a family. At the same time, I was working weird hours, odd shifts, and was often called to fill in on short notice. I would have been with them on this particular day, except that a coworker had called in sick.

"On their way home from shopping, an intoxicated truck driver veered onto the wrong side of the road and hit their car head-on. Dad, Mum, and Ruby were killed. The numerously-ticketed drunk barely received a scratch. This morning, Lark mentioned what had happened and offered his condolences. I don't know how he learned about my background. No matter. Peter and his wife, Beryl, came. They attended the memorial, helped me clean out the rental, and got me settled in an apartment. Our church generously picked up the tab for my apartment for six months and found me a better paying job at the college library. I also worked part time as a waitress."

Mercy sniffed. "Oh, Ve. You must have been devastated. I hope your family and friends checked in on you – often."

I shook my head. "We have a rather dysfunctional family. Six months later, Peter, Beryl, Charity, Jim, and their youngsters came to my graduation. They took me out to eat that evening and were gone by early the following morning. We didn't even eat breakfast together. I know Peter would have if he'd been alone."

I wondered whether to go on. It was so personal, private. I took a deep breath, let it out, and decided to continue.

"As you can imagine, I'd been struggling to stay focused, finish well, and not permit depression to completely overtake me. A couple of weeks after graduation, I was exhausted, but packed and had finished the final cleaning of the apartment. I was moving to a smaller place that was closer to work. I had had a few dates with a fellow named Paul, and we were supposed to go out again that evening, but I had decided I would call and cancel our date. Part of my reason was due to exhaustion, but in all honesty, I had come to realize we were not well-matched. There was a knock, and figuring Paul was really early, I opened the door without checking to see who was there."

I heard Mercy's sharp intake of breath and nodded.

Marilyn Stewart

"Much later, I learned that when Paul arrived, he was surprised that my door was unlocked. He found me barely clinging to life. The detective said he thought it might have started as a home invasion/burglary. It probably enraged the thief that I only had a flip phone and no credit cards. Weeks later, I told the detective the intruder was wearing a ski mask and had a faint odor of oranges."

I paused to take a long, slow drink of water before admitting, "I don't mind if you share the information I just relayed, if necessary, but this next part I'm about to share needs to remain hidden, as others are involved."

Uni's arm around Mercy tightened a bit as they both nodded. No wonder Mercy and I had felt connected right off. In the months since arriving, I learned about our commonality. I took the easiest item first.

"Mercy, I have come to realize we are alike in many ways. Despite our traumas, we stick to our belief that God does have good plans for us. A gift we have both been given is that of listening. You are a full-fledged EMT. Until a month ago, Ariel was here, acting as backup on emergency call-outs."

Before continuing, I handed them a laminated card.

"As you see, I am a full-fledged paramedic. When I arrived, I was totally burned out emotionally and mentally. Lately, I've realized I am finally ready to assist whenever needed. The general public will learn soon enough, but I'd appreciate my secret being kept as long as possible."

Mercy smiled, and as she leaned forward to hand back my card, said, "Totally awesome, Ve. Fabulous news! We can use another volunteer 'medic' to rotate on call-outs to fires, car wrecks, etc. I did wonder about your skills. Twice I have caught a glimpse of what is in your backpack. Several times at the Ghost Town you handed me something before I asked."

I nodded, grinned, then sobered.

"Cy, remember the day Roger broke your arm?" She nodded. I checked both their faces before continuing.

"That day, Sheriff Ben told Fe, Annie, and me about a church service during which you shared some of your 'secrets.'

21

Well, this next part of my story is sort of similar, but not in duration. Are you okay, Mercy?"

She nodded. I figured I'd warned them as much as possible since their own memories of 'bad times' would be triggered.

"To get back to my story. I recall waking up in the hospital and at first being very angry with the medical team for saving my life. I had been in a coma for weeks due to the head injury. I had sustained two broken ribs and a broken arm. Later yet, I became incensed. Thinking I might not live, they only did a swab for DNA and nothing else. Remember the words he said, Mercy, when he broke your arm?"

"Where is our child?"

"Yeah, well – until Sheriff Ben told us bits of your history, I thought the guy had mistakenly grabbed you instead of me. I was petrified. You see, seven weeks after my attack, I was shocked to realize I was pregnant. It threw me into a deep depression. My emotions fluctuated by the minute. I did not want a child who'd be a constant reminder of being raped, but neither could my beliefs permit me to abort. I'd been a virgin in spite of pressure to conform. Eventually, I realized that being enraged about numerous things rescued me from acute and fatal withdrawal. Paul disappeared, along with a few so-called friends. People at church began giving me pitying looks.

"Our family had loved going to garage sales, so I went to one and found a gold band. I never wore the ring to church or when Peter came to visit. It was like a security thing for when I was out and about."

I shut my eyes for a minute.

"Several times Peter came to see how I was doing. I swung wildly between keeping the baby and giving it up for adoption. Peter and Beryl repeatedly invited me to come live with them. I'd gone back to work, but knew I wouldn't be able to work much longer.

"One day, Peter and Beryl asked me, point-blank, what I was going to do. I sobbed out my dilemma and heartache. They told me their secret sorrow and made a request to adopt the twins I was carrying. Thus it was that Mark Marvel and Merry Mystery, were adopted by Peter and Beryl. They were there for their birth and moved here to Unique shortly after. To this day, I still begin to sweat when opening my front door."

Glancing between Mercy and Unity, I paused. Something was wrong. His jaw was clamped shut and his eyes were closed. I made my eyes shift to Mercy, back to Unity, and then back to her. She nodded and gently patted his hand.

"Honey, I know how difficult old wounds are to revisit. When we are chaplains we will hear worse. You've seen awful things overseas. Why this extreme response?"

He muttered, "It hurts to think about what you girls have suffered. I never dreamed – wasn't prepared for more devastation. You hide it well, Ve. Sorry. Please carry on."

"I know I did the right thing for all of us, but it has become hard to know how to interact. The adoption has changed our family dynamics – again. While Peter and Charity's families get together frequently, lately I feel as if I am not welcome. Our family has had some issues in the past, but I thought we'd worked them out. Peter and I do meet up for breakfast once in a while. This week, he told me that if something happens to both of them, they have it in their wills that the twins will return to me. It is freaking me out! I am invited to visit with the family briefly on Christmas, New Year's, and Easter. I was really happy to be working with the Welcome Huggers at your wedding on Thanksgiving Day. At future holidays, I plan to make myself available to serve meals, do clean-up, etc. It beats being unwelcome at family gatherings."

I took a quick sip of water and a deep breath.

"Almost done. Today, Larkspur made the comment, 'You are in my sights, honey.' It is as if everything is imploding inside me. Mercy, I remembered you said you felt this way most of last summer. The day Unity came home from the service, you helped find all those missing kids and your world got complicated. I needed to talk to someone who would understand, keep my secrets, and not judge. I really appreciate you both listening to me vent. Sorry to be so long-winded."

When I glanced again at Unity's grim face, he asked, "Do they know who it was? Is he in jail? Are you afraid he is hunting for you?"

"No idea who he was. Yes, I have bouts of fear that I will be found or that the twins could be kidnapped, or...."

Tears were streaming down Mercy's face, and then she smiled. "Oh, Verity. Ve, we do have a lot in common. Thank you for trusting us with your secrets. Now, how can we help?"

Now, my own tears flowed. "Your being available and willing to listen has helped immeasurably. Until three years ago, I never cried, but with the deaths and births, my emotions stay near the surface. I hate being such a cry baby."

We all heard the loud knock. Gem barked.

Unity stood. "Are we expecting anyone, Love? No? I'll go to the door. You girls might want to go into the kitchen and dry your eyes."

From there, we heard him say, "Good to see you, Lark. What are you doing here? Is there trouble at the Ghost Town?"

"Hello, Uni. Verity said she was coming here tonight. I see her car is here. I've been worried about her. Is she okay?"

Mercy and I listened to the guys talking and figured Unity would say something if things got too revealing.

Unity retorted, "Why wouldn't Verity be okay?"

"She's had some tough breaks, especially the last couple of years. Is she out on the back porch?"

Unity only got out one word, "Wait...," before Lark blundered into the patio door.

"Good thing I bounced off," Lark said. "Thanks for catching me before I fell. I'm certainly no Superman or ghost who can go through walls – or in this case, a glass door."

"Your sense of humor is returning; great to hear. Lark, what is going on? You don't seem yourself tonight."

"You didn't know me as a child, Uni, before life smacked us hard. I was outgoing and in charge, but being severely injured drained the last bit of laughter I had in me. I know I've been caustic and intolerable to almost everyone. Last August, Mercy talked to me about the kissing booth. Remember the day she was sitting on the ground in front of me and motioned you to leave? Five girls had requested to be kissed by me at the kissing booth. The time and work that you, Sam, Jeff, and Annie have invested in me, along with this knowledge, finally made me want to begin to live and not just exist."

My tears had dried. I decided we'd heard enough and walked out of the kitchen.

"Are you stalking me, Larkspur?" I demanded.

"Of course not! Ah, Babe, you've been crying. Is it about what happened after your folks died? Don't glare at me. I did some digging after your second visit to the Ghost Town. I even know the month, day, and year you were born."

I gritted my teeth and blasted him. "I am not on any social media network. I don't text and rarely email. Is nothing private anymore? I should have changed my name. I am not happy with you, Larkspur! And calling me 'Babe' is akin to referring to me as a child. Is that your way of saying I am being childish? Maybe you call me Babe like sailors often do, because they don't remember the girl's names from one port to another. I prefer to be called Verity or Ve."

"Okay, I got it, Babe, er, Verity."

Mercy chuckled. "Enough squabbling. Supper is ready. If you're hoping to eat with us, Lark, go wash your hands."

"Thanks for the invitation, Mercy. I am hungry, but will only stay if it is okay with Verity."

I hesitated. "Where does that leave me? Turning a hungry man out into the cold, night air? Oh, for goodness' sake, stay, Lark. But no discussing my personal stuff."

*****

I relaxed and held my tongue – well, for most of the evening.

"Thanks, Mercy and Unity. It turned into a fun evening with lots of laughs. I've played lots of games of Scrabble, but using your rules put a new twist on an old game! Thanks for an enjoyable evening. 'Night."

I looked back at Mercy leaning comfortably against Unity, who had his arms wrapped around her waist. I smiled, caught her eye, and nodded. She'd come a long way.

Mercy grinned. "Goodnight, Verity. You, too, Lark."

Walking away, Lark muttered loudly enough for Mercy to hear, "You might want to dirty that patio door or put on decals so no one else tries to walk through the glass."

She responded, "Thanks for the suggestion, Lark. If it were daylight, you would have seen the nose and paw prints."

Lark trailed me to my car. "I plan on following you home, Verity. I'll check to make sure your house is secure. Maybe then you will offer me a cup of hot chocolate, after which I will go home to my cold and lonely bed."

I was amused and answered him in kind. "Well, turn on either the electric blanket or heated mattress cover – that will warm you up. As for lonely, why don't you get yourself a dog or cat?"

"Sweet girl – you have a quick comeback. I know you're trying to keep me at arm's length through your use of smart words. See you in a few minutes."

Driving home, I reflected on the evening. Tears had turned to laughter and fun. I grinned as I recalled Lark's face when Mercy had announced their Scrabble rules: we girls would get double points for using plant or animal words, and the men for loving words. Unity had looked positively smug, while Lark had scowled. Unity had a head start on Lark with loving names, and I recalled hearing that the guys from our three towns had asked him to tone down his loving words to Mercy, as all the ladies wanted them to follow his example.

Halfway through the game, though, Lark began saying that he could call a girl anything if his tone was nice. It became guys against girls when he began spouting words such as 'star,' 'awesome,' and 'peanut,' then asking what his double score would be. We girls told him he was wasting his time, for those were descriptive, not loving, words. Suddenly, he had winked at me, grinned, and working off of an S already in place, put down 'precious.' While Mercy and I stared at the board, Lark was crowing over his gigantic score.

*****

Marilyn Stewart

"Thanks for checking out the house, Lark. As you can see, no one is here but us. The windows and back door are locked, and you now have a visual layout of my habitat."

There was a softness in Lark's eyes as he said, "Babe, I understand you might be a bit uneasy with me being here alone with you. While I am a little over six foot and you are only 5'7" or so, I would never use my size or gender against you. There is no reason for you to ever be afraid of me. I'll head out now and not overstay my welcome. 'Night, Ve."

I watched him drive away, then crawled into bed, pulled up the covers, and hoped, for once, to fall asleep instantly.

Four

Due to too many cups of strong tea and overstimulation with friends, my brain was not ready to rest. I began to mull over past sorrows and uncertainties regarding actions I had taken. A reoccurring question was whether my choices had been wise or prudent.

I had been wallowing in grief and loneliness when I got the call that landed me here. I'd jumped at the chance for a new beginning to rebuild my life, and once off the phone, I had exclaimed, *"Thank you, God, for this opportunity!"*

I have now been living in Welcome for over eight months. I am proud of 'our' library. It's on the main street with a parking area at the rear. When I first saw inside the building, I was dismayed, for it had been sorely neglected; however, later I realized that starting from scratch had been a blessing. The first two weeks, I put in sixty hours instead of twenty-four. Everything needed scrubbing, from the overhead lights to the floors. Then came the painting. I'd arrived in Welcome early on a Sunday and skipped church to stroll slowly through the small town. Stopping briefly to get a sandwich and water to go, I mounted my battered, but reliable old bike. Soon, one looping dirt path after another rolled under my tires. By the time I got back to my temporary home, two women were sitting on the porch with a tiny dog and a huge basket. They'd heard via the grapevine (aka gossip channel) that I had arrived. The Welcome Huggers Sunshine Committee was here to welcome me to their town and especially to the Welcome, Hope, Unique Girlfriends group known as WHUG. Mercy and Katie shared how their group of single women were now more often referred to as Welcome Huggers. While the main group met once a month, there were all sorts of interest groups meeting at different times and locations. Katie and Mercy were the Welcoming Committee for the month. Mercy's dog, a Pomeranian named Gem, was introduced as a therapy canine. He had happily permitted me to cuddle him. He was so soft. Katie and Mercy stayed for a half hour and invited me to join their group. I was given a phone number in case I needed any help or information. Before they left, both said they'd help with some of the cleaning – I was just to call and let them know when.

I recalled how after they'd gone I'd taken the basket into the kitchen, switched on the electric, automatic shut-off kettle, and peeked in the basket. There were packets of various teas, hot chocolate, homemade cookies, several cans of soup, a map of the area, a packet of tissues, a first aid kit, flashlight, pen, book in which to write, and a novel. I had strewn all the items on the table and felt truly welcome – almost hugged. I remember sitting down and sobbing, then switching on the radio and dancing around the kitchen to the beat of the music.

*****

Insistent thoughts popped up, demanding I sift through my feelings and actions – both recent and past. I knew sleep was far off, so donning a warm robe, I padded the short distance to the kitchen and fixed a cup of herbal tea.

I joined the Welcome Huggers and have attended each group meeting. For the first time since I arrived in the states, I felt welcome to interact with a group of my peers. Life suddenly became very busy and interesting. I loved my new job and most of the townspeople, despite their curiosity about me.

This single ladies entity is a loosely-run organization. Interest groups range from birdwatching to sewing. Over the months I tried various activities – from ice skating, to a retreat in which twenty girlfriends participated. I went fishing with several of the girlfriends, but didn't use a pole. Instead, I read a book, enjoyed the stillness, and watched a blue heron at the edge of the water. The three girlfriends who were fishing had smiled, but I knew I'd not be invited back.

Over time, I realized biking, hiking, birding, and rock-hounding were my favorite outings, along with visiting people – mostly those in the hospital. Early on, Mercy invited me to go with Gem and herself to visit patients, their families, and sometimes even the staff. We'd become close friends – it was like having a soul sister.

Welcome Huggers # 2 – Verity

Each day, I endeavored to keep busy and ignore my past sorrows and worries. Only shadow figures triggered by strange past events tend to shatter my nighttime hours. Strange as it might seem, I am glad the house is isolated, with no close neighbors to wonder or be disturbed by the lights and music erupting suddenly at all hours from my home.

I'd visited a quilting class and marveled at their work, but it definitely was not an activity in which I could relax when participating. Their products warm many hearts and bodies – be it a baby, young mother, family, or a wounded warrior.

I checked the calendar on the wall for upcoming events. First, Fe and Annie, who owned the local flower shop, were to demonstrate the art of flower arranging. The following monthly get-together, Daffodil and Heather would be presenting a fashion show. I had circled both. I wanted to learn the meaning and art of flowers and hoped to gain the skills of assembling a wardrobe and walking with confidence.

I had thoroughly enjoyed interacting with the Welcome Huggers during the three towns' yearly fair in August, then the Wounded Warrior Weekend held the first weekend in September. The townspeople did themselves proud – working long hours and doing it joyfully. I had been a gopher – going for this or that and working wherever needed. I got to know a lot of the townsfolk and thoroughly enjoyed myself. The townspeople and their dedication at volunteering to work one weekend a month simply amazed me. I considered whether, when my house-sitting time was up and the library handed to a qualified librarian, I would be willing to leave these people and the serene, scenic beauty. I was enjoying being a Welcome Hugger and member of a community.

Enough reflecting. I knew I was dredging up bits of stuff as a ploy to keep from thinking about a certain green-eyed man who unsettled me greatly. Thinking of men, I reviewed a bit of what I knew about Sam. Unity and Sam had known each other in the military. Sam had been a dog handler. He had lost a foot and his dog, Kong, to an IED. Over a year later, Unity had been injured in almost the same way. His dog, Degan, had died, while Boo escaped with lots of stitches and issues. Sam was now Boo's

30

guardian. Unity's cousin Katie met Sam at Unity's bedside. They had driven Unity home and dated for several months before realizing they'd never be more than good friends. I had heard Sam could be funny – as in witty – but he seemed to be struggling to regain his 'sparkle.'

My caffeine-laced brain skittered onward. I compared Mercy's and my past. Both had been victims of assault. Mercy many times; me, once. The difference was that I had been unconscious and harbored no fear of men. Mercy was not a hugger. After seeing her leaning contentedly against Unity, I wondered if her fear could be a bit situational: whether her face was against a chest or facing outward. Maybe someday I would ask her. Gratitude overwhelmed me. I did not have the frantic, instantaneous, escape-at-all-costs, reactions Mercy displayed at times.

I absolutely had to get some sleep, but it was still elusive. I tossed and turned frequently. I finally addressed what was teasing me and began thinking over Lark's parting words. I had never felt threatened by Lark, but maybe I should check him out. He knew way too much about me! Why me? Where was he getting his information? How much more did he know?

I whacked the pillow. This was not helping. Pulling the covers up tight around my face, I decided to pray for all the people I knew....

My eyes opened to sunshine. A new day had arrived. It was my life, and I had a choice. My options: be desolate or be cheerful.

Five

Yesterday, I'd had a thought. Today, I decided to test it with a call.

"Good morning, Sam. Verity here. I hope it isn't too early; I can call back."

"Hi, Verity. Nope, I'm good. What's up?"

"Sam, you know I am trying to get more people to use the library. I've been wondering if you have any free time when you could bring Boo so that kids having trouble reading could sit in a corner and read to your dog. I will also be calling Mercy about Gem's availability. On a side note, has Mercy talked to you about taking dogs from shelters, training them, and giving them to wounded warriors? I am willing to be a foster parent for a dog during their training."

"You are the third person to check with me about this – Mercy, Sheena, and now you. I guess I'd better check the 1pet4avet website. How about Uni, Mercy, you, and I getting together to discuss this program. Speaking of being available, how about going out on a date with me?"

"Sam? What about Marigold? I thought you were going out with her. I know you've had a couple of dates."

"Last week she told me she wanted to date other guys. 'Check them out,' she said, before she gets too serious. It's okay with me. We're just in the getting-to-know-each-other stage."

"So would this be a tit-for-tat, revenge, make her jealous type of date? If it is, then you've asked the wrong gal. I'd be happy to go out with you as long as you keep those boundaries in mind."

"You're very up-front, Verity. No ulterior motives. Is there a place or activity you enjoy?"

"Miniature golf, hiking, maybe bowling. Now, just so you know, I am a novice in two of the three. So if you have another option, I am open to ideas, Sam."

"So you like active stuff. How about going with me to some dog trials and then stopping for a bite to eat?"

Marilyn Stewart

"Oh, that would be perfect, Sam. Perhaps I'll pick up some pointers for when I am a foster dog parent. Maybe they will have literature available. Oh, before I agree, I should have asked, When does this event take place?"

"It's this coming Saturday. Is that going to be a problem? Is the library going to be open?

"This Saturday will be fine. The library will be closed then, but it's open the following Saturday morning. Will you and Boo come get me, or shall I meet you somewhere?"

"We will come early – around 6:00 am."

"I can do early, Sam, and if Marigold and you get back together, just call me. I would not want to break up a relationship. Shall I fix a picnic lunch?"

"Verity, I wouldn't do that to you. If Marigold calls and decides she wants to resume dating, I will be completely honest with her. Our date is on, regardless. If she has a problem with the truth, then I'd rather know now. A picnic will be perfect. See you on Saturday. 'Bye."

*****

When Saturday arrived, I thought back to the kissing booth at our fair. It was the last fund-raiser for and before the Wounded Warrior weekend. Mercy asked the ladies who had signed up to run the booth if they wanted to list five men they wanted to share a kiss with. My list had been: Lark, Rod, Jeff, Derek, and James. Lark was the only reason I agreed to kiss and kiss, but he never came. I'd decided that those I kissed who lacked sizzle, I'd not date. I had kissed four of my five with no sparks occurring. Today I was going out with a fellow I had no interest in romantically, but planned to thoroughly enjoy my time with Sam, the day, and the dog event.

"Thanks for picking me up, Sam. Mind if I ask a lot of questions while we travel?"

"Not at all. I hope I have some answers."

"I was glad you invited me to your first class last week on working with dogs. I had no idea of the different types and levels of training. I found it quite fascinating. I never considered the differences between a therapy (hospice dog) and one who 'works' in a hospital. Or a patrol dog needing one handler, versus sniffer dogs who need to interact around a lot of people. Thanks for sharing that, while a service dog can go anywhere, a therapy dog has restrictions. I now have a glimmer of the hours involved and the dedication required to work with dogs. Can you tell quite quickly a canine's ability – where he will fit?"

"Verity, the dog will, if you pay attention, tell or show you. I worked with Uni to help him train Degan. Fortunately, although both of them were newbies to the program, Uni had skills. Being a photographer with an eye for detail and having studied the handler and dog relationship in his unit, he learned quickly. Boo is a Belgian Malinois. Uni was Degan and Boo's pack leader, but they lived 24/7 with a bunch of guys who often needed to touch or hug them. After the blast, Boo was deemed no longer fit for combat. He is a trifle deaf and has some issues with loud noises. He still has the gift of smell. Boo can dispel nightmares and stop certain PTSD situations in record time. I think he smells or senses a chemical change in our bodies. Ve, I'm sure you know the spelling for dog in reverse is God. He, like a dog, seeks us out and always joyfully welcomes our company."

"Boo is certainly large, Sam. I remember laughing the first time I saw Boo and Gem together. Gem was walking in between Boo's front legs. Both had their heads up as they strolled down the corridor in the hospital. Everyone was peeking out their doors and smiling. Gem seems to also have a gift. I saw how he helped Sheena several days ago."

"JC and JJ told me how they checked out numerous different puppies before settling on Gem for Mercy. In my opinion, dogs, like people, are gifted with different abilities. Often, small dogs are noisy and get a bad rap. I've seen, at different times, a dachshund, a Pomeranian, and a Yorkie burrow under rubble to locate survivors. Golden retrievers with their mellow dispositions generally do excellent work in search and rescue and therapy jobs. Often beagles or terriers make good fruit and drug sniffers, and German shepherds are often the police dog of choice. Many dogs in our towns have surprised me by their unexpected and untrained skills."

Marilyn Stewart

"You mean like the two puppies who, by the time Mrs. Hatch returned home after five weeks away, were alerting her almost-deaf husband to the phone and doorbell?"

"Exactly, Verity. When we begin to select dogs for the 1pet4avet project we will need to look for certain qualities. Much behavior, of course, can be taught; however, sadly, some dogs have been so badly damaged, they would be too much work for a wounded warrior. Numerous agencies are doing great work in training dogs specifically for hearing, blind, medical challenges, and special needs."

"Sam, in the military as a canine instructor, did you have more than one dog? Care to share?"

"Dogs were always in training, but only one – a Belgian Malinois (same breed as Boo) – always worked with me. Kong was killed by the IED that took off my foot. First, though, he pulled me back about ten feet before collapsing. He saved my life. If I'd fallen forward, I'd have landed on a second IED. So, Ve, you might like to be a dog's guardian?"

I knew Sam wanted to change the subject, so I obliged.

"I've never had, or been in a home that had, a pet. I am basically clueless. What are typical duties of a foster parent?"

"Teach the dog to walk quietly beside you on a leash. Brush their teeth, rub their feet regularly – it makes nail trimming easier – and veterinary check-ups. Some dogs love hugs and tummy rubs. Keep your dog's mind working by teaching tricks. Go to 'school' with them. Take them with you to a variety of places. Just as exercise is important for us wounded warriors, so it is for dogs, especially ones recovering like Boo. A good idea would be to spend some time learning from Mercy and Gem or Boo and me – sign up for classes."

"Wow! I had no idea caring for a pet entailed so much. It is a lot like caring for a child; full-blown commitment, isn't it? Sounds rather scary and a lot of work."

"Nah, Verity. There are basically two ingredients: love and discipline. Dogs, like humans, need to know their boundaries and that they are accepted. You need to be the pack leader – the food source. Be consistent. Give them lots of attention. They will always give back far more than what you expend on them."

Welcome Huggers # 2 – Verity

"Thanks, Sam, for sharing so freely. Having lived in a third world culture, I know there are some dos and don'ts at certain events, so what is the etiquette at this dog show?"

"I'd forgotten you'd grown up in another culture and understand protocol can be very important. Follow my lead or ask me before acting, okay?"

"Okay, and thanks for quelling my anxiety. I am so looking forward to experiencing today as it unfolds."

"Is that the way you always look at life, Verity?"

"It used to be, Sam. I've had what I considered to be hard times, but with God's help, I worked through my troubles. Then, several years back, I met even more devastation head-on and lost my way for a bit there. Lately, I have been making a determined effort to choose joy and look forward to each new day. As I am sure you'd agree, some days can be a hard-fought battle to get up and look ahead, instead of back and to choose to see how abundantly blessed I truly am. I believe God's Word is true, and therefore have to trust He has good plans for me. Right now I am finally glimpsing bits of blue in the midst of my dark, gray life. Sorry, Sam, for such a long explanation."

"Don't be sorry, Ve. I appreciate your willingness to share. You are right about struggles. It has taken me a long time to accept my new self since I lost a foot in combat. Uni and Boo have been tremendous gifts from God these last six months. Soon after arriving home, Uni started a Bible study for us wounded warriors out at the Ghost Town. We share what works, what hasn't, and we pray for each other. Boo helps brings me out of my nightmares by laying his head on my chest. Often, lately, he has been waking me before they become full blown."

"So here we are, Sam – going to the dogs – and all set to enjoy our day. I forgot to ask if you and Boo are entered in any of today's events."

"What makes you ask?"

"You are wearing your military gear, and on the back seat next to Boo is a special-looking dog vest."

"How about you let us surprise you. Okay?"

36

"Works for me." We got out of the car and began walking towards the event.

"Look at all the canopies. It is almost like a mini fairgrounds. I would like to check out some of those booths before we leave," I said.

"We can do that together when they take a break to reset the course. Right now we have good seats, so for the time being, let's stay put."

*****

"So, Verity, what did you think of the day's events?" Sam asked me as we returned to the car at the end of the day.

"I will remember this day for a very long time. It definitely is in my top five dates as to originality, learning, laughter, and fun."

"What was your favorite thing?"

"It's too hard to pin down any one, Sam. I loved the search and rescue demonstrations. The agility course was so fast – well, most dogs were. Their skill maneuvering the weave poles, jumps, and tunnels was exciting. I kept thinking what a formidable amount of training is involved. The jumps went well, except for the little dog that went under instead of over. I was so pleased the trainers didn't fuss when their pets goofed. Watching the dogs and their guardians reminded me to keep going – not to fret over my mess-ups, keep my focus on the future, and finish well. At my end, I should leap with faith like the dogs did – with assurance, knowing I will be caught in God's waiting, outstretched arms."

"Good reminder, Ve, that I am the dog and need to obey my heavenly Commander. Glad you enjoyed our outing."

"I was so proud to be with you, Sam. Your presentation was excellent. Stating your qualifications as well as Boo's service record really showed you knew what you were talking about. Then, telling a story that made them laugh and having me hide and directing Boo to find me really captured their attention. Plus, when you finished with a plea for support for pets for wounded warriors – that was spot on. Well done!"

"Thanks, Verity, for coming and being so supportive."

Welcome Huggers # 2 – Verity

"It was a fantastic, fabulous day, Sam. What special memory will you take away?"

"The three year old kid racing after the dog, zig-zagging to cut him off, and trying to catch his tail."

"That was good for a laugh. I had a really great time, Sam. Thank you so very much for inviting me. Goodnight." I started to get out of the car, then hesitated.

"Wait a minute. I don't recognize that car over there, and no one is visible inside it. Sam, would you check who is visiting me at this time of night?"

Sam got out and took Boo out of the backseat. I followed, staying behind my guardians.

"Marigold!" Sam exclaimed as he got close enough to see the car. "What are you doing here, Marigold? I know it's your car; show yourself."

A sheepish Marigold came out from behind a bush.

"Hi Sam. Verity."

"Why did you come here? To spy on us, or to give Verity a hard time for going out with me?"

"Why don't the three of us – four with Boo – go inside, out of the cold, and get something hot to drink while we talk," I broke in, sensing Sam's irritation and wanting to defuse the situation. "Let's go sit in the kitchen. You must be freezing, Marigold."

I unlocked the door, and the four of us entered the welcome warmth of the kitchen. I put the kettle on while Sam hung our coats on the hall tree and Marigold settled herself at the table.

Once we all had a cup of steaming tea in front of us, we picked up where we'd left off outside, with Marigold leading the conversation.

"I came to see if you'd kiss goodnight, or if Sam would..."

"I would what? Try something on with Verity? You know I am not like that!"

Marigold turned embarrassed, pleading eyes to me.

"Verity, explain to Sam about the dating bit."

"Well, I'm guessing here, but Sam, I think when Marigold told you she wanted to go out with other guys, she was actually hoping you'd get a little pissed off and kiss her a good one."

Marilyn Stewart

"Yeah, Sam," Marigold picked up the thread. "Instead, you went and got all noble and walked away as if I wasn't worth fighting for, or that you didn't even care very much who I dated." Her eyes welled up with tears at this point.

Sam frowned, looking a bit bewildered, not to mention flustered. "So it was a test? How was I supposed to know what you were thinking? How many guys are you interested in checking out? I'd like the truth here, Marigold."

"Here's a tissue," I said, pulling one from the box on the sideboard. "Dry your eyes, M, and be honest with Sam. I know it is hard, but it is better than keeping a secret longing or love or hurt."

She took the tissue and dabbed at her eyes.

"Come on, girlfriend. I know you are capable and courageous. If you'd rather share with Sam privately, I will leave you two alone." I stood and said, "Lock the door on your way out."

Marigold grabbed my wrist. "No, Verity. Stay."

"Okay with you, Sam?" I looked in his direction, and he nodded.

"Right, then. Link hands across the table, Sam, so Marigold will feel your strength and acceptance."

Sam gently took her hands, and Marigold looked down at the table, then began. "I had a rotten four years after my mother died. I don't know which of the three men in my family would have been the father. They ensured I had an abortion. When I came of age, I moved to the town of Hope in search of a new beginning. I have major trust issues. Most men scare me, but Sam, you make me feel as if nothing could harm me while you are near. It seriously worries me, so I got mouthy and did a bit of verbal shoving back to see what you would do."

I hesitated to say anything. I knew something was off. Looking at their faces and then hands, I softly said, "Sam, are you okay? Loosen your grip."

"Sorry. I'd like to beat them to a pulp. Were they ever prosecuted, Marigold?"

I noted that she looked down and hesitated before replying.

"No. It is my word against theirs. The doctor kept no record and took no samples for DNA."

Welcome Huggers # 2 – Verity

I saw Boo's tail wagging near Marigold. He'd been lying near the stove, but sensed her tension and had moved to lean against her leg.

"Hello, Boo. You knew I needed a hug from you just now, didn't you? Thanks, pal." She gave him a scratch behind the ears, then looked over at me. "I'm sorry, Verity. I came over here with every intention of blasting you."

"Oh, Marigold, I'm not. Sam and I are friends – he is like a blood brother to me and nothing more. Much good has transpired here, tonight. Your burden has been shared with people who care about you. Anything else requiring airing? Sam?"

"I need to go punch something, go for a run, work out, or something. Give me a couple of days, Marigold. I will follow you home and check your apartment, but won't stop in for a coffee. Right now, I am enraged beyond measure on your behalf."

"I wish you both God's blessing, regardless of what happens between you. In future, if either of you need to talk, I am available to listen," I added as I saw them to the door.

Sam nodded.

Marigold said, "Thanks, Verity. Goodnight."

*****

I reflected on my day as I readied myself for bed. I loved living in this small town. I delighted in the Welcome Huggers group and their support. Even my pottery skills seemed to have more pizzazz with the added nature touches. At the next meeting, I would be giving a demonstration and a short devotional regarding clay. I was already thinking about a poem or write-up to be placed with each piece of pottery. I knew I was avoiding pondering about what Marigold had told us. Why had she....

As I drifted off to sleep, I refocused my thoughts on my lovely, fun, educational day with Sam and Boo.

Marilyn Stewart

Six

The library was only open part time; therefore, I'd been accepting small jobs to supplement my income. I liked diversity, from getting out and meeting people, to trying new things. I had answered "yes" to every job offered me, and as a result, I was beginning to feel chronically exhausted. I realized I needed to take some time off to relax – maybe do some pottery or take a long drive.

Tomorrow was the day off I had chosen. No amount of money offered would change my mind.

I often talk to God – especially when I can't sleep. Since 'tomorrow' was now today, I vented loudly, *"Where were you, God, in protecting me? I know Peter and Beryl now have two lovely little ones, but what about the awful traumas I have suffered and still have to deal with? I no longer have anyone who really cares about me! You know something about Peter and Charity that I am missing. Life for me just isn't fair! Why, of all the places in the world, did I end up in a town called Welcome? Some days, just hearing the name grinds at the wound inside me."*

I was not happy – with myself or God. What's more, I'd found out a few days ago that I was soon to be without a home – the couple for whom I was house-sitting had a change in plans and would be returning much earlier than they'd originally thought. So I'd been packing my things in between jobs and other distractions.

Today, I'd planned to sleep in and throw myself a humdinger of a pity party – and here I was, wide awake! It was my birthday, and no one would be allowed to interfere with my plans – no one! Yesterday, I had bought three favorite flavors of ice cream, as well as two types of pies.

I turned off my phone and alarm at three a.m., pulled up the covers, and murmured, *"Tomorrow, not today, I'll try to move back to being a survivor – okay, God?"* I decided, okay or not, that was what I was going to do, and promptly cried myself to sleep.

Ding-dong. Ding-dong. Rap, rap, rap. The light tapping soon sounded like a man's fist... pound, pound.

Peter hadn't said anything about coming around, and neither had anyone else. I tucked my head under the pillow and held it tightly against my ears, hoping they would just go away.

Ah, silence. I suddenly remembered leaving the curtains parted and the bedroom window a couple of inches down from the top. I lowered one hand, pushed up the pillow a wee bit, and raised the covers just enough to peek.... Two green eyes were peeking back at me.

I shrieked loud and long, and flipped the covers back up over my head.

I was stunned to hear a man's voice say, "Happy Birthday, Darling Verity. We're here to take you out to breakfast. Come on, girl, shake a leg. We're getting hungry."

I softly grumbled, *"Are you laughing at me, God? No pity party today, huh?"*

I groaned, then shouted, "All right. All right. Get away from the window. Go sit on the front porch."

"See, you get up, girl, or we will pester you until you rise and shine. The day is wasting away, and so are we, from lack of nourishment."

By the time I got into the shower, I was laughing. Impossible as it had seemed, I was sure those had been Lark's green eyes peeking in the window. So, for him to be visible, he was out of his wheelchair. As far as I knew, only my kin – Peter and Charity – knew my birth date, time, weight, and year. I grimaced. Someone had leaked the information. Or maybe that lousy Internet had divulged the data. Wait a minute. Lark had once stated he knew my birth month, day, and year. I dithered about wearing a dress or jeans and finally settled on black slacks, a multicolored blouse, and a warm sweater. Easing out the door, I looked around expecting to see people – not just one man.

"I thought there must have been quite a few of you from all the noise you made and your use of the word "we" several times. You are looking really chipper for being half-starved. Good to see you out of the wheelchair and walking."

"Seeing a person in a wheelchair can give an illusion of numerous things. Weakness, lack of height, and deficiency of

42

mental acuity being three inaccurate assumptions," Lark replied. "The others have gone to the restaurant. If we don't hurry, they will be done eating before we even get there."

"I think you tried to fool me into believing you were almost tied to the wheelchair and Tim. Why hide the truth, Lark?"

"Sometimes it is just easier. I can concentrate on making a movie without worrying about losing my balance, or falling with a camera, or some such mortifying action. As you can see, my vehicle is equipped with special controls, so I can drive with ease. I appreciate your act of faith, Verity. You got in without a look, hint of reluctance, or saying you'd prefer to drive. I like it that you trusted me. By the way, why did you, or do you have a death wish, my dear?"

I ignored the 'my dear' part. "You know my parents were missionaries, Lark. They were different from many who served. They taught us to accept what we were offered and trust God. This didn't mean we were to be foolhardy and take risks or make illogical choices. We were to size up the person, the situation and all the variables, and then make an informed decision. That is what I did just now before getting into your vehicle."

"They must have been real special people. They did a good job raising you."

The faces of my loving family flashed into my mind, and I couldn't stop the tears from springing to my eyes.

"Ah, Ve. You crying?"

"I didn't mean to — sorry, Lark. I miss them and my sister, Ruby, so very much. It has been hard to move forward, knowing they are no longer somewhere in the world doing good deeds." I blew my nose and asked, "Where are we going?"

"You'll know when we get there."

"Hmm, sounds a bit ominous — lacking information, Lark."

"Don't fret or open your worry box, Verity. We're almost there, and we will not be alone. Okay?"

I was so happy, I almost smiled. All these months, and he was finally conversing with me! I didn't want to blow it, so I quietly replied, "Okay. Thanks for the clarification."

He paused for a moment, then glanced at me.

"Verity, you have been on dates with Ben and Sam. I know Derek plans to ask you out. How about a date with me? I'll try not to push or pry into your life, but I'd like to know you a lot better. Right now, I know a lot of facts, but not the essential you. We have two short clips making a debut. Jake will represent us. I plan to go incognito. I'd love for you to be my date."

"I would be delighted to accept, Lark. How fancy is this shindig? Should I wear a dress, suit, or slacks? Maybe the question I need to ask is – what are you planning to wear? Military outfit, tux, suit and tie, or jeans?"

"I'll be wearing a dark suit and tie. I'd love to see you in a dress and high heels."

"I believe I have an outfit that will meet your specifications. What time will you stop by for me?"

"I think you carefully avoided the words, 'pick me up.' It is several weeks from now – on a Saturday. We'd need to leave at 5:30 pm since it starts at seven, and we have a ways to go. After the event, I'd like to take you to a nice restaurant."

"I'll look forward to the outing and being with you, Lark."

"Good." Lark parked the car and looked me full in the face. "Close your eyes, Verity. Wait for someone to open your door, then look to your right."

The car door opened, so I opened my eyes and saw a large sign reading, "HAPPY BIRTHDAY, VERITY!" posted near the entrance to the restaurant.

As we entered the building, people began singing the birthday song, and at the end, one man said, "Finally, we can get something to eat!"

I laughed and began, "Thanks for waiting," only to add, "Ah, it looks as if a lot of you didn't, and you are once again headed to the buffet."

Jeff laughed. "Busted for sure! But Verity..."

"Gals and guys – I am just blown away that you took time out to even be here. Thanks. Eat up!"

"It's nice that you aren't on any social media sites, Sis, for it allowed us to surprise you this time. Lark told Charity and me to get our buns over here and celebrate your special day with all your

Marilyn Stewart

friends. How did you like the sign out front? Here is a tissue; dry your eyes, Snicklefritz."

"That's what Dad always called me. Presents? For me? Do I get to open them now? Hey, girlfriends, I'm not going to be embarrassed to open any of them in mixed company, am I? Maybe I'd better wait."

Heather laughed. "Nope, no waiting. We will bring them to you. Now, relax, enjoy yourself, and be prepared to be spoiled."

Jasmine piped up. "So, you've never had a pet, and yet, you volunteered to become a foster parent for a dog."

Peter had filled a plate for me, but I barely had time to begin eating before presents were placed before me to be opened.

Tears trickled down my cheeks as I tried to smile and speak. Among the presents I'd opened were a collar, leash, dog bowl combo for water and food, roll of plastic doggie bags, food and treats, brush and comb, dog soap, tooth brush, a doggie crate, gift certificate for a visit to the veterinary clinic and for three sessions with Sam or Unity for dog training.

"I am totally blown away!" I finally managed to say. "I wouldn't have known to get half of this stuff. You all have overwhelmed me by your generosity! Thank you so very much. I will remember this day..."

Mercy interrupted. "We aren't done yet, Verity."

I was so flabbergasted, I blurted out, "More? No one has celebrated my birthday with me in seven years! This is like Christmas unrolling right now for the next ten years!" I sniffed, blew my nose, then beamed. "This is beyond...," I began, but was cut off by Peter.

"Okay, make way, coming through, I don't want to drop this cake. The twenty-five candles are lit, but sputtering. Make a wish and blow, Sister."

I did as asked, and Peter said, "So, what was your wish?"

"Hey, Peter, she can't tell, or it won't come true."

"My wish is for each of you to be blessed a thousand times more than I have been by all of you today."

"Hey, they're trick candles," someone said as the flames reappeared on the wicks. "So her wish can still come true."

Welcome Huggers # 2 – Verity

"Thanks, Peter and Charity and your spouses, for the gift certificate for clay. I was almost out."

Fairlyn handed me a card. Outside was a picture of a dog, and inside were the names of ten Welcome Huggers who had signed up to dog sit.

A voice yelled, "Hurry up, we need to head to work."

Mercy signaled me over. "Gem, out. Ve, peek in the crate."

Looking in, I whispered, "Is this my first foster dog for a wounded warrior?"

Mercy nodded. I turned to Sam. "What kind of a dog is it, Sam?"

"The vet says he is a mixed breed and about seven months old. He thinks he will probably end up under twenty pounds. It will be up to you and him to decide his ultimate destiny. You get to name him."

I looked around at all the faces – most were smiling. I grinned, and throwing up my hands, blurted out, "I'm overwhelmed by your kindness. I know you need to get to work. How about a quick hug of thanks for each of you as you leave?"

*****

"Verity-girl, you didn't have to kiss them as well!" Lark teased, then his eyes grew serious. "You look frightened. What's wrong, Babe?"

"There were six guys I didn't recognize. I can't believe it. Peter, four of them smelled like oranges. Is there an orchard nearby?"

"We're too high in altitude. I'm calling Sheriff Ben, Sis. Charity and I will head on out. It was a lovely party. Verity, I think now might be a good time to hold your puppy."

Despite her stiff stance, I lightly hugged Charity and kissed her cheek, as I had the others. As Peter hugged me tightly, I whispered in his ear, "Make sure you aren't followed home. Call me."

Mercy and Unity moved closer. I shared a look with Peter while saying, "Unity, Mercy, Sam, Lark, Annie, and Fe are still

46

here, so I feel secure. Thanks to both of you for making my day special by coming."

As they left, I faced the others to ask, "Would some of you mind staying a wee bit longer? I will explain when Sheriff Ben arrives."

I hadn't noticed that Lark slipped outside shortly after Peter and Charity had left the room. Marigold suddenly materialized near Sam. Fe opened her mouth, but noticing Marigold, hesitated briefly before proceeding.

Turning to face me, she quietly murmured, "Verity, here is a card Annie and I were going to give you later. We know you're house sitting for a couple who will soon be returning. Our birthday gift is a month's free board at our place. We have the big, old house on Spruce lane. There are three bedrooms no one is using. We'd love it if you'd consider moving in and staying with us indefinitely."

Tears filled my eyes – such kindness from new friends.

Annie added, "We hope you accept. Lark knows nothing of this invitation; however, being triplets, he might have guessed."

I murmured, "I thought he was your older brother."

"He is, but only by a few minutes. I wonder why he went outside, and why he is talking to Peter. You will move in today, right? You wouldn't need to worry about the dog, which might be a problem the guys didn't consider given where you are presently living."

I hadn't thought of that, either, and exclaimed, "You are so right! Sure, let's try and mesh our lives and schedules. This will be so much fun! No, wait. I might put you two in danger."

They laughed and wove their sentences together. "Verity, there is safety in numbers. You're moving in with us today! Woohoo! This should be fun! Three girlfriends living together."

Sheriff Ben came into the restaurant, and catching sight of me, headed over. "Verity, Peter called sounding very worried. Want to tell me what is wrong, or do you need some privacy?"

I glanced around. "I see only friends, Sheriff. About six months after my folks and sister were killed, I was cleaning my apartment, getting ready to move. I was alone, but expecting someone, so hearing a knock, I opened the door. I later learned

47

more than two hours had passed before I was found. I had a severe head wound. The hospital kept me in a coma for over two weeks."

Looking around again, I changed my decision.

"Sorry. I think I will tell only Sheriff Ben the rest."

He and I moved to an uninhabited corner. He lowered his head to catch my whispered words.

While he listened, I noted that his eyes scanned the room. Glancing briefly at me, he shook his head. "Verity, I cannot change your past, but hopefully we will be able to keep future mischief from occurring. I'd say Mercy and Unity already know about your past."

I was not comfortable with where this conversation was going, so in an attempt to take the focus off of me, I retorted, "You are sharp, Sheriff Ben, but if you were really sharp, you'd snatch up Sheriff Ann from the next county over."

His face flushed.

"Oh, look at your red ears," I sighed. "You are right. The other night, I shared some of my history with them."

"Is there anything else I should know?"

"Yes. There should be evidence of a bite mark on the perpetrator's lower arm, where I managed to bite him during the attack. Detective Dan Ragland has my file. The man's DNA was retrieved."

As Lark walked back into the restaurant, Sheriff Ben returned to the group and began asking questions.

"Did any of you get a good look at the six guys Verity didn't recognize? Were they sitting at a table together? No? Did everyone pay for their own meal? Stay here while I go talk to the manager and the servers." Sheriff Ben started to turn, then said.

"Wait a minute. Verity, what are your plans for today? Peter said the house where you are staying is isolated."

"Well, I am ashamed to admit that I stocked ice cream in three flavors and two of my favorite types of pies with plans to throw myself a huge pity party. The owners of the house are returning a month earlier than planned, so yesterday I packed most of my stuff. In between indulging, I planned to thoroughly clean the house."

"Sheriff, Ve is going to stay with Annie and me, so she will no longer be living alone. We can make some calls to help move her today." Fe smiled. "We will help Ve have a grand birthday."

A deep voice boomed, "Hey Sisters, I'll be happy to move permanently into the room on the main floor."

The sheriff chuckled. "Lark, I'm sure we could get more than enough guys to offer to live in a house with three beautiful, single young ladies! You have more right than anyone else, but I think your sights are focused on someone other than your sisters. I or someone from the Sheriff's office will check in with you later, Verity. Come down soon to meet with our sketch artist."

Thinking Lark might soon be living under the same roof unnerved me. The puppy moved and I responded, "This little guy must need to go outside. I think it will be best if I carry him since he doesn't have a diaper to catch a spill."

People hooted and chuckled at my comment until Sam intervened. "Good thinking this time, but in future, Ve, don't coddle him or he will quickly be running your life with his own agenda."

"Got it, Sam. Such a memorable birthday; thanks all."

"Dry your leaking eyes, Babe. How much stuff have you got to move? You said it is packed up?"

"Yes, Lark. Three large suitcases, two boxes of books, two pairs of shoes – not yet packed, several items on hangers, and a cosmetic bag in the bathroom."

"That's incredible, Verity. I find it hard to believe, at your age, that you're not loaded with lots more stuff."

"You said the magic word: 'stuff.' To be honest, relationships are what I deem valuable. I have lived in several countries, foster care, and dorm rooms, and the last two places I stayed were already furnished. I have never had either the money or any reason to buy much. The gifts for the puppy will about double my earthly goods!"

"You girls gather up the items here. Take Verity and the pooch to their new home. Sam and I will go to the house and get her meager trappings. You'll have time to settle on her room before we get back. The key, please, Verity. Later, maybe several of the Welcome Huggers can help you finish cleaning the house."

Welcome Huggers # 2 – Verity

I stared at Lark, but wanted to laugh. "Listen to the military taking action and organizing us. I noticed no offer to help with clean-up duties. Annie, Fe, do you have any freezer space? Good. Would you guys bring back the ice cream and pies so we can dig into them later today?"

They nodded, and I thanked them.

*****

Lark brought in a duffle bag crammed full of his stuff, while Sam and I made two trips upstairs with mine. What an eventful, crazy birthday! Later that evening, as the four of us sat at the kitchen table, talking over the last of the pies, I decided to share some information.

"I want to entrust you three with a secret. Unity and Mercy already know."

As I was lining up my thoughts, I hesitated and was shocked when Lark declared, "Besides the head injury, you sustained two cracked ribs, a punctured lung, and a broken arm. A different paper mentioned something much worse."

"I cannot believe you know all that, Lark! They had not expected me to live. Later, I found out I was "with child," as my mother would have said. I remembered the intruder had on a ski mask and smelled like oranges. I hugged numerous people today, and at least four of them smelled like oranges."

"Verity, honey, what about the child? What happened?"

"Is nothing private? So, Lark, you knew about that state of affairs, too? How humiliating!"

"No, that part was never in the papers. You just told us."

"You are right, I did; sorry. I had twins, who were adopted by Peter and Beryl." I ignored the girls' gasps.

"Thanks for the party, Lark. I know you were the power that made it happen. It has been many years since anyone celebrated my birthday with me. Holidays have always been a struggle, with parents and siblings so far away. Peter and I have always had a close relationship, regardless of how far apart we lived. I was delighted when he fell in love and married."

50

Marilyn Stewart

"I heard they've been married quite a while, and..."

"Yes, Annie, the adoption fulfilled their desire for a family. Five months ago, I noticed a shift in dynamics while I was in their home. Because of my background, I tend to be ultra-sensitive to nuances others might miss. I have never visited them without an invitation. Today, Peter confirmed my suspicions about underlying subtleties."

"You mean you are a threat in some way? I mean, not really, but an emotional, irrational kind of thing."

"Exactly right, Fe. Thanks for understanding. I am almost done rattling on. A couple of weeks ago, Peter and I met up for breakfast. He shared two things: first, they are thinking of moving away from this area. Secondly, if anything happens to the both of them, they have it in their wills that the twins will be returned to me."

"Oh, wow. I reckon you were in shock. I don't know what I would do in your circumstances."

"You are spot on, Fe. I have been praying and seriously considering leaving this area. Charity and Beryl meet regularly, and their five kids play together. The men are in the same Bible study group, and they all attend the same church. There are nine of them versus just me. We rarely even see each other."

"But...?"

"I'm sure you three can understand. I have struggled regarding the distances we have had to live from each other. We are all finally less than thirty miles apart. I can hardly bear thinking of being far apart yet again. I didn't move here because of the twins, but to be near family. My half-brother, Peter, has sound judgment, and is a sensitive, protective, and caring man."

Lark had been suspiciously quiet, letting us females talk. As he stood, he muttered, "Don't make any sudden decisions. We are here if you ever need or want to talk."

"Thanks. I guess it is time I take Puppy for a walk."

During our quiet stroll, I let my mind drift. I was suddenly aware of how little I actually knew about my older half-brother and sister. Had Peter ever been in the military? What had Lark and Peter talked about outside the restaurant today? Peter seemed to be out of town a lot lately. Had he been instrumental in my move

51

here? If so, why? So many things happened after our parents' death, but not here – not until this last month or so. I stooped low, baggie in hand to retrieve the puppy's deposit, then retraced my steps 'home.' Looking up, I saw a plaque near the front door and thought of how often this town of Welcome utilized its name. There was a Welcome to Dine; a Welcome Inn; the library had a sign with an open book – Welcome Paws2Read, and I was about to begin living at a place named Welcome Home.

Marilyn Stewart

Seven

I thought the three of us girls were blending rather well, but Lark seemed to have some issues, which we all tended to ignore.

Puppy was keeping me busy. He'd had several accidents in the kitchen, even though we'd taken him out numerous times. He followed me everywhere, causing me to almost fall. I'd just taken him for another walk and put him in his crate, hoping he'd nap.

I walked into the study to sit quietly, relax, and maybe read for a bit. Hearing a nearby throat-clearing caused me to jump. I spun around to leave, but froze upon hearing Lark's harsh query.

"You going to ask me how many people I've killed?"

I was appalled. Why would he ask such an insensitive question? Hands now on hips, I glared at him and tersely stated, "That's none of my business. That is strictly between you and God! I know you are hurting – struggling to balance the slicing your soul has endured with the acceptance of God's love of you, but why would you even think I'd ask such a grievous, hurtful thing?"

Lark hung his head, muttering, "I guess you'd be surprised to know how many people have asked me to share war stories and how I've killed people."

I all but moaned, recognizing this wounded warrior's stark revelation of additional harm inflicted on him by others. I stood still, staring at his bent head, until he looked at me. Then I spoke.

"Lark, you pounced on and prejudged me. There are a lot of clueless people out there. Maybe they just didn't know how to start a conversation with you. Regardless, I have enough strife and baggage of my own. While I grieve for the struggles you guys face, I'll not be asking stupid questions. Stop delving into my past, or I'll start mucking about in yours. Are we clear?"

He suddenly grinned. "Feisty, aren't you? I like that."

I don't know why I felt I needed to have the last word, but I did. "If you ever need a listening ear and closed mouth – that's me."

My stomach churned. Reading lost out to a long bike ride.

*****

For several days, Lark and I avoided each other. I was reminded of being left in a new home or school and 'walking' as if on eggshells. It always took time to suss out my 'place.' I wasn't a daughter, a cousin, nor a servant, but most often, more like the last than the first. I'd found it easiest if I kept my mouth shut and eyes wide open to the dynamics of the household. I had learned to be very flexible and not set my heart on going to any promised outing. Plans including me... oh, well. Enough negative thinking. I understood foster kids' fears and reactions better than most. Often inside, I'd felt like stomping and shouting, but knew my actions would reflect badly on my parents, so I bit my tongue. I became withdrawn – almost invisible – and thus, became privy to information that a blackmailer could only dream about.

I felt Lark was not only trying to find his place back in society, but also how to transition smoothly in this home.

As time passed, tensions eased between Lark and me, to the point where we could tease and be teased without taking offense.

Eight

Unlike most libraries, I encouraged 'indoor voices' rather than whispers. I wanted the children, reading out loud to the dogs, to read naturally and not be worried that people could hear them.

I moved around, monitoring each area for stray books, litter, and anyone needing assistance, while also working the front desk. Rosemary, my sole assistant, was shelving books. Puppy was sleeping in his crate in a nook under the counter.

Daffodil, one of the Welcome Huggers, came charging up to me. She had a determined glint in her eye and her 'outdoor voice' was at full throttle. "Word has it you have a date with emerald-eyes Lark, and you both are living with his sisters!"

I kept my smile in place while gritting my teeth. "Please lower your voice," I said. "Shall I post that information here in the library so the whole town won't need to quiz me on those facts?"

She blared on, "Tut, tut; that is no way to respond, Verity. He is hot, and he'd be smoking hot, if he only had all..."

At this, I, too, lost my 'indoor voice' and spat, "Don't you ever, ever say or infer something like that again. Especially about someone who almost died so that you can speak your mind. I'd like to wash your mouth and mind out with a keg of soap. What if you lost a limb, and someone thought of you the way you obviously regard wounded warriors? How would you like to hear someone saying 'if only she were....' I am ashamed of you. Look at your inner self as in a mirror, and..."

Daffodil muttered, "Sheesh, lower your voice, girlfriend. You aren't Miss Perfect, either."

She had me there. I immediately lowered my voice and said, "You are so right. I have lots of flaws. No way am I perfect. I often have to ask forgiveness, and God looks at me through Jesus's sacrifice for my sins. I am able to smile and have joy in my heart – all because of Jesus."

"Good for you, Verity. I didn't think there was anything that could ruffle you. Just now, your eyes smoked, almost blackening my essence into a crispy critter. Are we still friends?"

"Yes. We both had our say. I'm good, if you are."

"I'm chastened and better for it. Now, have you heard the latest? Remember..."

"Girlfriend, please. No gossiping!"

"You are funny. I'm talking about me, Verity."

I shook my head. "Sometimes, Daffodil, I have trouble understanding western culture. Are you wanting to share something with me or stuff people have made up about you?"

"Okay, Verity, I'll make it simple. You know Kenneth and I are going out. Date number seven is coming up this weekend. It started at the kissing booth!"

I chuckled. "That kissing booth certainly has triggered a lot of extra smooches. I reckon you are bursting to tell me about your upcoming date."

"As you often say, Ve, 'spot on' at first guess. We're going to visit his family, who live five hours from here."

"You look so happy. I wish you both a delightful time."

"Thanks, Verity. See you around town or at the Welcome Huggers meeting in a couple of nights."

After she hurried on her way, I found Rosemary and asked her to monitor the front desk for about twenty minutes. I needed to take the dog for a walk and have a cuppa tea.

Stepping outside, I saw Lark leaning against the wall. As I came even with him, he silently joined me. I guessed it was up to me to begin a conversation.

"Were you waiting for me, Lark?"

"Babe, you need to give your dog a name. If you don't do it soon, he will only answer to Puppy!"

"I am working on it, Lark – trying to get it right. Growing up in another culture might have me thinking a bit differently. Sometimes a child in the tribe might not get a "proper" name for two years. Of course I don't plan on waiting that long. You know I do not like being called 'Babe.' Want to hear the names that have either been suggested or that I am contemplating?"

"Okay, my champion defender, share away."

My face flushed, and he noticed.

"Yep, I heard you, Verity, and I'm sure half of the people in the library did, too. For a few seconds, it looked as if they were all going to start clapping. My dear, you look even more beautiful when you blush."

"You must have kissed the Blarney Stone."

"Nope, but I can hardly wait to kiss you, Verity!"

"Yeah, right. I don't think so. I have lived in Welcome for nine months. You had your chance at the kissing booth over five months ago and ignored your opportunity."

"It was too public a location in which to share our first kiss, Babe. There will be a proper time and place."

I gulped. "Oh. Ah. Back to the names for Puppy: Rascal, Happy, Jewel, Hugs, Sunny, Pressie or Present, Comfort, Treasure, Mr. L (which could stand for Listen, Loyal, or Lively). Treasure might be shortened to Tree, which wouldn't be good. Another one was Ragamuffin, but that might give him a complex. Rascal might make him act up. It needs to fit him. Did you guys think of a name when you picked him out?"

"No, we didn't. This past week I've been wondering if 'Angel' would fit his calling."

I stopped walking and so did the dog. "It might fit his calling, but so far, not his personality. He hasn't exactly been angel-like – stealing and shredding boxes of tissues and chewing on shoes. But he is a puppy, so… Angel, sit."

The puppy sat.

"Angel, down."

The puppy lay down.

"Angel, come. Good boy, Angel! Heel, Angel. I do believe we have a winner. Thanks, Lark! Now I need to get back to work."

"Verity, tonight is my turn to fix the meal. Maybe you and I can take a walk afterwards, before it gets dark."

I nodded, but wondered why the sudden frown crossed his face?

*****

"Annie, Fe, I saw Lark today. He's going to fix supper tonight. We named the puppy 'Angel,' and he seems to respond to it."

Welcome Huggers # 2 – Verity

Annie grinned. "Care to share with us what took place at the library between you and Daffodil?"

"Nope. I think you both already know anyway. Now what I'd like is to talk straight with the both of you."

"Are you upset over something we've done, Ve?"

"No way, Fe. You two are the best housemates, ever. I think we need a schedule for such things as cooking, cleaning, TV programs, down-times, laundry – you know, things to make this household run smoothly. I realize it has been just the two or sometimes the three of you, but now Angel and I are added to the mix. Let's start with menus. Do you make them for the week and change off who cooks? Do you pool your money and take turns shopping? Do you usually eat breakfast together, pack your lunch on week days, and have supper together? You have been spoiling me. I want to fit in and do my share of the work."

Fe began, "Before you arrived, there was mostly just the two of us. In five days, we start a new month, so tonight let's work on filling out a calendar to help us get started. Lists will be helpful as to what groceries we need, foods each of us does not like, and who cooks on which days. It's a start. We can address other concerns as they show up. Your honesty and suggestions will always be welcome, Verity."

"Thanks. Another question. Are you two going to the same premiere Lark and I are attending?"

Annie muttered, "Um, we are still thinking about it."

My tongue got ahead of my brain censor. "No dates, you've seen it, or...?"

"Wow, girl. You do cut to the quick!" Annie continued. "We'd like to go, but don't want to go alone or with the men from the Ghost Town. As you know, neither of us have a boyfriend, so we might just go together."

I glanced at them, grinned, and boldly said, "I've heard JC and JJ, Mercy's twin brothers, aren't dating anyone. Why don't you call them? First, though, might I recommend you talk to each other to make sure you don't want a date with the same guy? I heard that has happened once already with two of the Welcome Huggers. Clear the air between the two of you, then call them at

58

the same time. That sounded rather bossy, eh? Sorry; just a suggestion."

Later, I heard the sisters calling to me as they hurried down the stairs. "Verity? Ve, we did as you advised. Are you sure you aren't in the matchmaking business?"

Fe giggled. "Can I hug you? They both said yes without even hesitating! I'm going with JC, and Annie is going with JJ. Thank you! You gave us the courage to ask."

My mind was elsewhere. I was holding Angel, absently petting him as I tried to decide where he should spend the evening on "premiere night."

"Good. Do you think I should call and find out if Angel can have a play date with Gem, or do you think he should get used to staying home alone and in his crate? I would hate leaving him in the crate. If he chooses to be given to a wounded warrior, I doubt he will ever live in one."

The sisters laughed. "You are so funny. I can just see it all now: you making Lark bring you home early because Angel might be lonely. You know something crazy, Ve? We can actually envision Lark doing it for you, too."

I shook my head. "Don't you dare even hint at such a thing. It is Lark's night, and no dog, however tempting, would make me sabotage his triumph in this new venture."

Mercy and I had talked about how Annie was finally beginning to relax and enjoy life. I smiled as she reached out, saying, "Here, let me hold Angel. You are so fiercely funny, girl. It is so great having you here." We laughed as Angel gave her nose a wet kiss.

"I love hearing you three laughing," Lark's voice interrupted.

Three of us shrieked, and Angel barked.

I frowned. "Don't creep up on us! You scared us half to death. You military fellows seem to be able to tread so softly, it is scary. Maybe we need to put a bell on you."

Lark ignored my comment. "If someone would nuke the potatoes, I'll soon fire up the barbecue and cook the steaks and corn." He twisted the lock on the door, then said, "I thought you always locked the doors."

Welcome Huggers # 2 – Verity

"We do, but you're right; we need to be more careful. By the way, our WHUG group – Welcome Huggers, that is – will be meeting here two nights from now."

Fe softly queried, "Why did you volunteer our place, Annie? You know we have to clean and make goodies and then when they are gone, clean again."

"Fe, we aren't very busy at the florist shop right now. Since it is just once a year, I figured we'd better get it over with."

"Sorry I was cross. You're right, sister. Besides, we now have extra hands to help!" Fe said, flashing a smile at me. "But right now, I'll fix the salad. Annie, how about setting the table? Ve, put ice in three of the four glasses, and fill a pitcher with water."

As I followed Fe's direction, I saw Lark heading out the door and hollered, "Hey, Lark, would you please put my potato on the grill? I like it crispy on the outside."

*****

As soon as we were seated around the table, the steaming food before us, Fe announced, "Let's pray. *Heavenly Father, we are grateful for Jesus, who died and rose again so that we can live with you forever. We are thankful for all who have served or are serving our country so we are free to sit down and enjoy this meal together in peace. Please bless this food by strengthening our bodies. Thank you for friends and family and sending Verity to live with us. In Jesus's name, Amen.*"

As we dished up, Annie broke the silence. "What have you been up to this day, brother, dear?"

"Making the final cuts for a commercial and looking at a few new scripts. I did some research at the library and helped give pups the name 'Angel.' Since I fixed supper, you females get to do the clean-up. Oh, yeah, one more thing: I made sure Sheriff Ben knows I am living here – permanently."

I almost laughed at his tone. It was as if he'd expected some dissention from me. I caught Lark's eye, then asked, "Do you have nightmares or tend to walk in your sleep?"

60

He frowned and growled, "That's a sucker punch. Why do you ask? You afraid I'll come uninvited into your room?"

I gulped. "What? No – not at all! I was thinking that maybe I should put Angel in his crate, but leave the door open in order to see if he will go assist you in the way Boo or Gem might."

Lark hesitated, obviously debating whether or not to share his thoughts. We three waited quietly.

He finally admitted, a bit sheepishly, "I just can't wrap my head around your thinking sometimes, Ve."

I looked at him, grinned, then calmly stated, "It is called 'communication,' Lark. Talking back and forth until we each grasp the other's meaning. Oh, my! Look at your sisters' faces. Their eyes have been flying back and forth between us and each other. Care to share what is going on with you two?"

Annie said, "Neither one of you raised your voice. We expected fireworks out of Lark. He actually listened to what you were saying; he didn't get huffy, shout, or get up and walk out."

I laughed. "Maybe he is too hungry to leave. My personal theory is that men like just facts so they can 'fix' things. Remember, this is just my opinion, but we females often tend to go by our gut feelings and emotional responses. I've worked with both men and women in various jobs. I personally have found, for the most part, that it is easier working with men."

"Yeah, but you do lose it sometimes, Verity – like today," Lark broke in. "I was astonished at your verbal attack on Daffodil on my behalf."

Feeling the intent focus of six eyes, I changed the subject.

"Lark, are we taking that walk before dark that you suggested? If so, we need to move – now. We won't be too long, ladies. I'll be back to help with the dishes. Then, it is lists and planning time for the four of us."

I had noticed Lark had a wee bit of trouble with stairs, so I deliberately slowed my pace to match his. I tried to disguise this fact by working with Angel.

"Sit, Angel. Heel. So, Lark, what did Sheriff Ben want you to share with me?"

"Just a minute. What or who caused you to take the sheriff aside at the restaurant to have that private word?"

"Two things: my gut instinct, plus Sam catching my eye and moving his head just a tad."

"I'm not following. Be more specific. Exactly what tipped you off to keep from divulging your secret in front of everyone?"

"I will tell you, but only if you promise not to share it with your sisters. They would act differently towards a certain person at the Welcome Huggers meeting. Promise?"

"If you think it is serious, Babe, of course I promise not to tell them."

"Marigold said some things to Sam and me that I know to be false. I don't trust her. At the party, Sam was looking over her shoulder as she texted. He caught my eye and twitched, or shook his head a smidgen. Later, when I was near her, I smelled a faint scent of oranges. But to be fair, that scent might have been on my own clothes after those guys hugged me."

"So you watch, listen, and pay close attention to your instincts. What do they tell you about me?"

I noticed a limousine driving very slowly down the street, but the tinted windows were too dark for me to see inside. Angel noticed it, too, his ears pricking up as he stared in the direction of the vehicle.

"My gut is telling me it is time to go home," I said to Lark. "Look at Angel; he is on full alert. I've never seen a limo driving down our street before. It certainly is going extremely slowly."

"Ve, why did you let go of my arm? What are you doing?"

"Taking the loop from the leash off of my wrist so I can hold it in my hand. I want to be able to drop it rather than get it entangled around our legs."

"Right – a survival tactic. You are hurrying me," he said as I rushed towards the house. Angel stopped at a nearby bush, much to my dismay.

"I know. I am extremely uneasy. Whew, I am pleased to be almost to the porch. Angel stop!"

"Babe, you are so funny. You can't tell a dog to stop peeing on something!"

"Should I have used the words 'leave it'? Guess 'stop' is not yet in his vocabulary." I looked down as Angel stepped away from the bush. "Look, Lark. There is twine and a note attached to a rock. Angel compromised the evidence." I pulled out my cell phone and punched in the number for the sheriff's office. After finishing the call, I said, "Now, while we wait for a deputy to arrive, what did the sheriff want you to tell me? I know that's why you moved in with us so quickly."

"One question first: have you talked to the sheriff about your suspicions?"

"Not yet. I am hoping Sam will talk to either me, Sheriff Ben, or you. I don't want to get between him and his girlfriend, although I don't think they are connected anymore. I have never thought she fit his personality as well as two others would."

"Right. Okay. The sheriff said there have been a couple of reports from some bartenders and shop owners. Since Mercy's abduction, they keep their ears open for the slightest hint of a problem concerning any female in our three towns. Someone described you, but seemed not to know your name. Another reported a guy claiming to have been a friend of your brother, but said he had lost track of him. Your birthday party sort of blew your cover, so the sheriff is taking this very seriously. One of the deputies will be moving in with us and staying until this is resolved."

"Please share this with your sisters. We are – you included – making shopping lists, duty rosters, etc. for the next month, and need to program whoever it is into the mix. Do you know if it is a male or female deputy? I reckon you'd prefer a male, or maybe not. Four females in a house with you might just be a dream come true – or a nightmare."

"Wouldn't you like to know?" Lark replied with a sparkle in his eye.

"Yeah, I would; however, I'll soon suss it out from your demeanor. Should be intriguing times!"

Shortly after that, Sheriff Ben himself approached us.

"I decided to come myself to bag the evidence. Neither of you touched it, did you?" he said, squatting down to examine the rock.

"No, sheriff, we left that for you."

Nine

This home was noisy and fun, but rarely at rest. Some days, I found it a bit overwhelming, due to years of being a loner. Angel brought a lot of laughter and comfort. Each day, he required time dedicated to grooming, playing, and schooling. I often wondered who the teacher was – Angel, or me. Acceptance, patience, and a willingness to learn were three of Angel's positive attributes.

Sam surprised us by arriving in uniform with a badge, a gun, and Boo by his side. While we congratulated him, I wondered if I could question Sam now that he was an official lawman. I wanted to talk about Marigold, but now felt that I couldn't.

"Why are you here, Sam?"

"Boo and I are to be your bodyguards, Verity."

"So you are the deputy moving in with us?"

"Affirmative."

I clapped my hands. "Oh, good, you can guard the house and babysit Angel while we all go out Saturday night."

Sam retorted, "Just a minute, now."

I rushed on. "Look at it this way, Sam. You will have time to check the house from top to bottom, figure out our weaknesses and strengths. You and Boo can work a little with Angel, plus there will be a huge steak waiting just for you. Otherwise, you can put your feet up, vegetate, or arrange your stuff."

He relaxed and grinned. "When you put it like that, what's not to like? Is Lark around? Am I rooming with Lark, or...?"

"Well, Sam, you aren't rooming with any of us girls!"

Lark piped up. "That is good to hear! Are they trying to give you a hard time, Sam?"

"Nothing I can't handle, Lark. They remind me of my sisters. I'm glad you're here; we need to talk."

I wasn't about to be ignored. "Hey, if it has to do with me, Sam, then I want in on it. If it is other stuff, count me out."

Marilyn Stewart

"How about Lark and I talk, then all five of us will get together. Right now, why don't you girls take the dogs and work with them in the backyard."

Fe proclaimed, "I think we were politely told to get lost. Time to exercise the pooches. Annie and I need to leave for work soon, but a bit of fresh air will do us all good."

We worked with the dogs for a bit, running through commands such as sit, down, stay, come, no, fetch, bring, out, drop, and heel. As each command was obeyed, we praised them with a hearty, "Good boys!"

I said to the sisters, "I've noticed that Boo, being military trained, versus Angel, who's been house-trained, understand the word 'out' differently. I plan to stick with the one-word military-type commands, but use 'drop' rather than 'out' since Angel will think he'll get to go outside. Boo will just need to learn one more word. I'll check with Sam."

"Don't they ever tire of fetching the balls, Ve?"

"Hey, you two, I'm new to this, but so far it is as if after they rest for a second, they become totally recharged."

"Wish I could do that, especially on long days with lots of orders to fill," Fe said. "Annie, I want you to know you have been a double answer to prayer. I certainly missed you and Lark all those years. Just at the time when I desperately needed encouragement and help, you two arrived back in my life."

Annie reminisced. "Katie and Jeff coming to the Ghost Town on their first date was a miracle. A God thing. Katie calling out your full name Fe, still gives me goosebumps. The hard, missing years of struggle fade a little more each day with all the joy we are experiencing right now."

During the lull in conversation, I said, "One of these days, I hope you will share your stories with me. You know about a large chunk of my life. I'd really like to get to know you two better."

"Right, Ve, is this with an eye to learning about our brother? We'd love to have you for a sister. We have already become like family. Angel even obeys us!"

"I really like you both. I figure if I want to know anything about Lark, I will ask him straight out. If he is not forthcoming, I might just have to ask you two."

65

"Good to know!" a manly voice broke in.

I jumped. "You guys are so sneaky! That is what Annie and Fe's eyes were trying to tell me. I saw them glance behind me, but was concentrating on Angel obeying my hand signals. I can see I need to respond quicker and not focus so intently on only one thing."

"Some good concepts of survival are developing situational awareness," Sam replied. "Trust your gut, be ready to change direction quickly, and never take anything for granted. Thus ends the lesson. You three have done a good job with the dogs. I am starting a class next Tuesday night where we will work to further your skills. Angel will be a puppy until he is two years old. He needs to have short, ten-minute lessons, mornings and evenings. Remember, to me, it is always 'bad owner,' rather than a bad puppy. Some breeds are harder to train, but not impossible."

"Thank you, Sam, for that information. Now, what do you plan to share regarding my situation?"

"Everyone needs to go about their normal activities. Today, Boo and I will go with Verity and Angel to the library. Hopefully, some kids will be there wanting to read to Boo and Angel, which will make everything appear normal. Your Welcome Huggers meeting will take place here tonight as planned."

Annie coughed. "You know those girlfriends are going to want to snoop through the house. What can we make off limits? The guy's room and the study, maybe? To satisfy their curiosity, we'll have to take them upstairs. Do we fix up the spare room, make the bed, and add some clothes? Sam and Lark, are you both going to be home tonight? Do you plan to put in a brief appearance so everyone knows you are nearby, or...?"

Fe looked at the men and softly admitted, "We have single women from all walks of life in our group. I am sorry to say this, but a couple of our most cruel of tongue are church-goers." The sorrow and truthfulness with which Fe, the gentlest of souls, reported the facts kept the men silent.

Annie added, "I hate to add to your disillusionment, but for your protection, there are three who are definitely on the prowl. They would be happy to put either or both of you in a compromising situation. You might want to stay together and keep both dogs with you."

Sam shook his head. "That is so depressing. Really? No lie? Nah, you three are just yanking us around."

I casually stated my views. "Men can be so very naive about women." Sighing, I stood. "Come, Angel. See you all tonight, and you, Sam, in a bit at the library."

*****

"Being on edge certainly made for a long day. I wish I knew who it is, what they want, how they found me, and after all the months I have been here – why now? Sam, is there anything you can share with me, or should I call the Sheriff?"

"Feel free to call Sheriff Ben."

"Right. Sam, I have two questions I hope you will answer truthfully. Have you told the Sheriff what Marigold was texting at my party, and has the Sheriff shared with you what I told him?"

"The answer to both is 'yes,' but I can't tell you what was in her text. We don't know who or why you are being targeted."

"Sam, I have been conjecturing some wild scenarios. I wonder if it has less to do with me, and maybe more to do with the twins. Could it be possible they are heirs or leverage in some way, and thus in jeopardy?"

"I suppose it is a better reason than we have come up with, which is that the rapist wants you dead."

"That is crazy. He knows I didn't see him, and that his DNA is in the system, so why harass me?"

"We'll do our best to find and neutralize the threat as quickly as possible. I won't be too far from you – even tonight at your meeting. And Ve, be careful what you eat or drink."

"You are scaring me, Sam. Honestly? Food, in our home?"

"Maybe I'm being extra cautious, but existing in a state of alertness might someday save your life."

*****

Welcome Huggers # 2 – Verity

It was amazing how having Sam and Boo living with us had changed the atmosphere in our home. Lark was more relaxed, and Angel promptly copied Boo's actions – no more piddling inside!

Ten

I exhaled. "Thanks for fixing the lunch sandwiches for us, Fe. The guys said they'd be home by five tonight to barbecue. Do either of you remember if there was a discussion question for tonight at our Welcome Huggers get together?"

"Ve, I think it was left as a free-for-all, so we can chat about anything. Something on your mind?"

"I really liked the retreat format, where each person gave a short talk. I learned a lot with all the different themes covered and would love to hear more, as well as from some of the new ladies."

"Last night, you cooked treats for tonight, Ve. So we had time to move Annie into the room across from me. Now, the girlfriends will learn each bedroom is occupied and not ask to move in with us. If one of them wishes to stay overnight sometime, we can set up the extra single bed. Ve, what do you think of our brother, Lark? We know you are going out with him soon, but how well do you like him?"

"That was a quick switch of topics, Fe. I am conflicted. I feel like we have a connection – a bond, but he can't seem to permit his mouth to say what his eyes suggest. I know he is in a lot of pain, which makes him a little surly at times. He can be funny, endearing even. He seems like a really nice guy. Ah, well, early days. I hope if nothing blooms between us, we girls will remain friends. I like living here and wouldn't want to jeopardize our arrangement."

"Of course you can stay here regardless, but Annie and I have talked about it, and we'd love to have you for a sister."

"Let's talk about something else. It is as if the walls have ears sometimes. I was wondering if you two might like to go hiking or biking some evening or weekend. Saturday can be a busy day, so that might not work. I could help deliver flowers, if things get busy. I am feeling really antsy about staying so close to home."

I did the lunch dishes so Fe and Annie could return to work for a couple of hours. With that job done, I moved slowly up the stairs to my room. I snuggled with Angel, then sat at my desk to work on my library 'wish' list. My mind kept wandering to things that needed doing. I had briefly consulted Brenda, a Welcome

Hugger and lawyer, upon my arrival over a trivial matter. After much thought, I realized she didn't need to know my secrets.

Finally, the Welcome Huggers began arriving, and the meeting was called to order.

"Welcome, ladies," Jasmine, the current president began. "In the last eight months, we've lost three members. Tonight, we need to elect new officers. As you can see, we have the names of three or four ladies for each position. Please mark your ballot, fold, and place it in the basket."

"Don't we get a say in taking our name off?" one of the ladies asked. "The committee never asked me, or I would tell them I am dyslexic. For me, being the secretary would be a nightmare."

"I'm so glad Connie spoke up. I can barely balance my check book. I would really like to help out where I am needed, but you truly don't want me as your treasurer," another remarked.

"Hmm. Anyone else need to share a glitch in our ballot? No? Okay, strike through the names of Connie and Amie Lynn. We'll find other tasks they will be able to help with in the future."

Jasmine announced, "Our President for the next six months is Brenda; Vice-president, Carolyn; Secretary, Lacey; and Treasurer, Jewel. Let's give them a round of applause. As of the next meeting, Brenda will be in charge. Our cruise is scheduled to take place in three months. Next week, we will be calling all the single ladies in our towns. The following week, all will be expected to give a firm yea or nay and pay a third of the payment. Now is the time for questions, comments, get-together suggestions for this coming month, and our discussion time."

As I got up to go into the kitchen, I heard, "Verity, get back here. I have a question for you."

I replied, "I will be right back. I promise, Marigold."

"No. I want you to answer right now as to why Sam is living here. Now he is a deputy, does he look better to you than he did before? Is it not enough for you to get your hooks into Lark, but now my boyfriend is living in the same house as well?"

I let out a relieved sigh when Fe took over.

"Marigold, Annie and I invited Sam to stay here. You know when he arrived in town, he lived with the Unique family. Once

Unity was married, Sam no longer felt comfortable living there. You know he has lived briefly at the Ghost Town; however, since his new job, living in town makes sense. Yes, our brother Lark is living here, also. Sam and Lark are sharing a room since they both suffer from PTSD. Boo helps them."

Annie added, "Marigold, you told Sam you wanted to go out with other guys. Doesn't sound as if he is your boyfriend any longer, now, does it? Maybe you want him back now he has a new job and is living in a house with three available Welcome Huggers."

"Fe, you and Annie have all the answers, don't you! It doesn't mean Verity is not..."

Jasmine spoke. "Enough. Open discussion does not mean slander, Marigold, and you are nearing the edge."

"Sorry. Things lately have been terribly upsetting for me."

"Let's break for refreshments. When we come back, we'll discuss ways to make our club better and gain more members."

As Heather stood, she asked, "Would you show us your home, and when we regroup, how about sharing tips on how the five of you seem to live together in apparent harmony?"

Since the house belonged to Fe, Annie and I made a deep bow and a sweeping hand wave in her direction. Fe started up the stairs, followed by all the girlfriends. I didn't realize I was frowning until Annie asked, "What's wrong, Ve?"

"What if one of them is a scout? You know, here to get information – especially the house layout?"

"When they come back down, we will invite them to the kitchen for goodies, tell them the rest of the area is off limits, and escort them back into the living room. Shouldn't be too hard. They can use the restroom since the stairs block it off from the study and the guys' room. We three can rotate near the stairs and block any attempted access to the men."

"Good idea, Annie. How about after they are settled, you begin by sharing how we started with discussions and lists. We can share about the puzzle here and our once-a-week quiet evening. Fe and I can add tips and bits to clarify. I guess this might be called a 'teachable moment.' Let's make the most of it. Will you clue Fe in so we present a unified front?"

Welcome Huggers # 2 – Verity

A manly whisper came from the 'forbidden' zone. "Good, girls. When there's time, planning ahead is a wise strategy."

In the end, it turned into a profitable time of questions and answers. We stressed the importance of words, as in using 'please' and 'thank you.' The last critical ingredient in a peaceful home, Fe concluded, was attitude. A point of interest was whether or not the guys cooked and did laundry or the dishes. The girls were happy to know they did all three.

The Welcome Huggers were preparing to depart when we heard a man's voice outside. He was loudly proclaiming, "I need to speak to Marigold. I was told she'd be here."

We heard Sam boom, "Who are you? State your business. Wait until their meeting ends in a few minutes."

Marigold pushed by me, then elbowed and wiggled past everyone. Hurrying out the door, she eagerly said, "Hi, Ronnie. Are these your kids, Daniel and Pansy? What are you doing here?"

"Goldie, do you respect me?" the man queried.

"Of course! I love you, Ronnie. I've loved you since junior high, when you kissed me on a bet."

"What I asked, Marigold, was not 'do you love me,' but 'do you respect me?' I heard a preacher a while back talk about the difference between men and women when it comes to love. He mentioned how in the Bible it talks about a woman respecting, not necessarily loving, her husband. The preacher said, 'If she can respect a man, only then will she truly love him. It is not a question of whether he can make a lot of money, but of his integrity, his character, and work ethic. It is not the color of his hair, his eyes, or his looks.' So I will ask you again, Goldie, do you respect me?"

"Ronald Tryon Bakers, I respect the way you cared for your wife when she was dying; the way you make your children a matter of priority; are hard-working; love to help people, whether they go to your church or not, and besides, I do think you are good-looking."

"In that case, I desire to make our home one of communication, commitment, honesty, and peace. Marigold Amber Harworth, will you marry me?"

"Oh, Ronnie, for sure? YES! YES! Let's go home."

"Not so fast, Goldie. We messed up when we were younger, but this time we are going to get it right. I have a minister waiting to hear if we are coming tonight to talk. Afterward, we will set a date, go to counseling, get married, and only then will we live together, as man and wife. Understood?"

"I can hardly believe it. Hey, girlfriends, never give up on your dreams. Mine are coming true. Sweet man, I love you! Let's go see that preacher."

"Marigold, do you need to do anything before we go?"

"Nope. Well, yes, I do. Verity, I'm sorry I blasted you – sorry for my unruly tongue and jealous heart. Please forgive me and try to forget my words."

I nodded, saying, "Yes, I forgive you. Congratulations and the very best of wishes for your future."

Marigold sucked in a deep breath. "Ah, there is one other thing. What I told you and Sam about my background wasn't true. I was actually raised in an orphanage."

"We know you lied to us."

"Well, I want a clean slate. Ronnie is an upright man, and I do so love him. I am truly sorry, Verity."

"We each have vulnerable areas in our lives, Marigold. You are now aware of yours. Remember, girlfriend, it is God who makes us clean and forgives us totally."

Sam cleared his throat. "Before you leave, I need to know where you got your information that I am a deputy and living here. It is extremely important. The truth, the whole truth, and nothing but the truth, please, Marigold."

"Sam, I'm sorry I lied to you several times. I got a text message this morning. Honest."

Sam nodded and raised his voice. "Did any of you ladies get a text about me, and if so, do you still have it?" A number of women raised their hands. Sam checked their phones to see what time they received the message.

"So, seven of you got the information around noon. Did you respond? You three, please take your phones and go immediately to the police station. Ask for Tom. Thanks, ladies. Safe travels home."

Welcome Huggers # 2 – Verity

When all the ladies had gone, I dropped into a recliner. "Whew, what a night. I am exhausted. Annie and Fe, you were magnificent. Thanks for pitching in on my behalf with calmness, reason, and sanity concerning Sam." I looked around. "Speaking of Sam, I wonder how he is doing. He went out with Katie, but that didn't last more than a couple of months. He begins to date Marigold, and in one breath she says he is her boyfriend, and almost the next, answers yes to a proposal of marriage from an old flame."

Fe smiled. "It certainly looks as if Marigold will soon be absent from our group, and for her, I am pleased. Ron appears to have her number, yet love her unconditionally, if we base our assumptions on the words and kiss we just witnessed."

I nodded and admitted, "Life has certainly perked up since you invited me to live here. One more thing done – as in hosting the girlfriends group for this year."

"Are you not happy to be with us, Ve?"

"Oh, Fe, don't fret. I love the interaction and fun we have been enjoying these past weeks. It is adjusting from extreme quiet to people, bustle, and Angel, that at times is a tussle to my emotions. Speaking of Angel, we'd better go outside for a bit."

"Not by yourself, my dear," a man's voice stopped me.

"See, that's the thing, Lark! You popping up unexpectedly and overhearing stuff – it's like being monitored. It is unsettling. If I don't hear you, then I am likely to miss hearing a prowler."

"Babe, don't you know Angel would alert you in a second to a stranger? The five of us are family to him, and he knows it. You've seen how he acts when a stranger arrives. He is learning from Boo, who is large enough to scare the wits out of anyone. Now stop fretting."

"That makes sense, Lark, thanks; however, that word 'Babe' has got to go. Excuse me while I take Angel out. Please do not put on the porch light – it would give a prowler or shooter a perfect target and destroy my night vision, which by the way, is excellent."

74

Fe waited until I had shut the door behind me. I found out from her later what the family discussion had been about.

Fe said, "Lark, what is it with you and Verity? Annie and I thought you might love her. You don't seem to have made a move in the, what, seven months you've known her? She's lived here for almost three weeks. Andrew and Bret are set to ask her out. They're only holding back due to you. She'll go out with them – maybe just to check your reaction."

"I like getting to really know her – here at home – don't want to mess that up. Besides, I have other reasons. Remember, we're having an official date on Saturday."

"I hear a 'but' coming – like you don't even have a plan for a future date. Oh, my goodness, Annie, do you realize Lark has yet to make a move to even kiss her?! No wonder she doesn't know if they are headed in any direction except as friends."

"Ah, come on sisters, she could have any fellow. I am biding my time, staying close, waiting and watching."

"Good grief, you guys can be as dense as a wooden fence post! Remember the kissing booth last fall? Why do you think she put you down as the number one guy she wanted to have kiss her! Maybe you are just too chicken to share a smoking hot kiss with a beautiful lady."

"Maybe I just want to get it right, Annie. You know, the right place and time for our first kiss."

"Ah, brother, that is so sweet, but you are missing the point of kissing. Instead of planning for perfection, you should practice enjoying an impulsive, instinctive, heart-blowing smooch. You'll lose her if you don't soon make some sort of advance."

"Don't laugh. I feel that when I kiss Verity, I will never let her go. She has had so much grief. I ache for her and know for a fact I'd die rather than let anything else bad happen to her. I haven't even held her hand, yet I want to cherish her forever. Now, are you both happy? Leave us alone."

"We're not laughing. We're thrilled that love has a tight hold on you. Tell her your heart, not us. We want her for our sister-in-love. Fe and I think there is something else, far more serious, holding you back that you don't want to think or talk about, let alone face."

"Yeah, brother, dear, we are of the opinion that neither you nor Verity have yet accepted your present bodies. You'd both like to go back in time to around three years ago."

"I know I would for sure, but Verity is perfect."

Fe sputtered, "Really, Bro? I could scream. Of course, she is lovely in every way. Now, don't interrupt, just listen. She has carried twins, without...hmm...how do I put this delicately...?"

At that moment, I walked back into the room.

"I heard that," I said. "I'm glad you think I'm perfect, Lark. My body changed significantly due to being pregnant. I much preferred my old shape. Some days I struggle not to hate this new me. Where is Sam? Two people are in our backyard. One is sitting up on that wooden platform, and the foot of another is visible by a tree trunk."

"I'll call Sheriff Ben and see if these are his people."

"Thanks, Lark. Angel and I are headed for bed. Don't worry, I'll not put my light on. 'Night, all."

*****

After I'd prepared for bed, I kneeled by my bedside to pray.

"God, I'm so tired. I'm scared someone will get hurt because they are near me. Please protect each of us. Everything is so vague about why or who... I look around and see family groupings, and I so miss my family. Many days, it is really hard to be cheerful and upbeat. Now, God, I am thankful for Angel, Peter, Charity, and their families; Annie, Fe, Lark, Sam, Mercy, and the Welcome Huggers. I haven't a clue if Lark is Your intended for me, but I like him – a lot. Do you think Lark might be scared of the slim possibility that I might have to raise the twins? Thanks for loving me – always. Give my love to my family up there with you. Amen."

I wiped my eyes and climbed into bed. "Up, Angel. I should have named you 'Comfort,' for you certainly help me relax and feel loved."

Angel gently growled, then I heard a whisper. "It's Lark, Verity. I know you are crying. Can I get the girls for you, or maybe we could share a hug?"

Marilyn Stewart

I sniffed. "Go away. Mind your own business."

"I climbed the stairs for the first time, just for you. Why won't you come out? I just want to give you a hug, Verity. You could pretend I am your father or brother."

"Are you crazy? You aren't either one. No way could I stretch my brain to think of you in that way."

"Verity, girl, please come out. I saw the tears running down your face as you climbed the stairs. I can't leave you to cry yourself to sleep. Put on your robe and come out – please."

"Sit, stay, on guard, Angel. So you are willing to hug any female in the house who is crying?" I demanded when I threw open my door.

"Hush, my dear. Just relax your head against my chest and lean against me. I will lightly encircle you with my arms, then I want you to go quietly to bed."

"Thanks, Lark. Good night."

"I knew you'd not be able to leave without talking. Hug Angel, and good dreams, Verity, love."

As I once more crawled into bed, I savored the reluctant withdrawal of his arms and his kiss on top of my head.

Eleven

Tonight was one of those nights when the weather cooperated, everyone was home, and we girls had persuaded the men to sit on the porch. On nights like this, we enjoyed the sunset – some nights in silence, but more often, we shared events from our day. I treasured each of these special times. It was Sam who first referred to one of these interactions as having a clarifying moment. Fe had laughed, saying the guys' future wives would owe us, big time. As I checked the men's faces and body language, I often became privy early to topics they wished to avoid. Tonight, we arranged our chairs in a curve. The sky was filled with clouds, so we expected to witness a magnificent sunset.

I suddenly had a thought – no one had checked the mail. Even though I rarely received any, I jumped up and dashed down the steps, hollering, "I'll check and see if the Postie left us any mail." I ignored Sam's concerned comment and kept going.

The mailbox itself was enclosed inside and near the top of a four foot high, three foot wide brick structure. Visibility from the porch was mostly obscured due to a tall hedge that ran from the brick structure to the right for fifteen feet. Just before reaching my destination, I briefly wondered if this might be a bad idea. Tossing my head, I told myself that fear would not deter me.

For the last ten years, whenever I opened a mailbox, I always did the same thing. I stood to the left of the box, pulled down the lid, and only after a few seconds had passed would I move to where I could peek inside. I did this now.

An object flew past my head, and my survival response kicked in. I squatted, placed one hand on the ground, ready to spring up, and glanced over my shoulder as I heard a grunt, followed by a shriek. I slowly stood up to face a very unhappy young woman who had sneaked up behind me, and I was barely able to stifle my laughter. I heard my housemates racing towards us.

Annie, with a grin on her face and hands on hips, said to the newcomer, "Well, that plan certainly backfired on you, didn't it, girlfriend! It's going to be you instead of one of us who is covered in green… for a long time."

Casey, a Welcome Hugger, muttered, "Yeah, just my dumb luck to have it hit me."

Fe sputtered, "That was some dye pack. Where did you get it, and why? Which one of us were you aiming to splat?"

Casey raised her head. "I found it on the Internet. It's all Verity's fault. I told you to stay away from Ian. He is mine!"

I protested, "How many times do I have to tell you, Casey, I am NOT interested in him! He keeps mooning me."

"He'd never do that! He is not a pervert. You lie, Verity!"

I was adamant. "No, I do not! He does so."

Fe and Annie began to laugh. "Verity, we think your lack of understanding American slang is again causing a problem."

I was sure I had used the correct word, so sought to justify myself. "My dad once said that Peter was mooning around Rose like a love-sick calf."

I glanced at Sam, then Lark. They were trying to hide their grins. Suddenly, Casey began to laugh. Annie leaned over and whispered in my ear. I could feel my face heating due to the image now in my head. Deciding mirth might help, I laughed, then sighed, saying, "Oh dear, not again. Sorry, Casey."

Casey began to lament. "I read the instructions and cautions. This green will take ages to wear off. It will certainly be a daily reminder of my sin of jealousy. I'm glad there's only a bit on you, but I'm sorry it probably ruined your blouse, Verity."

As I studied the full extent of the damage Casey had done to herself, my lips twitched from the effort to withhold the giggles. Casey would be horrified when she saw herself in the mirror. She was just plain green – from her hair, all the way to her shoes. Too bad she was wearing shorts and a sleeveless blouse. A thought popped into my head and right out my mouth. "Casey, if I were you, I'd immediately find Ian and confess all. By the way, I think he likes me only because I listen to him."

Several high fives and giggles later, Casey dashed over to her car. Over her shoulder floated the words, "Really, really sorry, Verity."

We watched to see if she'd check her face in the rearview mirror – she didn't. I hoped she wouldn't see it while she was driving, nor anyone else, before she found Ian.

Now that she was gone, we girls burst out laughing. "She is greener than the 'Hulk' on TV."

I sputtered, "Wow! Glad it missed me. I'd sure like to witness Ian's face when he sees her."

Annie moaned, "Too bad none of us had a camera! Maybe we should call Jeff at the paper – or maybe not, as he'll hear about it soon enough." She noted my stillness and followed my finger.

I turned to see that the men had begun walking back, and yelled, "SAM!" I signaled him to return. While there were several letters on the ground – all now green – there was also a small box. In spite of the dye, we could all see a deeply etched V. In order to preserve what evidence the dye had not destroyed, we kept Angel and Boo at a distance. Sam was tempted to permit Boo to sniff it; however, caution prevailed. While the guys stayed by the mailbox to meet the forensics team, we took the dogs with us. As they fetched and played, we giggled about how Casey's 'prank' had backfired.

Meanwhile, Lark asked Sam, "Does Verity always open the mailbox like that – standing off to the side?"

"Yes, she does. Verity has an inch long, thin scar at the top of her right shoulder. She was lucky. It was ten years ago. She was a lot shorter. Someone had called her name, so she stepped a little to the left as she pulled the mailbox lid down. The explosion only gave her a glancing blow."

Lark looked appalled. "Why? Who? Were they caught?"

"Hey, man, you were in the military. Her family didn't always live in the most secure of places. When I questioned her, Verity shrugged and answered, 'Probably someone was trying out a homemade pipe bomb.' And yes, I've seen her scar – looks like an amateur stitched it."

Lark murmured, "It's a wonder she even goes near a mailbox. I'm continually surprised by Verity's strength of character and ability to face her fears. Here's the forensics team. I'll go back to the house and check on her."

Marilyn Stewart

My shakes had calmed due to chatter, petting Angel, hot tea, and biscuits so that when Sam arrived, I was able to calmly apologize.   I had been truly humbled. In future, I promised to follow his advice regarding threat assessments and suggestions.

Twelve

I was just leaving my room when I heard Sam calling, "Ladies! Breakfast is ready. Come and get it while it's hot."

Fe asked, "To what do we owe this treat? Smells great."

"Sam and I decided to start the morning with a good breakfast in the company of three beauties. Where's the third?"

Sam's voice was loud and clear, "Flip you, Lark, to see who gets to go wake Sleeping Beauty."

Annie quipped, "Here's a quarter. Shall I flip it for you? I dare one of you to go wake Verity with a kiss."

I'd eavesdropped enough and entered the room.

"I heard that, Annie. Something smells really yummy. It's still dark out and my day off, but I couldn't pass up the chance to check out the culinary expertise of our male roomies. I can always go back to bed after you lot go to work. Hi, Sheriff. Thanks, Sam, for sitting guard in the eucalyptus tree the other night. Who was near the tree on the left?"

"For a bit, I was, but we moved around during the night. We now have three suspects to interrogate. Sam tracked each of them to their residences. I'm starved. Bring on the food. Been a long time since I was on a stake-out."

"Wow, Sheriff Ben, you take protecting and serving seriously. I mean, way beyond what I'd ever expect. It is all so nebulous. Maybe I should be used as bait to draw the person or persons out and get this situation resolved quickly. I could be a danger to everyone here, including Angel and Boo."

Fe interrupted. "Verity, it is your turn to give thanks before our meal. Everyone link arms with the person next to you."

"Dear Heavenly Father. Thank you for these three men and their gifts of serving and protecting. Thank you for Fe and Annie, and their open hearts and home. Thank you for Boo and Angel and their gifts of comfort and defense. Thanks and please strengthen our bodies due to this lovely food. Help us to find ways to help others today. In Jesus's name. Amen."

"Maybe next time ask Verity to give thanks before the meal is dished up and while it is still hot, or after we've eaten."

I grumbled, "That's harsh, Sheriff. I think God prefers a few words of gratitude more than us having a super-hot meal."

Sheriff Ben dug in. After loading his plate a second time, he smiled and started to talk.

"Great breakfast. Thanks, Fe, for refilling my mug. Now for a few updates. Thanks to Angel peeing on the earlier evidence, forensics was not able to retrieve any information at all; maybe this time, we'll get lucky. Today, the forensics team will begin work on this new package. The text messages to some of the Welcome Huggers about Sam were sent through a generic computer program. One of the persons who came by late last evening is staying at the hostel in Unique. I had a word with the owners – Unity's parents, Eb and El Unique. The fellow checked in as 'Paul Ward,' he's staying in room nine, and he pre-paid for four days."

The shock of hearing Paul's name had caused me to flinch. I had no idea that anyone, outside of Peter, Charity, and the people I had house-sat for, knew where I now lived.

"I saw your reaction, Verity. You obviously know him," the sheriff said, drawing all eyes in my direction.

I debated as to what or how much to share. I took a deep breath and dove in.

"I went out with him about five times, Sheriff. The day I was attacked, I had planned to cancel our date and sever future ties. I was exhausted. I had recently graduated, had been working extra hours, and just finished packing to move closer to work. Paul and I went to the same church, but it had become apparent we did not share the same moral code. He kept pushing for more than I was willing to share."

I lowered my eyes and murmured, "To put it bluntly, I value my psyche and body. I know I wanted to wait until I married to intimately enjoy God's design for sharing." I knew my face had turned red, so I swiftly continued. "I have wondered, Sheriff, if maybe my assailant was not a stranger."

"Verity, I know this is hard for you to revisit. I've talked to the detective, who said that so far, they have no matches for the foreign DNA found on you. Do you know if Paul was tested?"

"No, I do not. Are you going to talk to Paul? Maybe I should leave town for a while. The last thing I want to do is to endanger anyone."

Annie giggled. "Naughty, Angel! Sheriff, you shouldn't have started giving tidbits of bacon to Angel and then eaten the whole last piece yourself. Look by your chair."

The Sheriff looked outraged and boomed, "He left a turd!"

Whew. The focus was off me. I laughed. "Guess he knows how to make a point, huh? That is so funny. I wonder if we could teach him to do it on command. Good thing it wasn't from Boo."

Fe joined in, "Hey, in future, maybe we can teach Angel to leave a nugget if he doesn't approve of a guy. He certainly let us know he wasn't happy with you." All three of us burst out laughing.

Sheriff Ben was not amused. "Ladies, enough silliness! What are your plans for today, Verity?"

"Working at home for a bit on posters for the library. Later, I will go throw some pots – working with clay helps calm my nerves. If I don't answer the door or phone, I should be fine. Don't you fellows need to catch up on some sleep?"

Lark cleared his throat, then announced, "I'll stay home and work here, where it's quiet. I've got a commercial in critical need of modification. If anyone comes, I can either not answer or go to the door. I'll follow your lead, Sheriff."

"Just follow your gut, Lark. Good idea you being here with Verity out of sight, but I'm sure she'll not be out of your mind, huh Lark? Verity, I am ordering you to stay home today."

For a second, I pouted then responded, "Sheriff, I don't want to know, but maybe we should. Who were the other two people who came snooping the other night? Was one of them Mr. Sheppard from the Willis RV park? He told me he is a retired police detective. 'I'm looking into things for you, Verity,' is what he told me before hurrying away."

The Sheriff's cell phone rang, and he took the call. When he'd finished, he shared what he'd learned.

"That call was about the last snooper. It was a woman who evidently heard Sam is now living here. How she thought she'd connect with him in the middle of the night, though, is a mystery. Guess she was a little drunk, didn't know he was up a tree for part of the night, and already had a roommate. I'll go talk to Sheppard. Keep in touch, everyone."

I got up. "Thank you, Sheriff Ben. Fe and Annie, you need to get to work. Since Sam and Lark fixed the lovely breakfast, I will do the clean-up and dishes."

"Sam needs a nap. I'll help, Ve," Lark broke in.

I was surprised, but didn't plan to pass up an opportunity to learn more about Lark. I smiled and happily proclaimed, "It will be lovely to do them together. Do you wish to wash or dry?"

I expected a grunt, but heard, "I like that about you, Verity. You ignore the fact I am missing a hand, and yet welcome my participation in doing things jointly. Today, I choose to wash. If I need help, which I doubt, I will ask for your assistance."

"Fair enough. If something needs to be put up high, then I will ask for your help."

The others had gone about their business, and we were alone in the kitchen with a sink full of suds.

"Care to share a bit about yourself, Lark? Everyone can see you have gorgeous green eyes and were badly injured; however, I know nothing tangible about you. For instance, I'd like to hear about your values, what you did in the service, where you grew up, how you three became separated. If those things are too personal, then how about sharing regarding the script you are revising. Or is that top secret, too?"

"Why do you want to know about me, Babe? You trying to slot me into a certain category?"

"Ouch, Lark, you've gone all spiky again! You suddenly are reacting like when you first moved in. So don't share! Yesterday, after the mailbox incident, you came into the kitchen, leaned against the door jamb and just stared at me. You were brooding about something – not that you shared what it was that upset you. Are you now, or have you been married? You don't mind pushing my hot buttons, but I'd better not touch any of yours, is that it?"

"I'm sorry, Verity. You're right; I can be very difficult and thin-skinned about certain things. I'll tell you this much – my emotions were in a turmoil yesterday, and I still don't know how to explain it to you. I know communication is important – to you."

"I am positive that communication in the service is of vital importance. It is not just a female trait, it is a God thing. Remember in Genesis, where it tells of God coming down and walking and talking with Adam and Eve. God showed by example that in a relationship, talking as well as listening is very important. Tell you what, Lark, I will table my questions to allow you time to mull over what, in future, you will willingly share."

"What's your favorite color, Verity?"

"If I tell you, then you have to tell me your favorite. Deal?"

"Yeah. Deal."

"Years ago, my favorite color was yellow, then for about five years, I loved everything blue, and now I am growing to favor green. Your turn."

"That is so convoluted. I've always liked red."

"Why am I not surprised? Men seem to be enamored with red. You think maybe the fruit Eve offered Adam was red in color?" I realized I was getting off topic. "Sorry. My turn to ask a question. Which musical instrument do you prefer to play or listen to, Lark?"

"These days I can't play anything properly. I like the sound of a saxophone."

I let his comment pass, briefly. "Hawaiian electric guitar is my first choice, with a close second being an organ with all the bells and whistles. So what do you play, but just not, in your terms, properly these days?"

Sam came around the corner as we were finishing up the dishes. "Good to hear you two getting along so nicely. Lark used to play the trumpet – very well. Still could, I reckon, if he'd put in some sweat equity."

Lark scowled and growled, "Butt out, Sam. If I'd have wanted her to know, I would have told her."

I smiled. "Thanks for the information, Sam. I thought you might be taking a quick nap. Are either of you up for a bike ride or a game of racquetball if we can get a court? I feel as if I am in jail, except of course for the really excellent breakfast, guys. Fixing it for all of us was very thoughtful."

Sam grinned at me. "Verity, why don't you get to work on your projects? Instead of thinking about what you can't do right now, focus on things for which you are grateful."

I was not amused at his pointed remark and tossed the dish towel onto the counter. "Getting a kernel of information out of you two is like squeezing a rock hoping for some water, but all one gets is dirty hands! I am out of here. Are you going to exercise Angel and Boo since even the garden and backyard for me is now forbidden territory?"

"No use in getting snarky, Ve. We are not avenging angels sent to keep you inside. We are here for your protection."

As I headed up the stairs, I loudly proclaimed, "I have never had much use for staying indoors when the outside world beckons." I quickly felt remorseful. "Sorry, guys. I'll behave and am glad you care enough to try to protect me. Thank you."

Later, Sam knocked on my bedroom door. "Ve, a text from Sheriff Ben. It appears Paul is headed over here. Are you willing to meet him?"

"Yes. Let's do it. Shall I talk to him on the porch, invite him into the kitchen, or...?"

"Have Lark answer the door. Get the water boiling for tea and spread some papers on the kitchen table. Keep Angel with you. I will be out of sight in the alcove off of the kitchen."

I ran down the stairs, lists in hand, shouting Lark's name. I whipped into the kitchen, checked that the coffee was still hot, and flipped on the electric kettle. By the time Lark arrived to learn what my shouting was about, I had added goodies on a plate. I breathed a quick prayer for wisdom and calmness. The doorbell rang – repeatedly. Lark went to answer it. We'd decided to pretend we didn't know anything about Paul's being in town.

Lark shouted, "Verity, where are you, girl?"

"In the kitchen, Lark. Who is it?"

"Babe, do you know a fellow named Paul Ward?"

"I did – a long time ago. Has he had an accident, or...?"

"Why don't you come to the door, Ve?"

"Okay. The coffee is ready, Love. Heel, Angel, Boo."

The dogs and I joined Lark at the door, and I steeled myself to see someone from a past I'd rather forget.

"Wow, Verity, you look really good!" Paul exclaimed.

"Paul? How did you find me? Why are you here?"

"We need to talk."

"Let's go into the kitchen," I said as I turned way.

"Two dogs, Verity? I never knew you liked animals."

I ignored his comment. Coming through the doorway, I headed over to the chair where Lark was now sitting. I reckoned I was becoming quite the actor. Placing a hand gently on his shoulder, I leaned down so that my head blocked Paul's view, looked into Lark's eyes, and pretended to kiss him on the lips. I almost spoilt it all by bursting out laughing at his intense, transfixed gaze. I saw a definite spark of powerful heat flood his eyes. Straightening up slowly, I pretended to reluctantly release eye contact with Lark.

Boo laid down near Lark, while Angel sat staring at Paul. I almost giggled as I recalled the earlier conversation. For a second, I wished Angel would leave a turd by Paul. Mum would not have approved of that thinking. For a fleeting second, I berated myself, then took a deep breath, gathered my thoughts, and began introductions.

"In case you didn't exchange names at the door, Paul, meet Lark and the dogs, Angel and Boo. Lark, this is Paul. Would you like a cup of coffee or tea and a cookie?"

"So, you can now say cookie rather than bickie. I want to talk to you in private, Verity, not in front of a stranger."

"Whatever you care to share can be said in Lark's hearing. Now, why are you here?"

He cleared his throat. "I came to ask you to marry me."

"No way. You are joking. I do not believe you. Where is the ring? There is something else going on here. Before you go any further, maybe I should call the sheriff."

"NO! Someone is looking – trying to find you, Verity. I had to locate you first – to warn you."

"Well, you found me and have probably led whoever it is right here. Do you know who it is or why they are hunting for me? What do they want?"

He didn't respond, so I decided to air my own suspicions.

"I think they paid you very well not only to come, but to make sure I was the Verity you knew several years ago. How much are you being paid to act as a Judas goat, Paul?"

"Of course, I'm being paid, Verity. It is what I do in my spare time. I find people – for a fee."

"Who is looking for me?"

"Telling you is not part of the deal."

"So, what agreement did you make?"

"I wasn't supposed to warn you. Just locate you, make sure you are the Verity I knew, and see if you are open to their deal."

I remembered Paul hated silence and would chatter freely to fill a void. I caught Lark's eye, twitched my head from side to side a wee bit and remained silent, waiting for Paul to reveal all. It wasn't long before he obliged.

"It's not as if they want to kill you or anything – at least, I don't think they do. They just don't want you to inherit everything. They want you to divide it up evenly so all of you receive the same amount. Otherwise, fewer heirs mean more for those remaining, if you get the meaning. I'm here to take back your answer. Here are the papers they want you to fill in, sign, and date. I'm supposed to give you one day, two at the most. They said to tell you your mother would wish you to do the right thing," One of the papers on the table sliced his finger. "Ouch! I hate paper cuts."

"Here is a serviette – sorry, napkin. I'll get a Band-Aid," I said as I opened a cupboard. "Salve and this covering should alleviate the pain. Paul, would you push up your sleeves to your elbows, please? Thank you. Now, care to share who the 'they' are that you were talking about?"

"Actually, Verity, I don't know. The person on the phone said 'they,' so that is the term I used. I need that paperwork ASAP." Paul paused, then softly added, "Funny thing happened right before I left to come find you. Another 'they' called, asking for information regarding your location and if there had been a monetary settlement recently awarded to you."

I stared at him. What were the odds of two groups of people...? I shook my head. "I will get back to you about the paperwork no later than Tuesday. Do you have a number where you can be reached?"

He handed me a piece of stationery from the Unique Hostel. "Oh, you don't have a cell phone number. Lark, please show Mr. Ward out."

Lark came hurrying back. "What do you think, Ve?"

"We may finally have a clue. Did you hear what was said, Sam? Let's call the sheriff. Fe and Annie should be here soon for lunch. Should I call Peter and my lawyer, Brenda?"

"I heard everything, Verity. I'm calling the sheriff, but don't call anyone else, as there is nothing concrete to share."

"Okay, but while waiting, we can look at the papers."

Later, after the sheriff arrived, we went through what we'd witnessed.

"So you had a chat with Paul, did you?" Sheriff Ben said.

"Yes, Sheriff. Lark was with me in the kitchen. Paul got cut while handing me these papers. This is his blood on the napkin. I'm wondering if Sam or Lark would tell what they heard, then I will tell you what I think is a possible answer. Also, Sheriff, I'd appreciate you checking over these papers. It looks as if they want me to fill in some very personal information. I do not plan to do that – especially without knowing who wants it and why."

Knowing Sam was an actor in our local theater, and having witnessed his ability of "spot on" mimicry, I was a wee bit apprehensive. Sam ignored my pleading look. I was about to get roasted a bit due to how I had referred to Lark. I turned my back, dished up bowls of stew, and set hot corn bread on the table. Fe and Annie looked at me and smiled at one point during Sam's perfect performance. Then, while the five of them dug into their food, I nervously cleared my throat and launched some facts.

"Paul had no scars on either arm. Now that you know what was said today, I will fill you in on some background information. I told you Peter and I have always been close; however, there have been family complications. Peter and Charity's mother died when they were six and five. Their father married again before they were

90

eight and seven. I was born within a year, and Ruby, three years later. Peter accepted us unconditionally; however, Charity...." My voice trailed off as I tried to think of a way to express my thoughts.

Annie blurted out, "Verity, Beryl is causing a rift now because she has taken Charity's side. Charity is offended that your mother married her father, and thus your very existence grates on her."

Fe continued, "Beryl now has kids because of you, but emotionally, she... in a crazy way, it makes sense."

"Yes, Fe and Annie. I am glad you grasp the basic situation. Over the years, my parents shared bits of their lives. Dad's missionary parents died of typhoid when Dad was over here in college. Mum was from a rich family. Her grandparents loved the fact that she was a missionary, but her parents threatened to cut her out of their will. She was a skilled nurse who loved God and serving people. As far as I know, she was an only child." I paused.

"Wait a minute. Mum said, 'I am the only daughter,' which might mean she had a brother. I took a brief look at the papers before you arrived. Peter could probably tell us whether this is related to the insurance settlement regarding their deaths, or maybe my mother's relatives' estate. At my birthday party, Peter whispered to me that both are being processed. I wonder how.... Then again Sheriff, this might be the identity thieves at work." I paused and gulped as a horrible thought hit me.

"I wonder if what is going on could possibly involve my half-sister, Charity? We have had a stormy history. To get a balanced view, Sheriff Ben, you need to talk to Peter."

"Good idea, Verity, and if you don't mind, I'll take these papers to the office. To set your minds at ease, I have assigned a deputy to be alerted to follow Paul if he leaves the hostel. The Unique family and staff have been given a heads-up to call us regarding visitors to Paul's room. It is a miracle Paul was given the room right across from the office."

I had to know. "Sheriff, could I go down to either the library or my tiny studio and work with clay this afternoon? If you say no to those, please let me go for a run or a bicycle ride – anywhere. Saturday evening, the three of us girls have dates to go to Lark's movie premiere. Will I be allowed to go?"

"I'll let you know, Verity. Right now, I will escort Fe and Annie back to work." A sparkle came to his eye, and he smiled as he said, "Two good meals here in one day! Thanks."

I sat at the kitchen table with my hands clasping a warm cup, feeling like a drooping flower. I knew the guys were waiting for me to speak, but I was all talked out. Silence felt healing after all the commotion and the dredging up of another secret sorrow.

I made my mind drift to the library and things to incorporate: reading to therapy dogs every afternoon after school; girlfriends meetings to be held there; book signings; people from the RV park to give talks on their fields of expertise; grief support; wounded warrior information. These were a few dreams.

My mind seemed to be trying to catch something about those papers, but nothing clicked in. I finally looked at the two men, sighed and said, "Anything either of you care to share? Any brilliant words of wisdom?"

Sam asked, "Would a nap do you any good?"

Ah, yes, typical in my experience. Men prefer to fix it and move on. My past was not fixable, and the threat very vague.

Lark abruptly pushed away from the table. "Come on, let's go into the living room."

My soul ached as I watched his slow gait into the next room. He put in the CD we'd used a couple of nights ago. All of us were endeavoring to learn to line dance.

I perked up, smiled, and began to enthusiastically move my feet. I loved the stomping part! Angel came near. I picked him up and continued to move. None of us had perfect footwork, but it was fun, and at least for me, released some tension. I definitely needed to grasp and savor every small dose of joy offered.

Soon Angel wanted down, and the guys quit. Just as I was about to stop, my cell phone rang. Before I could answer, Sam thoughtfully stopped the music.

"Hi, Essie. I am so sorry. I cannot come, but I will send Sam right over to help out. Don't worry about it. I am positive he will be delighted to assist." I ended the call to see a frowning Sam.

"What do you mean, I will be delighted to assist Essie? You didn't even ask me, Verity!"

Marilyn Stewart

"Sam, I'm not sure if you've ever really met Essie. You have probably had her as your waitress at Welcome to Dine. She looks after her grandmother, works three hours over the breakfast rush, three hours around noon, or the three and a half hours in the evenings, five to six days a week. Sam, please look at me. I know you've taken a bit of an emotional hit with two girls in our towns. I suggest you take a long look at Essie, or better yet a certain Welcome Hugger whose name starts with an F, if you are looking for a lasting relationship. Essie lives a mile down the road. Don't forget to take Boo. Sam, please smile and enjoy yourself."

Lark murmured, "You set him up, didn't you?"

"I did. So what? Sam is a very special man and needs to be reminded of real love in action as well as to feel welcome to participate in giving of himself."

"Verity, Sam is my friend and military brother. You need to clarify what exactly he is going to be asked to do."

"Oh, ye of little faith. Sam is my friend, too. It's really none of your business, Lark, but Essie's grandmother misses hearing her husband's voice. Sam is going to read to her while Essie takes a little break. Sam will get a new appreciation of Essie."

"So you are matchmaking."

"Not really. I am trying to open his eyes and mind to possibilities of future joy."

"Semantics, honey. You have a kind heart. Verity, I find you intriguing, interesting, and intuitive. You often remind me of Mercy – of her insight and caring attitude."

"Good to know there is a bit of mystery left in me. What a lovely compliment to be compared to Mercy." I grinned and added, "I wish I could say you are like Unity, but maybe you can learn."

He did not take the bait. "Babe, do you realize for once we are home alone? Just us two? Plus, it is quiet – a double rarity."

"Not exactly alone. Angel is with us, and of course, God is watching, probably listening, too."

Lark smirked. "Right. Funny girl, you certainly know how to put the brakes on before an idea is barely formed."

Since he was talking for once, I pushed on. "Well, Lark, you are a puzzle. Your eyes say a whole lot more than your mouth

93

is willing to release. You perplex me on several levels, but for now I need a cup of tea and to get back to listing dreams for the library."

He softly asked, "What about your own dreams, Verity? You must have at least a few unfulfilled dreams."

I snarled, "Why should I talk about any of my dreams with a man who is like a clam when it comes to sharing anything of himself with me?"

His mouth remained closed. With my mug clenched in my hand, I noisily stomped out of the room, hoping Lark realized I was not at all happy with him.

The sheriff decided that I'd be permitted to go to the library, as long as I didn't stray far from Boo, Angel, or Sam.

It had been a long, tense day. Arriving home, I wanted to ask for something before I forgot.

"Mr. Sam," I began, in the way the little kids spoke to him at the library. It had come out a little hesitant, just as, at first, a request did from them.

"Yes, Miss Ve?" He responded as if we were at the library.

"Would you share a hug with me?" My eyes were 'leaking' a bit, which caused Sam to ignore the fact that Lark was now in the kitchen doorway, watching us. Sam immediately responded by lifting and opening his arms wide. It wasn't a long hug, but one enjoyed by us both.

I stepped back and said, "Mr. Sam, you need to write an adventure book – not too scary – for kids dealing with wounded warriors. You know what I mean. You were 'spot on' when answering that child's questions about your foot. You even let him pull up your pant leg and have a long look. I've been wondering if one Saturday morning you would be willing to be the guest speaker, followed by a question and answer time with the kids. We have featured an author before. How about you? You work with people and dogs, the drama group, and now are a deputy."

I hurried on before he could say no. "You are a multifaceted man. A theme could be 'accepting ourselves' and how you trained Boo. Please think about it. Today you not only helped a child, you reached a struggling daughter and mother."

"I didn't do anything but answer the kid. The mother didn't look as if she was having any issues."

"That's where you are wrong, Sam. In a few days, everyone will know. Her father, a veteran, will be arriving to live with them. He is not a happy man. She is concerned about the impact it will have on each family member."

The frown left Sam's face.

"Oh, in that case, Lark, Uni, Jeff, Jake, Zeke, Derek, and I, or two of us at a time, could take turns visiting them."

"How about making sure the visits include Angel, Boo, or Gem? And Sam, thanks for bringing laughter and balance into this home." I smiled, went up on tiptoes, kissed his cheek, and then darted past Lark to run up the stairs with Angel.

Lark walked towards Sam and quietly ground out, "Anything growing between you and Verity that I should know about?"

At first Sam was inclined to do the 'man thing,' and blow it out of proportion or tease Lark. The pain in Lark's eyes, however, revealed how much he loved me. Sam told him the truth.

"Lark, the girl's eyes were tearing up again, which she hates, for it is against the culture in which she grew up. These last three years, she hasn't been able to stop the sudden, brief leaking whenever her emotions are tweaked. Now, you know that is a fact. Um... I guess I'll share a bit more. Verity is contemplating driving back to the town where her parents and sister are buried. She needs to 'talk to them about things,' is how she put it. Angel won't be with her for long, for he has chosen to be a wounded warrior companion. She is scared and feels very much alone. She is falling in love with you, but you are not helping her see any future with you. Those are critical issues she is mulling over. You have to give her a glimmer of hope. I'd say we need to keep a close eye on her, for she might just do a runner very soon. She is also worried that one of us will get hurt because she is living here. Verity and I are the outsiders in this home. You three have made us feel very welcome, but we are not family as are Fe, Annie, and you. Care to share why you are letting this lovely girl swing with uncertainty?"

"Her brother has stopped me twice. The first time was at her birthday party. He made me promise not to 'mess with her' until she has been here for at least a year. Like a fool, I agreed. It has and yet has not been easy to be so close. I'd already asked her out and she'd accepted, so he okayed this one time. Now, if I can just make it through the next two months...."

"I'm sure he didn't mean you couldn't share bits of your life. I think it was any kissing. and.... I'll get Fe and Annie to talk about when you were all young."

"Thanks, Sam. I'm afraid she is soon going to begin dating other guys in our three towns."

"She is moving in that direction. Think seriously about clearing the air with Peter. You two are certainly old enough."

"It's been on my mind. I'd hate to lose such a special girl. Any clarity about who is making Verity a target?"

"Nothing concrete, but...."

"Yes?"

"The FBI has confirmed our findings of an identity theft group working in our area. They hide in small towns and target people who might inherit land or money. Maybe it is them, and they are trying to scare her into revealing her full name.

"How about Paul and those papers, Sam?"

"We're still checking, Lark."

"Keep me informed about how I can help look after her – without her knowing we are truly concerned. I hope you guys have talked to both Peter and Charity and their spouses."

"Sheriff Ben is doing that today."

"Okay. I'd appreciate being kept informed."

Thirteen

I was at the library front desk, and as always, when someone entered, I looked up. The man appeared to be exhausted – barely able to put one foot in front of the other. Grabbing a bottle of water, I hurried over to help him into a chair. Unscrewing the lid, I said, "Drink. Then talk." As he obeyed, I smiled – not so much at him, as realizing I had sounded exactly like my mum. Still kneeling by his chair, I softly said, "How can I help you?"

I was stunned when he replied, "Verity, you look just like your mother. This is going to sound a little weird, and it's quite a long story."

I interrupted him to keep him from sharing further. "Let's go to Welcome to Dine, where we can eat and you can share – my shout, okay?"

He nodded, smiled, and admitted to being hungry. The fact that he knew "my shout" was a Briticism that meant "my treat" was intriguing to me.

I found Rosemary shelving books and told her I would be gone for an indefinite amount of time and was leaving Angel in her care. When I returned, he stood, reached out a hand, and said, "My name is Joseph Caltron." We shook, then walked out to my car.

As I went to open the car door, my cell rang. It was Sam. I had totally forgotten to check in. When he found out what I was doing – well, to put it mildly – he was not pleased. He told me he would meet us shortly at the restaurant.

Joseph refrained from getting in the car. "Have I created a problem? I couldn't help overhearing. The man seemed really upset with you."

"Get in, Joseph. Nothing for you to worry about."

He looked unconvinced at my statement. "Call me Joe."

*****

By the time we had our order, Sam arrived, but chose to sit at another table – behind Joe. Seeing his choice, I realized that I had unconsciously positioned myself to be able to see who came and went, which placed Joe with his back to almost everyone.

"Joe," I began, "Are you now ready to share your story?" A strange look flitted across his face. He hesitated, looked down at his empty plate, then back at me, as if he were reluctant to proceed.

"Four years ago, your parents came to our church to share about their work overseas. They stayed overnight with us – such a delightful couple. We all mourned their passing."

He halted once again and looked down, not at my face. This was weird, because earlier he had remarked on how I was not focusing on his face except to glance and look away. I had explained to him that in the culture in which I grew up, it was respectful not to stare for a prolonged period into a person's eyes. Now that I was paying attention, I realized that, since beginning his story, he was having trouble meeting my gaze.

With his head down, he resumed, "While with us, your mother had shown us pictures of you four kids, telling us about each of your interests and skills. She had looked rather surprised at her own words and admitted her actions were not normal. I'd noticed your Dad had a funny look on his face while she'd talked."

Here he glanced up and briefly met my eyes. "The morning right before they said goodbye, your mother stopped and asked us to pray specifically for you, Verity. She'd shaken her head and said, 'This is so strange, but I have to tell you. If your town ever has a catastrophe, get in touch with Verity.' So here I am."

My mouth must have been hanging open, because he relaxed, nodded, looked me in the eyes, and grinned. "I know exactly how you feel, Verity Tracker."

It was so lovely to hear from someone who had interacted with Mum and Dad. I began to feel great excitement welling up inside of me. I watched him lean towards me, his lips parted, appearing eager to receive my words. Just as I was about to tell him that our three towns were scouting out a place in the USA to go to on a mission trip, when he softly said, "Oh, by the way, my middle name is Aaron. What's yours?"

He witnessed, but didn't realize the reason for my distress. Shock and devastation engulfed me. I'd been conned. He blurted out, "What's wrong? You look as if I knifed or betrayed you."

Marilyn Stewart

I was shaken to realize that hearing about my family had lowered my guard. Sam, in full uniform, appeared beside Joseph and took over.

I later learned that Joseph was an actor. Two weeks ago, his agent had accepted the role for him – over the phone. Upon his acceptance, three hundred dollars in cash had arrived in the mail.

Joseph begged Sam to permit him to apologize to me in person. Realizing he was innocent, I forgave him, but fear, suspicion, and lack of trust set up home in my spirit.

Fourteen

I was surprised to wake up humming. It was not a hymn or even a contemporary song. I had heard Hank, Mercy's dad, whistling it last week. It had brought back good memories. My father had trouble staying on key, but loved to sing. I had heard the song enough times to remember all the words; however, the "Be my love..." just kept on playing in my head, as if it was caught in a groove. Here I was humming it for the first time ever, and today was to be my special 'dress up' date with Lark. Since the song kept recycling endlessly, I decided to make the most of it. I would don a secret smile, which I hoped would bug Lark. I put on my robe, picked up Angel, quietly opened my bedroom door, and tiptoed down to Fe's room. Last night we had decided to meet for a confab early this morning. We wanted to talk through the logistics of us girls going out on the same night to the same place.

I tapped and opened the door. "Good morning, ladies! I was wondering if the four of you twins are traveling together."

Fe smiled. "Actually, for a day or two, we talked about whether Annie and I should call them and offer to pick them up individually. After all, we were the ones who asked them out."

"You both look content, so what did you decide?"

Annie chuckled. "They called us personally, asking to make this a regular date. They would drive, plus they would be picking up the tab for the entire night. JJ and JC both stated firmly that this would not be a 'twin' outing – no four-some."

I was thrilled for them and clapped my hands. "Oh, Fe and Annie, I do like it that they are treating you as individuals. In a way, I feel left out not, being a twin or triplet. I have been wondering, since your senses are wired for togetherness, if we might all wind up at the same place to eat after the previews."

Fe admitted, "It certainly is possible, Ve. We thought about asking Lark where he is taking you, but didn't want him to think we didn't trust him or that we wanted to be with you two."

I nattered on, "What about the other people from the Ghost Town who helped make the movie? Did anyone ask if they might like to have everyone celebrating together?"

Fe sighed. "What do you think, Annie? Should we check to see if the guys would welcome JC and JJ? It might bridge the gap between the men who served and two who didn't."

I again interrupted. "Fe, I think by now, both JC and JJ have already made eating arrangements. I have been doing the 'what if,' etc., trying to control things myself. How about we let the guys work it out and just be flexible and supportive?"

Annie broke in, "Ve, it looks like Angel needs to go to the backyard. I'll pop him out the door, then let him in again while you go and get dressed, get things ready, and set the table. Remember, we said we'd fix waffles and eggs this morning."

Later, most of us were sitting at the kitchen table, when Lark came into the room and sat down.

"Angel feels cold. Have you been outside, Babe? I thought you were going to help with breakfast. Don't wrinkle up your cute little nose at me."

"One of your sisters put Angel out. Coffee is ready. The eggs are out, batter is made; table set; skillet is warming; syrup and butter are on the table. Annie and Fe will be doing the actual cooking. Sheesh, Lark, what is wrong with you? You nervous about our date and maybe want to back out?"

"No. No way. I'm really looking forward to tonight. Hope we eat soon. I'm really hungry."

"Hmm. You only answered two of my three questions. So, Sam, care to share?"

"Not before breakfast, Verity. Don't start a controversial conversation before a man has food in his stomach."

"Good advice. Okay, then. Sam, I forgot to ask how it went with Essie and her grandmother the other day."

"That is one sweet old lady. She really misses having a masculine voice in the house. Losing her son, and then two years later, her husband, certainly has taken a toll. She wanted me to read from a book her husband hadn't finished reading to her. As I was leaving, she asked if I'd mind giving her a hug. She told me that there was just something special about the scent and feel of a man's arms. Got to be hard on Essie, too."

Lark smirked. "So, we guys are good for hugs, huh, Sam? Did you see the girls' faces? You had them nodding and smiling."

I snuck a look at Lark, then proclaimed, "There are hugs, and then there are hugs. Oh, yeah, each hug has its own message."

"Any of you girls care to explain that in more detail?"

I said, "Come on, Lark, you direct movies. A hug can stake a claim; be healing or offensive; bring comfort; be too long, too tight, or confining; be impulsive; delightful; therapeutic; perfect in length and in sharing an exquisite moment in time with another person. It can create a glow of pure contentment. Just like yours, and later, Sam's, did for me."

Sam grinned. "You get all that from a hug? For real? So a hug could make or break a relationship?"

Fe piped up, "One hug can reveal a person's character."

Sam nodded and smiled. "About the comfort and glow thing, I witnessed it firsthand the day I arrived. The short story is that Uni's, Katie's, and my plans changed overnight. The next morning, we were on the road, driving like crazy in an effort to arrive in time for the early spring, three-town picnic celebration. We arrived after the picnic had started, but it was perfect in God's timing. Hours before, Mercy had been instrumental in locating five missing children. Due to her past, she was ecstatic, shattered, and emotionally a wreck. Katie, Boo and I went to the picnic, which had been moved to the tarmac area at the Willis place. Hank told Uni that Mercy was on the verge of collapse. Now, Uni could barely lift his left leg, yet he somehow climbed the stairs to the second floor, even though he doesn't remember it. Mercy needed him. This is where the hug comes in.

Uni knocked on her bedroom door, then braced his back against the wall, along with his cane. Mercy saw him, laid her head against his chest, and sobbed uncontrollably. He loosely wrapped his arms around her in a reassuring embrace. As you know, she's been known to throw punches and kicks when a man touches her. That hug marked the beginning of her healing. I was there when

Marilyn Stewart

Katie took a picture of them sharing that embrace. So, their very first hug was the beginning step towards their future together!"

Three of us wiped away tears. "What a special memory. Thanks for sharing. Another waffle, Sam?"

"Yes, please, Fe."

Annie caught my eye. "Hey, Ve, what hugs did we miss witnessing? We will be talking with you later!"

Lark mumbled, "Sam, you'd better tell her."

"Verity, I've talked to both detective Dan Ragland and Sheriff Ben. Ben, in turn, has been in touch with Special Agent Marcus with the FBI. We don't yet know who hired Joseph, but computers are humming. This is bigger than just you. There is an identity and extortion ring targeting possible heirs. The FBI informed us there have been two kidnappings sixty miles from here, which they believe to be linked to this group. It seems Paul is on the fringe and maybe crucial to the network. He works in a courthouse in the records division. The Sheriff was told he monitors hatches, matches, and dispatches, which translates into births, marriages, divorces, and/or deaths."

"So I am not in imminent jeopardy, and we girls can go to the beauty salon today, as planned?"

"We aren't sure, therefore a beautician is coming here, as well as someone to take your fingerprints, Ve."

"Check with the file clerk at the police station, Sam. My fingerprints are already on file."

"What? When? Why?"

I shrugged. "It just made sense. Knowing I would be working with children, it was one of the first things I did. Now, I have two questions: Is a member of my family involved? Am I going to be permitted to leave the house tonight with Lark?"

Sam studied my face. I was sorry I had blurted out a worry. "Verity, what do you mean? I doubt you are referring to Peter. So far, we have found no link to Peter or Charity. We are working on tonight. They tell me you are to get ready, but...."

I huffed. "It just doesn't make any sense. Here, in town, I am a virtual prisoner, and tonight, I could be free to wander at will amongst movie-goers, where not only I, but Lark also could be extremely vulnerable. With the dress I will be wearing, a bullet

103

proof vest would be extremely visible. It would be beyond bearing if one of you were injured, kidnapped, or killed because of me. I truly want to go; however, if it will put any one of you in danger, then I will be content to stay home."

Lark muttered, "So you think I can't protect you, Ve."

I shook my head. "NO! I do trust you. But none of us know who the villain or villains are. It is your premiere, Lark! I refuse to undermine your special moment." I finally looked Lark in the face. As soon as I did, Lark spoke as if only to me.

"Verity, you are way more precious than a stupid movie debut. We could have our own screening here at home. Hey, Babe, stop giving me that disapproving look of yours."

Sam's cellphone warbled. "Sheriff? Oh, you're headed here now? Yeah, I told her. Oh, okay, right away." Sam put away his phone and announced, "Paul is headed in this direction. They missed seeing him leave Unique, but saw him entering Welcome. Fe and Annie, quick, help clean off the table, then go upstairs, please. Lark, answer the door. Verity, stay in the kitchen. Sheriff Ben is coming. I'll unlatch the back door so he can enter without being seen. Once again, I'll be out of sight around the corner."

Lark paused. "Stand up, Verity. Come on, girl, let's share a therapeutic hug and have a quick prayer. *Lord, this situation is way beyond our control. We don't know how to proceed. We're asking for your protection and our discernment. Amen.*"

Lark kissed the top of my head. As he released his arms, we heard the doorbell and a shout.

"Verity, its Paul. Let me in – now. I have urgent news."

I heard Lark say, "What's up, Paul? Verity is in the kitchen."

"I need to see – speak to her."

I stood to face him. "What do you want to tell me, Paul?"

He shuffled his feet, then began. "After I get done telling you, I'll go talk to the Sheriff. I started off finding a lost heir for a rich man. I work in records, you see. It was like I was a detective and it was fun tracking down people. I got a finder's fee. I learned how to search for a person via the Internet, and I swear I never went into any confidential files. Anyway, about three months ago, I

104

heard a woman at work mention your name. A month ago, she offered me five hundred dollars to find you. I had no idea where you'd gone after you got out of the hospital. I became curious and finally located you by finding Peter. She told me to come here and make sure it was you. I started to get a little worried when I called to tell her I'd found and given you the papers, but didn't yet have your signature on them. She not only yelled she wouldn't give me the five hundred she had promised, but the hit man she'd hired for you would be taking me out, too."

"Okay, young man, what is the woman's name, and do you have any idea who she might have hired as a hit man?"

Paul jumped and weakly said, "Hello, Sheriff. Her name is Wanda Witkins. She is my boss. I'd just be guessing, but knowing her, I'd guess it would be her really nasty brute of a son. We all steer clear of him when he comes to visit her."

"Do you know where he is, Paul? What kind of a vehicle he drives? Does he have any firearms?"

"Sheriff, according to Wanda, he is coming here. He has a blue BSA motorcycle and a car. He brags he was a sharp-shooter and a bomb expert in the military."

"What is his name? Describe him."

"I've heard him called Bubba, but I think his real name is William. He has brown hair and eyes, is about 5'10" and has a longish, scraggly beard. He has a scar on his arm that looks like a bite mark, and a tattoo around it of a vampire with two long teeth, poised to pierce the scar. I overheard Wanda telling him he'd better be clean-shaven when he came back from the job. She was on the phone to me, but yelling at him. I'm really sorry, Verity. I didn't mean to create trouble for you."

"Any idea why Wanda wanted to find Verity?"

"I don't know, Sheriff Ben, but a co-worker called yesterday. She overheard Wanda telling her son to be careful, and that Verity could 'put us all in jail.' We don't know what she meant."

"Sam, call and give the description to our office for an all-points bulletin, and ask them to text the business owners in our three towns. I'll call detective Ragland. Lark, call the Ghost Town.

I'm sure you must have a code word to use as a warning. He might be hiding out there."

I said, "Don't forget, he might have a scent of oranges."

Paul stared. "You're right, Verity, he does. How did you know? He's always eating oranges and drops the rinds wherever he is standing. Sheriff, that detective comes to see Wanda."

"The man might have been at my party, but I do not remember any bearded gent."

The sheriff made a call.

"Tom, Sheriff Ben here. Search DMV records for a Wanda or William Witkins, for any vehicles owned by them. If you have any trouble, call the contact number we have for FBI agent Brand. I will be at the office shortly."

Sam commented, "Sheriff, do you recall the bear that Zeke, Boo, and I tracked? Uni, Jeff, Lark, and Jake are also highly skilled trackers. Gem and Boo are the two best sniffers in our search and rescue group. I hope you have us on speed dial in case we're needed."

"Good idea, Sam. We might need all of you. Hang in there, Verity, we hope to get this moving thanks to Paul's information."

I had to speak. "I might be wrong, but Paul, I believe you lied to us about Detective Ragland. Everything else rang true, but you have a habit I noticed on a couple of our dates. When you fudge the truth or outright lie, you betray yourself as if you have to prepare your mouth to utter the falsehood."

"What, Verity? I never!"

"Sam, you have an excellent ear and perfect mimicry. Replay in your mind what Paul has shared and you will find a nervous anomaly. I think you will confirm my theory."

"Wait! Wait a minute," Paul back-pedaled. "All right, yes, I made up that bit because the detective has caused me some problems, and I wanted him to feel a little heat."

"Paul, come with me," the sheriff said. We need to put together a composite drawing of William. Sam, I will call you later."

After Paul and the sheriff had gone, I turned to Sam.

Marilyn Stewart

"I have two questions, Sam: first, why are there two different FBI guys? I remember Marcus, who came here when the kids were found last year, but who is Brand? Secondly, would you, or maybe Lark, take the dogs out back for a quick game of fetch?"

At that point, the doorbell rang again, and Lark answered it.

He hollered, "Fe! Annie! The hair stylist is here!"

"You don't need to shout, Lark," Annie replied. "We've been sitting on the stairs, listening to everything. Come on up, Megan."

Before Sam took the dogs out, he told me that Brand worked on identity thieves and Marcus, threats and kidnappings. I shuddered.

With just the two of us now in the kitchen, Lark queried, "Verity, honey, how are you really holding up – emotionally?"

I was not going there. "How are you coping with the lowly, boring job of babysitting me, Lark?"

His face lit up in an unexpected and sweet smile. "Honestly, Babe, I am happy – content. I wouldn't want any other fellow to have this privilege. Don't look at me as if you think I'm stretching the truth. I really like being with you. Honest. I really do."

I figured I would admit to something also. "Lark, I appreciated the prayer and hug earlier. It was spot on. Psalms 23:4-6 have been floating through my mind for several days now. The verses are about walking in the valley of the shadows, eating in the presence of my enemies, and dwelling in the house of the Lord forever. I have been troubled, uneasy, and yes, rather panicky. While I am still on edge, the core, chilling fear is gone. I need to remember that God is *with me* wherever I am – and trust Him."

"Babe, I quoted that Psalm many times in battle. There were times I walked in the valley of the shadow of death, but because Jesus was with me, I learned to trust Him and not fear. I'll admit, many times I've wished God had decided it was time to beam me up. I wanted to be done with inner conflict, pain, and loss. Many days, I've found it a struggle to look forward, with joy, to another day here on earth. You girls have, time and again, overlooked Sam's and my bad spells with total acceptance. Thanks."

"Wow, Lark, that is the most I have heard you share. You guys are the ones who inspire us. If I were in your shoes, I would be whining all the time that life is not fair. I admit, I tended to worry – more the last couple of years than ever before. Daily, I try to remember I have the choice to be as happy as I choose to be at each given minute. It keeps me praying – a lot – for God's help."

We heard, "Ve, your turn! Go do some work, Lark."

I yelled, "Coming!" Then, I decided to tease Lark. "What is the going rate for babysitting an adult female?"

He smirked. "I'll tell you sometime, Verity. Thank you for setting an example to the Welcome Huggers about wounded warriors. Now, think how good my hugs feel. See you later, Ve."

I laughed. "Yes, you will, Lark. You certainly will!"

I passed Sam and heard him say to Lark, "Verity trying to get a rise out of you? Get you to 'communicate,' as she calls it? What hugs?"

I stood still to eavesdrop on their conversation.

"Let's go to the study and work on a plan for tonight," Lark replied.

Sam chuckled. "So you're not going to share about the hugs – more than just one, huh?" Sam then raised his voice. "You can leave now, Verity."

Upstairs, Fe greeted me with, "Verity, did our brother hit on you once we all cleared out?"

I shook my head. "No, he did not, and if he doesn't show significant interest tonight, I am going to start accepting dates every night of the week. Well, you know what I mean. Of course, I first have to be invited and then permitted to leave the house. I am feeling claustrophobic. Enough of my whinging, or as you two would say, 'whining.' You both look totally 'hot' and for sure will set the Willis twins on their heels! If their hearts aren't stolen by now, tonight should do the trick. I can hardly wait to see their faces light up when they see each of you."

"Your turn, Verity. What do you want done?"

"I haven't a clue, Megan. Why don't you three talk over what would suit me and do it."

"For months, I've been wanting to get you into the salon, Verity! When I'm done with you, Lark won't stand a chance."

*****

As we were finishing our date preparations, we heard a knock.

"It's Sam, and I'd like to talk to all of you. Woohoo! Awesome, ladies. What I'd like to do is escort you one at a time down the stairs to your date. When we leave tonight, the Sheriff will be in the lead car, followed by one of the twins. Lark and Verity will be in the next car, then another set of twins. I will be in the car guarding the rear."

Annie and I grinned while Fe exclaimed, "That sounds terrific, but we three wish to see the expression on each of the guys' faces."

Sam grinned. "Ladies, ladies – have a little faith. I've rigged up several cameras and will make a DVD for each of you – as a wedding present. I'm not in the drama group without reason."

Fe clapped her hands. "Oh, Sam, you are a treasure! Thank you times three! What a grand way to begin a festive evening."

I was happy, but needed clarity. "Wait a minute. What about leaving the house empty, and where will the dogs be?"

"Don't worry so much, Verity. We have that all covered."

Ah, yes I thought, trust. Lately I had not trusted anyone other than myself and God. Well, I had to admit my trust in God had taken a huge hit three years ago. When I looked at it from this perspective, I suddenly realized I was doing the Creator of Heaven, Earth, and myself, a grave injustice. Sometimes I found that believing God had good things for me was hard to accept. I looked down at my clenched fists and slowly stretched out each digit until my hands were open and empty. I breathed slowly in and out. *"Okay, Lord, please fill my hands and heart with what pleases you."*

I vaguely heard, "Are you okay, Verity?"

I nodded, then spoke. "Yes. I am good, thanks, Fe. Let's have a fantastic celebratory evening with our dates."

Fe continued, "No matter how late we get in, we agreed to meet in Annie's room and share our adventures."

*****

I had never seen Annie so lit up and serene. Her eyes sparkled, and her smile grew. "We have our hot drinks, jammies on, and Angel to snuggle. Are we all going to share or hold it close? Verity, are you willing to be open with us? I can hardly wait to see the movie of the guys' faces as we came down the steps."

"JC and JJ were totally oblivious to us bystanders. They only had eyes for their own dates! I caught Lark beaming and nodding his head – he approves! Now, since I really want to know how you two fared, I'll share. Looking at your smiles, I'd say you both already have future dates scheduled."

Annie looked at Fe and me. She was beaming brighter than the high beams on a car. Her face was telling us everything was super-terrific. She thought back to the kissing booth, where she had wanted JJ to kiss her; however, he was off on a bus tour to pick up wounded warriors. Right before he left on that trip, he'd come into the store to pick up some flowers he'd ordered for his mother. She'd asked him if he'd like to write a note to go with the bouquet. JJ had stopped fiddling with the vase, as if he'd been stalling, looked at her, and said, "Maybe."

"Maybe?" she had responded.

"This time of year, our mother gets sad. Micah, Mercy's twin, was only seven when he died."

JJ then picked up a pen, jotted a few words, put the pen down, squared his shoulders, and left. Now she remembered he'd stopped, turned, given her the sweetest smile, and said, "Thanks, Annie." So even then, since Fe was the owner, he knew which twin he was talking to, and it made her smile grow. Annie beamed as she shared these past events with Fe and me.

"JJ kissed you!" I exclaimed, "And on your first date, too!"

Annie explained. "Remember, JJ was out of town the day of the kissing booth, so I'm guessing that when he said, 'this kiss is long overdue,' he was referring to missing that event. I never dreamed I'd be so blown away by a kiss. My whole mental perception shifted in emotional understanding. After our kiss, JJ and I sat stunned. I'm sure we both had silly grins on our faces. 'Never had a kiss like that before,' he whispered."

Annie admitted, "I had to clear my throat before I could say, 'me neither.' Monday night we will be going ice skating."

I teased, "Need something to cool you off, huh? Oh, Annie, I am so very pleased for you."

"Me, too. Thanks, Ve, for your suggestion to call him. He is a keeper! How about you and Lark?"

"I had a great time. I loved the short clips and was thrilled when Lark and Jake came in second."

Fe was shaking her head. "Oh, Ve, I hear a 'but' coming."

"We went to Rivers Edge restaurant and talked about the photography, plot, dialogue, and what the fellows are working on now. Lark's eyes said one thing, while his mouth shared nothing personal. He politely danced around all of my questions by turning them back to me. When we got home, he asked me to stay in the van and let him open my door. He helped me out, but before he shut the door, he reached for me. We kissed like it would never happen again, and I could tell he was as physically responsive as I. As we moved away from each other, he put his forehead against mine and groaned, 'Oh, Babe, I'm so sorry. You're awfully hard to resist.' I asked him, 'then why are you resisting?' Without another word he walked me to our front door, then went back and got in his vehicle. Do either of you know what is wrong? I asked him once if he was or had ever been married, and he never answered me. Well, I am a little hopeful that all will be revealed when the time is right. Now, Fe, what about you and JC? Give, girl!"

Annie lent her voice to mine. "Yeah, Fe, spill."

"First, Ve, I'm sure Lark has never been engaged, let alone married, and I know he deeply cares for you. Now, that being said, let me just take a deep breath, okay? Wow, JC is so nice and such a gentleman. We talked about everything and nothing. I told him things no one else knows; not even you, Annie. We could relate in everything from being the youngest triplet or twin to dreams and places we'd like to visit. We laughed a lot. He really listened and asked me insightful questions. He took a deep breath and appeared to be shy as he quietly said he's been praying for the wife God has for him. He then asked if I thought it was too early to share a kiss."

Welcome Huggers # 2 – Verity

"Nice! What did you say? As if we don't know."

"I told him it wasn't as if this was a blind date. I knew his sister, Mercy; for months, I had seen him around town; and in church and in our towns, he had a good reputation. By this time, he was laughing and said, 'So then, is that a yes?' I told him, 'Yes, I'd really like to share a kiss.' JC grinned at me and admitted, 'I would really like to, also.'

"You two know I've kissed a lot of guys, but none moved my world like JC. Can you believe I licked my lips and said, 'Oh, my, smoking hot. Can I please have another?' JC whispered, 'Happy to oblige.' What a special night! After church tomorrow, JC and I are going out for lunch and then for a hike. Our schedules are super-busy, so we are trying to fit in outings whenever we can."

My heart was so full, I felt like I might explode if I didn't share my thoughts.

"Do you realize I have lived here for almost five weeks? I can never thank you adequately for inviting me into your home and lives. This has been a healing place for me."

They both smiled and said, "We love you being here."

"By the way, Fe and Annie, a while back Mercy shared how, in less than a six-month period, she had to cope with many changes and what a toll it took emotionally. I wanted to say that you two are being very wise to start separating now. I know it happened because of the girlfriends wanting to see the house. If we have company, you both said you'd double up again. You have realized how important it will be to totally focus on your mate and not on your twin. You are taking different seats at the kitchen table and going to different girlfriend events, which in my opinion, shows you are intent on growing your futures with these men. Well done."

Fe stated. "I like that phrase, Ve: growing our futures."

I hesitated, then said, "Um, will you help me with something? Most of the guys who were in the service tend to use the word 'Babe' a lot. Unity never does. I've noticed lately that Lark is reverting to using it more often. I've asked him not to. You see, it makes me think of sailors – you know, a girl in every port. As long as they say 'Babe,' they won't say the wrong name for the girl they are with. I worked for a time with servicemen, and it was 'Babe this' and 'Babe that.' I don't like being called 'Babe.' How about Monday morning we start using the word 'Babe' instead of Lark or Sam whenever we address them. Do you think it will work? Will you give it a go? You can tell JC and JJ if you need to."

"What fun! We'll pretend we are actors and just slide it out of our mouth as if 'Babe' is what we've always called them. Hey, Verity, well done! You used four contractions!"

We all yawned, and I got up. "Come, Angel. Last minute pop outside, and we can retire."

"Verity, you shouldn't go out alone."

I frowned. "Fe, I've got to get my life back. I'll tap once on each of your doors when we come back."

*****

Why couldn't he just tell her what was in his heart? Yeah, he knew. One defense was fear of rejection if she actually knew the extent of his wounds in body and mind. But honestly, it was the promise extracted from him that kept him silent.

Lark heard the clicking of Angel's toenails on the wood and saw the dog moving towards him. He was busted, but so was Verity for she was disobeying orders to stay inside. She obviously knew it was a friend Angel had sniffed out, for he had not growled. Boo had taught Angel well as to when to growl, bark, or be silent. Verity whispered, "Fetch," and threw the ball a short distance. Angel flew off the porch and brought it back to be thrown again. After a few more soft throws, she and Angel disappeared through the door, but not before she whispered, "Goodnight, Lark. Sweet dreams."

Sweet dreams? He contemplated as to why she had chosen those words. Why couldn't she have said 'pleasant dreams,' 'sleep well,' or just remained silent? It seemed that Verity wished him to have a good night with sweet dreams in spite of his almost-rejection of her. What were sweet dreams anyway? Thinking back, he figured it was at about age thirteen when his sweet dreams had ended.

He thought about Philippians 4:8 in the Bible, where it mentions filling one's mind with noble, honorable, pure, admirable things. He needed to cultivate this habit. He was sure his dreams would be replaying the awesome, heart-stopping kiss they'd shared. He just hoped his dreams wouldn't turn into a future-fulfilling nightmare of her walking out of his life.

He suddenly realized he would never want to weigh her down with his black thoughts. What had she said to him the other day? Something about being as happy as she chose to be. Lark sat up straight as he realized he needed to change his attitude. No one else could do it for him.

Verity was never far from his thoughts. He desperately desired to spend all of his days – and nights – with her. She might not realize it, but she made him want to be a better man. He shuddered, as if cold, at the thought that he might exact a toll on Verity for his loss of limbs. Right. It was critical he begin working, as of tonight, on his attitude.

"God, please help me not to dwell on my losses, but choose daily, minute by minute, if necessary, to determine to live for You with joy in my heart. Thanks for bringing us kids back together. Please let Dad, Mother, and the Grands know we are doing fine. Help me to live with expectation, in hope, believing You have good plans for me. Uh – I hope Verity is the wife you have for me. I really love that gal. Amen."

Marilyn Stewart

Fifteen

Lark knew I usually visited a church I hadn't visited before one Sunday each month and asked me at breakfast if we could do so together today.

Oh, yes, we had definitely made an impression. People in that church certainly had more than roast preacher to discuss over their noon lunch. It started with his daring invitation to me at breakfast to go to with him to the church two blocks from our home. After I had agreed, Sam decided, as my bodyguard, that he and Boo needed to tag along. Looking at each other, Fe and Annie said they'd come, too, since the church was close and they had plans with their guys after church. Well, I couldn't leave Angel home alone, and thus, it had escalated.

The five of us and two dogs entered the building early in order to pick our seating arrangement. Annie moved down the pew, then Angel (on the floor), me, Lark, and Fe. Sam had taken his place in the pew squarely behind me, with Boo lying on the floor to his left.

We discovered later that, early Sunday morning, Mercy called her brothers, asking if they would come support Unity, who was to fill in for a sick pastor. Their unexpected appearance surprised and pleased Fe and Annie. They quickly shifted along the seat to let JC sit next to Fe. Annie walked around to the pew in back to sit near Boo (taking up three places on the floor), while JJ took the aisle seat next to her.

As if all the above jockeying wasn't distracting enough for the church members, a young lady named Serah came and sat down next to Sam. We all learned later, from Annie, that Serah and Sam had been holding hands. Apparently, since it was obvious that the other couples were holding hands, Serah had reached over and taken Sam's hand in hers. He'd looked at her briefly, rearranged their hands, and with a smile and a little sigh, relaxed and leaned back.

When our group caught sight of Mercy, her brothers told us Unity would be preaching. He entered from the side door. Taking a couple of steps and without looking around, he sat down next to Mercy on the front row and bowed his head.

115

Welcome Huggers # 2 – Verity

Right before Uni was to share, the song leader asked all of us to stand, bow our heads, and sing an old hymn. Everyone had closed their eyes. Some raised open hands towards heaven, while others did not. The song began softly, but gained in volume as the three siblings suddenly began to harmonize.

My arms broke out in goosebumps. I realized they were unaware of the astounding, joyful effect they were stirring in hearts. I peeked at JC's, then JJ's awe-struck faces, then at my housemates. The three, with chins up but eyes closed, sang with enthusiasm. Tears ran down my face, but I didn't let go of Lark's hand for fear of spoiling a heaven-enabled treat. With the song over, we all slowly, quietly, sat and savored a moment of pure worship. Unity finally rose, moved to the front, and without looking at anyone, bowed his head and prayed. Our thinking had been transformed by the words in addition to the pure notes sung by the Lane family.

Raising his head to preach, Uni appeared stunned at seeing friends and in-laws sitting in the pews, smiling at him. At first, Uni had difficulty harnessing his own attention, let alone his congregation's.

I knew I dared not look at anyone. Between my hand being held firmly, the awesome song, and the general quirkiness of the morning, I was sorely tested to remember we were in church. Once or twice, I tried to move an inch or two away from Lark, only to have him shift as well, so we touched at the shoulders and hips. My stomach had butterflies due to Lark's nearness and his fingers intertwined with mine. Lark seemed happy to share my Bible with our united hands supporting one side and my other hand keeping the Bible steady. Time and again, I had to refocus my thoughts back to what Unity was sharing.

His theme was God's ways in view of eternity. All my extraneous flights stopped when he looked at Mercy and said, "Sunshine, are you sure you are okay with me sharing this information?" At her nod, he proceeded.

"Most of you have lived in one of our three towns long enough to know a bit about Mercy's difficulties. When she was nearly sixteen, she was kidnapped and held a prisoner for seven months. As a result, she has lots of physical scars and mental issues. During this last year, Mercy has prayed for healing. She studied the scriptures regarding people like Joseph, Daniel, Esther, and others. Their lives and attitudes challenged her to move forward by trusting that God had good things in store for her.

"The day she made the choice to really live, she spotted a youngster on her bus with a mark on one wrist that was similar to hers. Weeks before, she had considered leaving home to drive for a trucking firm. She drove for them one day and will probably drive again on a part-time basis. The morning of the day that I returned home, she was involved in locating five children. Five year old memories returned. She was on the verge of total collapse – feeling she'd break into a zillion pieces. In the middle of that night, she realized she was and had been exactly where God needed her to be, so that she could be the answer to three sets of parents' desperate prayers. Joseph was sold, then left in jail for years. Esther was taken for a king's pleasure due to her physical beauty. In both cases, God turned evil intentions around in order to save many lives. Let us grasp a new perspective of God at work. We will not have a perfect or maybe even a safe life, but He is always with us. Every day, we must ask for His help in all things. He wants a personal relationship with us to bring glory to His name. The ripple effect of your obedience and deeds will only be fully revealed in eternity. Think of the awesome privilege of going on adventures – unwanted as some may be – with the Creator-God of this awesome universe, you, and me."

At the end of the service, we probably shook hands with everyone except the babies. Each of us stopped to thank Unity and Mercy for sharing the how – the reality of living, looking with expectation towards God's leading in each new day.

We had left church uplifted and thoughtful, but one stray remark after we'd gotten down the road a bit set Fe, Annie, and me off. We exploded, doubled over with our long-held nervous laughter. We laughed, giggled, and snickered – we just couldn't contain our hilarity. One or two of us would stop, only to hear another snicker, which set off another burst of giggles. The men looked at us, smiled and shook their heads.

Welcome Huggers # 2 – Verity

Finally, Sam said, "If you females can stop laughing, how about we all go out to lunch together? We should treat Uni and Mercy for what they had to put up with today. You want to come with us, Serah?"

She smiled, saying, "Yes, please, I'd love to."

Lark had enjoyed watching his sisters interacting with their beaux. He realized that, before the end of the year, he might be related by marriage to even Mercy and Uni. He saw Verity giving him quick glances and realized he'd grown extra quiet. The possibility of being even a shirttail relative of Hank and Mel overwhelmed him. He never spoke of it to his sisters, but he sorely missed their parents. He certainly could empathize with Verity.

I noticed everyone around our round table except Fe, Annie, and Lark, who still seemed unaware of what had happened at church, were dying to comment.

Lark finally looked at me and said, "Okay, Ve, what are you wanting to say or ask? You're biting your lip and glancing at me. This means you want to say something, but are not sure if you dare. Out with it, Love."

Around the table came, "Yeah, out with it, Love!"

"Lark, Fe, and Annie, did you three as youngsters, sing together in church or with your parents? You each have a fantastic gift that you shared with us today."

"We did?" Annie queried.

From around the table were nods and statements: "Definitely!"

"Oh, yeah!"

"Awesome."

"You guys rock!"

I nodded and challenged them. "I expect to hear a lot more of it at home. Humming is fine, but your singing is incredible."

Fe surprised everyone when she gave a little chuckle. "I've been praying for quite a while for that song to be played in a church when we three were close together. You see, that was the last song we sang together before our parents were murdered and we were split up. I hadn't known the title. This morning I was surprised, but so thankful. I deliberately leaned against Lark as I used to and sang loud enough to pull in Annie behind us. As we sang, Annie leaned forward and gripped part of both of our shoulders. I could barely sing for thinking, Thank you, Jesus!"

Tough Annie surprised us. Tears flowed down her face as she leaned forward and touched Fe's cheek. "I blocked out a lot of stuff that I found too painful to recall. Thanks, Sis. I wasn't sure how I knew the song, but it just rolled out of me like water being pumped out of a fountain."

Lark cleared his throat. "Guess I'd better add my two cents. Thank you, Fe, for making today special by giving us a new memory and testimony of God answering a prayer."

JJ grinned at Annie. "You blew me away! No more, 'I can't sing' from you, my girl! You or the three of you can sing with my band anytime. In fact, let's make it this next weekend."

JC leaned in to whisper something in Fe's ear, which caused her to blush, then giggle. No one had the nerve to ask what he had said. Mercy and I glanced at each other, having noted how red his ears had become, and grinned.

Unity cleared his throat and caught Lark's eye. "When you began to sing, I recognized your voice, but not that it was you. Years ago, I heard you at a talent night when we were in the military. You also played the trumpet. I'm pleased you made the decision to sing with your sisters. It's obvious you've finally decided to accept you're alive and chosen to live with intention."

Sam stood. "I hate to eat and run; however, I have to take Serah home and then go on duty. See you all."

At that, we began to move. JC and Fe were going hiking; JJ and Annie up to Scenic Lake. Unity and Mercy were headed to the hospital. Lark asked if I'd go with him to the park. Walking hand-in-hand along dirt foot paths, watching the birds, and enjoying the quiet was therapeutic. I loved the sound of the breeze dashing through the trees. Time and again, Angel made us laugh. Whenever a chipmunk dashed by, he froze, but was very curious about the little lizards sunning themselves on several large rocks. He eased up, gently put his nose on one, then pulled back. If it stayed still, he'd move to the next one. If it moved, he darted in and placed his nose on it, but never opened his mouth. It was like a game of tag. Lizard moves, Angel touches it, then backs up to wait for it to move again.

What a fabulous morning – memory-making, fun, uplifting, and emotional. Walking quietly with Lark in this park was nice. I welcomed the much-needed break from fear and uncertainty, and therefore pretended ignorance as to why Zeke and Jake were strolling in the park on a Sunday. I was tempted to say their names and wave, just to see what they would do, but refrained.

*****

I, Lark, knew today I'd pushed past the line of my promise to Peter, but am in no way sorry. I knew Verity was puzzled by my behavior, but I had more than one reason to keep my mouth shut for right now. I just hoped in future, Verity would recall my touch every time she went out on a date. Four of us roommates knew Verity's touch since she often brought relief by massaging our shoulders. As I slid into bed, a chuckle escaped. It had been years since I was happy to be alive. I was sure Verity had seen our escorts in the park, but since she hadn't said anything, neither had I. It had been a wonderful, fun, spectacular day. I fell asleep with a smile on my face, reviewing the events.

Sixteen

"Good morning, ladies."

"Hi, Babe."

"Good morning, ladies."

"Hi, Babe."

"What's with this 'Hi, Babe' greeting?"

"Shush," I said as I answered my ringing cell phone. "Hello, who's calling please?"

"Verity, this is Jeff Daylight, from the newspaper. Oh, sorry I hadn't checked the time. I didn't wake you, did I?"

"No. How can I help?"

"You can help by being my plus-one at an event two weeks from now on Saturday. I think you'd relish the venue, and I would certainly enjoy your company. If you're now a twosome with Lark, then just tell me I am out of line."

"Tell me more. As for the other, I don't seem to be."

"I get it. Someone is listening. It would be a seminar on writing, followed by a meal, and ending with an awards ceremony. We'd need to leave by noon and would get back around ten."

"I'll think it over and call you in a day or two. Okay?"

"Perfect. Thanks, Verity. 'Bye."

"'Bye."

Without saying anything further, I placed the hot toast on the table. Four pair of eyes focused on me. I ignored their silent question and instead said, "All is ready, if you care to sit down." After saying that, I felt silly, for Sam and Lark always waited to push in our chairs. Everyone stayed silent after Sam asked a blessing. I knew they were waiting for me to tell them who called.

Normally when answering my cell, I always said the caller's name. In fact, they liked to tease me about this habit of giving myself a bit of time and alerting people as to the caller. As we ate, my mind drifted. I hoped the men would get the message without us having to explain the 'Babe' campaign.

I broke the silence. "I plan to head down to my workshop this morning, Sam. I need to empty the kiln, do some paperwork, and take the finished pots to Ben at the gallery."

"But that wasn't who phoned was it, Verity? Are you trying misinformation to divert our attention from asking who called?"

I sighed. "Well, nosy, I guess it didn't work, did it? But I really do need to be in my workshop. I can hardly wait to feel the silky-smooth clay and endeavor to create something useful."

"After breakfast, I'll check with the Sheriff for you, Ve." Sam stated, then added, "I heard some giggling long after lights should have been out on Saturday and again on Sunday night."

"So, Babe, were you, like, doing a bed-check or listening to hear where we were or what we were saying?"

"I thought about it, but I didn't eavesdrop. I heard Verity tip-toe down to your bedroom, Annie. Did you all have a good time Saturday night? What's this 'Babe' business?"

We girls beamed, shared high-fives, and mischievously announced, "Oh, yeah, smoking hot dates, that's for sure!"

I witnessed Sam raise an eyebrow at Lark and observed Lark give a tiny nod and a rare, happy grin.

"So, Babe, are you going to ask Serah out now that you've been to church and out to eat with her?"

"I might, Fe. Now, girls, stop bugging me about dating. If I need your input regarding a girl, I'll ask, okay?"

I blurted out, "I'm curious. When you all were growing up, what did you eat for breakfast? Or what is your favorite food?"

They looked at each other. Fe was the first to respond. "I remember having strawberry jam on toast along with my cereal."

Annie countered, "I preferred honey and peanut butter on my toast, and as you can see, I still like that combination. Nowadays, I love pears, corn on the cob, and steak."

Sam laughed. "In our home, we had a variety of things. My older sisters preferred those gooey things you put in the toaster to heat and eat. When they were in high school, they only permitted themselves to have toast and tea or coffee, except on weekends. Either on Saturday or Sunday, and sometimes both, we got bacon, eggs, potatoes, or pancakes. I really liked the weekend meals. But usually for breakfast, we ate oatmeal and toast."

Sam looked pointedly at Lark and asked, "What do you like or remember eating for breakfast all those years ago?"

"I've always liked eggs, bacon, and hash browns; however, I remember having a whole lot of oatmeal and toast."

My turn. "To break our fast, we had oatmeal, or oatmeal and toast with vegemite or a rare treat, jelly." I had decided the only way to learn things was to ask lots of questions.

"So, which one of you three is the oldest triplet?"

I glanced quickly at Lark and away, but not before seeing a knowing look enter his eyes.

Annie responded instantly. "Lark was born a couple of minutes after midnight. I came next, which makes Fe the youngest. Why are you shaking your head and frowning, Lark?"

"I didn't realize you both still think we are triplets. You two are twins, but we are not triplets."

Annie protested. "No way. Of course we are triplets."

I noted Fe smiling sweetly at Lark as she said, "Now it all makes perfect sense. I've always wondered if it was your gender or you being the oldest that made the difference. You never seemed to share as much of our heightened sense of awareness and weird connectedness. Have you always known, or when did you learn you were older? We shared the same birthday cake. Dad and Mom always called us their terrific triple threesome."

"After our folks died, I lived with a family and worked on a farm. I then joined the service rather than pursuing a college education. I thought our grandparents would need to sign the papers, but then I got my birth certificate. I, too, had often wondered about things. Why, for instance I was ahead of you two in school. I knew it was not due to being super-smart. I located the Grands in a nursing home. With all our losses, they told me not to hunt for or say anything to you girls about not being triplets – at least not for a while. Since it wasn't important, I forgot about it."

"But you really are our brother, aren't you, Lark? How much older are you than us?"

"Yes, Fe and Annie, I truly am your blood brother. I am a year older to the very day."

I couldn't resist a tiny smile along with a sigh, thinking the dam was breaking. I again quickly glanced at Lark, only to be caught by his twinkling eyes and knowing grin. He drawled, "I know what you are doing. Are you satisfied, my dear?"

Annie and Fe looked at me in surprise, then laughed. I nodded, saying, "Yeah, Babe, I am." I met his stare and decided to accept Jeff's invitation. A little more nudging, and I might find out why, while his eyes spoke volumes, his mouth stayed shut.

Sam broke the silence. "Verity, think hard. What odd things have happened to you in the last five years? Actually start from the accident in which your family members, but not you, died."

His words hit hard. Was it me who should have died? They had been driving my car. I shut my eyes so that no one would see the shock I'd received. My mind finally settled enough to review the years. College; roommates; work; bosses – nothing stood out. My parents' return; the funeral, then... Paul; the assault; then....

Lark spoke sharply. "Verity, stop; go back. You flinched, skipped ahead, then again seemed to pause briefly."

I hesitated. My mind warred over possibly incriminating someone, versus the fact that Sam needed to know everything in order to protect me. I sighed, nodded, took a deep breath, and opened my mouth.

"The first incident happened at the cemetery a couple of weeks after their deaths. Every so often, I'd go check the flowers at the grave and sit and talk. I know they couldn't hear me, but being so alone, it helped. Hearing what I was 'telling them' assisted me in realizing what I could do to move forward. Anyway, one time I heard strange sounds nearby, got spooked, and headed for my car, which I'd parked around a corner. The police had arrived and were standing near my car. Someone had called to say a man was smashing a rock into the back of it. Of course, he was nowhere to be seen. A week later, I went back to the cemetery. On my parents' grave was a piece of cardboard with R.I.P. and my initial. The plastic flowers from their grave had been used as an anchor to keep it from blowing away. That was the second time I met Detective Dan Ragland. The first was in regard to my parents' 'accident,' and the third was when I was in the hospital after the assault. I talk to him now and again, asking for any updates."

I dropped my head and stopped talking – I had whined enough. I'd share the rest later. I heard Sam state firmly, "Go on,

Verity. Tell us now. All the rest of the strange happenings, regardless of how small."

I shrugged my shoulders and began to talk really fast. "Well, soon after that, I went on an outing with the singles group from church, but surely it couldn't be connected. Anyway, we were in wooded area near a creek. Lucky for me that I don't like heights and was back a few steps from the edge. I thought I was the last person to leave, but heard a twig break behind me. For some reason, I grabbed the small tree trunk next to me. I was suddenly struck by a tree limb with lots of leaves on it. You know how someone in front of you lets go of a branch – that sort of thing. I lurched forward and down onto my knees, but not into the water. When I finally stood up and turned, no one was in sight. That night, after I doctored my scraped knees, I looked in the mirror at my back – red welts were still visible. Months later, the day before I moved out of an apartment, I had a bit of a scare. I always locked my door, but it was unlocked, there was a faint smell of cigar smoke, my mail was inside, on the floor, and the word 'deceased' had been stamped multiple times on each envelope. That's it, folks. Honest." As I began to relax, a thought popped into my head.

"Wait a minute." I raced upstairs and retrieved some papers.

"Remember the paperwork from Paul? I made two copies before giving the originals to Sheriff Ben. See? They've checked three places on each page to print my name and underlined the middle one. Maybe we are looking at two sets of people – one being the identity thieves. I have never, ever used my middle name or initial on any document. My middle name has always been a secret – just between my Dad, Mum, and me."

Lark burst out. "Don't you realize, Ve, that you have been harassed for a long time? I'm amazed you've coped so well."

I shrugged my shoulders. "I was taught not to complain, to take precautions, pray, and trust God. What else could I do?"

"But why haven't you told anyone? Does Peter know?"

"Lark, what can anyone do since there was 'no crime' to my person? I took pictures and told a detective about those events, but he said I probably did it myself for publicity. After I was attacked, Detective Ragland entered my life. He believed me."

Sam interrupted. "Go back, Ve. On what part of your car was the fellow pounding?"

"The detective said it was the lock on the trunk and the left rear taillight, and that he probably just wanted in out of the cold."

"You still have the same car, Ve?"

"Yes, Sam. The dents in the back are still there, but I did replace the taillight."

"Would you mind if we check your car?" Sam said, as his phone rang.

"Excuse me. Sheriff? Yes, they are all here. Interesting. I hope to have some possibly pertinent news when I see you in about a half hour." He turned back to us.

"The sheriff says we can relax regarding the four fellows you hugged who smelled like oranges. There is a new deodorant for men in its trial phase. It has a faint odor of oranges. The company is sending the names of the men in the study to the sheriff. He said you can go to your shop, but keep the door locked, and let someone know before you leave for the day."

"Oh, this is great, Ve! You can ride with Annie and me since we'll only be a couple of doors down from you. We'll go to lunch and come home together."

I handed my car keys to Sam, saying, "Thanks, Babe!"

I kissed Sam on the cheek, then dashed out of the kitchen into the backyard, with Angel and Boo at my heels. I felt mildly guilty about not sharing one other thing, but Peter was still out of town, and I needed to discuss it with him first.

Meanwhile, back in the kitchen, Sam turned on the girls.

"Girls, I'll ask you again: what is this 'Babe' stuff?"

Fe answered. "Guys, figure it out. No wonder Verity lets us answer the door and seems to be ultra-aware of her surroundings. I was surprised when she went to the mailbox the other night. Now, what is going on with Verity and you, Lark? Annie and I want the three of us to get married, on the same day, time, and place."

"Dear sisters, as much as I love you two, I am not going to marry either or both of you."

Marilyn Stewart

"Very funny, brother. You are evading our question with semantics, smarty-pants. We don't care if we aren't triplets, we still want to share our special day with you and Verity."

"Nice of you to give me a heads-up. There's still time for you to do the dishes before you head to work."

*****

A brisk cleaning of my little workshop helped calm me. I'd been surprised by an unexpected surge of rage, then fear. Who was harassing me? Why? As I took the last piece from the kiln, Angel laid down on his mat. His example had me sending a "help me, Jesus" prayer, then I deliberately relaxed. Right. Everything I did today would free me up to work with clay tomorrow. While my fingers itched to feel the firm, smooth, slick, mud-like substance, I forced myself to not go near it. Spreadsheets, ordering supplies, and other such mundane things had to be done today. Tomorrow, my personal therapy could begin. My mind drifted towards creating new designs and settled. Looking at my watch, I realized there was only a half hour until lunch. Since I had time and privacy, I called Jeff.

"Hi, Jeff. I need you to be straight with me."

"Okay, Verity, what do you want to know?"

"Rumor has it your heart has been lassoed by Katie. Something, other than her grandmother needing her, caused her to flee. You don't need to share the particulars. Is asking me out a way of getting back at Katie to make her jealous? Are you setting me up for trouble? What are your expectations here?"

"You're certainly forthright, Verity. I'm crazy about Katie. I am hoping she will fall so deeply in love with me, she'll accept me despite my war-related injuries. As head of the library, where words are key, I thought this seminar would interest you. I know you are attracted to Lark, thus, we can have a great day together without complications. Katie should be back home in two weeks."

"Thank you for your candor. I will be delighted to be your plus-one. We can have an educational, fun day. It will be lovely to have Katie back in town. Okay, Jeff – it's a date."

I had not liked hearing Jeff reveal he knew who held my heart. I put my head in my hands and quietly reflected on what I had just set in motion. I knew my motives weren't pure. My goal was to make Lark jealous enough to make a move on me. I was hoping to force him to break his silence. I would date and date and maybe even kiss.... I snickered recalling this morning. I thought Lark would break his neck, whipping his head around so fast upon hearing me call him 'Babe.' I had ignored his shock over me also calling Sam 'Babe.' It had been hard to hide a grin when the sparkle in Lark's eyes had fled and a scowl had swiftly covered his features.

Stepping out of my wee shop, I turned, locked the door, and froze. Angel was sniffing at a potted rose bush near my shop door. I hurried Angel down the covered boardwalk to Fe and Annie's flower shop. Bolting through the door, I checked for customers, then blurted, "Do you ever sell potted plants?" They shook their heads.

"I thought not. Did you place a rose bush by my shop door?" At their 'no,' I touched 'send' on my phone.

"Sam, did either you or Lark put a plant outside my store today? No? Neither did Fe or Annie. Angel kept sniffing the pot; I could hardly drag him away. Fe, Annie, and I are headed to Welcome to Dine for lunch."

During lunch, we avoided what I had shared this morning. Fe and Annie told me a bit about their parents. They'd loved nature – plants and rocks – good thing since they'd owned a nursery. Now I understood the names they'd bestowed on their kids. Fe told how the three of them walked to and from school together. They always checked in first at the nursery. This is the reason they all had the same visual imprinted on their brains. A few weeks after their eleventh birthday, they'd found their parents lying amidst trashed plants – murdered. Their massacre had never been solved. After sharing this sadness, we moved on to a lighter topic.

We were still giggling over the reaction the men displayed this morning regarding the 'Babe' campaign when we saw Casey come into the restaurant. I was stunned. Despite a week having passed, she was still colorful enough to drop jaws. I moved my hand to hide my grin. Catching sight of us she hurried over and flung herself into the available seat next to me. Before we could say anything, Casey stood back up and loudly invited everyone to have a good look at the results of her sin of jealousy. It definitely stopped conversation for a few seconds, but glances and chuckling continued to break out. Casey shrugged her shoulders, sighed, and then, to everyone's surprise, began to laugh hilariously. Stuttering through her mirth, she proclaimed, "Actually it is rather funny. I'm certainly being noticed. Did you know I've gone viral?"

I was curious. "Casey, did you find Ian before he heard about it via our gossip channels? Is he communicating with you?"

Casey wiped her eyes, drew in a deep breath, and leaned in, so we did likewise. With our four heads nearly touching, she whispered, "At first he just stared at me, then asked how I could do such a stupid thing, and shouted at me to leave. I thought I had blown it with him for all time, but guys began to tell him that he was one lucky fella. We've been talking on the phone and texting. He admitted that, at first, he hoped I'd stay hidden and away from him, but his thinking has changed. This weekend we are going to play miniature golf and go to a restaurant – not to a dark movie theater." Casey hurried away, and we hop-scotched from topic to topic.

Fe and Annie wanted to invite JC and JJ to supper, soon. We discussed inviting someone for Sam. For a second, I wondered about a date each for Lark and me, but quickly realized, in their minds, we were a twosome. While we thought about who to invite for Sam, we moved on to create a man-friendly menu. No casseroles. A roast, green beans, mashed potatoes, gravy, a salad, and for dessert, apple pie and ice cream. I would do the shopping. All three of us would help with the cooking. Annie would make two of her fantastic pies. Fe would decorate the living room and table. When I recommended we invite Fairlyn for Sam, Fe and Annie stilled and studied my face.

"Do you have 'the gift,' like Mercy does in matching people up? Fe softly queried. "You were 'spot on' for Annie and me."

I laughed, then shrugged. "I just use my eyes, ears, and assess character traits."

Welcome Huggers # 2 – Verity

The rest of the day was uneventful. After supper, I saw Lark hovering near the stairs – obviously waiting for me. With no one around to overhear, Lark quietly asked, "Verity, love, are you afraid it could be a family member who is harassing you?" I stilled, dropped my eyes, and hesitated. Then, looking at him, gave a tiny nod and hurried past. As I crawled into bed, I prayed not only for freedom from fear, but for protection for everyone in the house. I loved the way the five of us had become a 'family' unit.

Marilyn Stewart

Seventeen

After a couple of days, the guys "got it" and swore off using the word Babe when addressing me. I was looking forward to tonight, for we would all be home for supper and free to spend the evening together. It had been a while. Fe and Annie had had three separate large flower venues, back-to-back. I had found myself helping by running errands, cleaning up, taking orders, etc. The library now stayed open two nights a week until nine. Sam bounced between his deputy duties, once-a-week dog training class, and acting in our local theater. I knew I probably should tell Sam about the fellow I saw at the Ghost Town, but Peter and I had yet to talk. Lark had been busy editing his latest commercial. This morning, his client would have viewed the completed project.

As the guys came in, I heard, "Smell that, Sam? My favorite. Meatloaf!"

I smiled at the happiness in Lark's voice. Yes, I had made his favorite. With the thought of greeting them face-to-face when they entered the kitchen, for a change, I was facing them. My smile wobbled. I tried to hide my response, but to no avail. Both men queried, "Ve, what's wrong?" I ignored their question. "Welcome home. I need to see both of you in the study after we eat. It won't take long." Fe and Annie missed the interaction and came in full of what had happened in the shop, and of course, sharing the latest concerning JC and JJ.

*****

Lark looked around and thought about how love was the glue that seemed to be saturating the air in this home. His sisters were so conspicuously content with the guys they were dating. The subject of love had come up numerous times since Sam and he had moved in. In a way, it was rather fun to provoke the girls with crazy outrageous statements, just to get them going.

I could see Verity chewing her lip. We all knew it indicated she was debating whether or not to blurt out something. She was probably thinking about sharing a "Verity truth" one of us might

131

not appreciate hearing. For some reason, I was always interested in what she divulged. It kept things very interesting. The last couple of times we'd all been together, Sam and I had been bedeviling – teasing Ve and my sisters. I briefly wondered if we'd gone too far – they were just such easy targets. Verity was a lovely girl, female, woman, lady – whatever she might like to be called, I wasn't really sure. I knew it wasn't 'Babe.' The single females in town talked about girlfriends; guys had girlfriends, but some people thought calling a female over a certain age a 'girl' was just not right. I wasn't sure what to call Verity, except 'dear' or 'honey' or 'precious.' I hadn't tried that last name yet, but time was on my side. I smiled at my sisters and said, "Am I going to have to go over to the Willis place and ask your young men if their intentions are honorable?"

They pretended to think it over, then broke out laughing, sputtered a bit, but didn't say yea or nay.

It seemed as if harmony in the house was a matter of priority to the ladies. I vividly recalled the last time the subject of love was raised. Verity had gotten up to get something during one of these exchanges. With her back to us, she'd responded to either Sam or my leading statement by retorting, "One can 'love' with only their body, but not using their mind, heart, or soul. A purely physical thing, which is not giving and forsaking all others. That person withholds themselves from total commitment. Is it a form of lying or lust? Could it ever be categorized as love?" I suspected a hidden barb directed at me for my unwillingness to share.

My sweet sister, Fe, always wanted to believe the best of everyone. "Maybe it is an acceptance problem of themselves. Selfishness maybe. Maybe they have never had a loving home life. Maybe a lack of willingness to share. Maybe lack of trust?"

I'd chuckled hearing an explosive, "Baloney!" Annie was adamant. "That was a lot of maybes, Fe. If two people love each other, trust, and desire to share their lives, they'd better first be willing to talk freely. They'll not make it if they aren't open and willing to share their innermost secrets. To me, love is forsaking all others, even your twin,, in favor of your spouse. Love is risky, as in scary – being a total commitment – emotionally thrilling,

132

terrifying, exhausting, and yet surprisingly splendiferously glorious."

There had been a long moment of stunned silence. I had finally smiled at my sister and said, "Wow, Annie, tell us what you really think, huh, girl! What has happened to our tough, fierce, secretive, no-guy-will-ever-trap-me Annie?"

"Well, brother, after living in foster homes, I know I said no marrying; too painful; messy; heart-breaking, not for me. JJ happened. Love totally caught me by surprise. Lately, I've been thinking about Dad and Mom. I know, Lark, you've been supportive, yet skeptical, since JJ comes from such a different environment from ours. If he asks me, I plan to say 'YES' and no, it isn't just because I'll get Hank and Melody for in-laws. I have to admit though, they would be powerful incentives. You feel it, too, don't you, Fe? As you know, we have been out formally, snatched meals together, enjoyed fishing, and gone for long walks. This last time out, JJ shared how when Mercy was in the hospital due to her arm being broken – you all remember that awful day...."

Fe mumbled, "Too clearly. We were right behind her!"

Annie continued. "As she regained consciousness, she heard Unity praying for her – for them. His prayer, according to JJ, changed Mercy's attitude and the possibility of a 'them.' She shared with her twin brothers that they needed to start praying for their future wives and be true men of God. JJ said it changed both JC and himself. Before we parted ways this last time, JJ prayed for me, for us. I've been wanting to cry every time I think of it. It for sure changed me. Sam and Lark, I challenge you to pray for your future wives. Don't forget to pray for yourselves as well."

I had smiled. "Thanks for sharing. I'd like to know if there is anything you don't like or love about JJ?"

"Funny, funny. Of course there is, and I'm sure there are things he doesn't like about me. We are humans and not perfect, which I'm sure comes as no surprise to the four of you."

"I wondered if you thought everything was impeccably perfect and reality had flown out of your head."

"Ah, brother dear, we do have some issues which would or will need to be resolved; however, I plan to enjoy one day at a time and not jump ahead to worry over things which may never happen.

Welcome Huggers # 2 – Verity

This fragile, extraordinary feeling inside me is growing stronger and more confident each day. I feel like a tight bud opening."

Nodding at her, I replied, "Glad to hear it. Remember, this may be old-fashioned, but I expect any fellow who wishes to marry either of my sisters to come talk to me first."

"So, brother, are you going to hint, inform them, or tell Unity to pass on the warning?"

"Thanks for the good suggestions, Fe. I'll wait on events, monitor the situations, and then proceed."

Annie grinned. "Wow. That was fun!"

Fe agreed. "We are like a true family. Secrets are safe as in all for one and one for all. We have knit so tightly it is going to be really hard when we have to part."

I tuned back into the present to hear Fe say, "You've been quiet, Sam. Anything to share with all of us?"

"Yes, Fe. I've invited my folks to visit. I want them to meet all of my many friends."

"Well, Annie and I would be delighted to go back to sharing so they could have a bedroom. Let us know if or when they might come so they can stay with us."

"I really appreciate your open invitation, Fe. You, too, Annie. I now have several options since Eb and El Unique have also invited them to stay."

*****

I was surprised when Lark broke up our chatting with a suggestion. "We've sat long enough. Everyone choose a task."

Sam nodded. "Let's mix it up. Lark, you go throw the ball for the dogs. Verity and I will do the dishes after Fe and Annie clean the table, scrape off the plates, and sweep the floor."

I immediately said, "Works for me."

Upon hearing Lark say, "Sam?" in a quiet, steely, questioning way, the three of us girls stood still. After checking the guys' faces, three of us moved to follow Sam's suggestions. After Lark, Annie, and Fe left the kitchen, Sam and I looked at each other, grinned, and burst out laughing.

134

"You stirring the pot a bit? I got the idea Lark wasn't happy with you. Wash or dry, Sam?"

"Trying to help get Lark to open up. I didn't realize how insecure he is about you. How about I dry this time? I reckon Lark is going to make short work of the dogs fetching and find a reason to return to the kitchen."

"So what did you want to talk to me about, Sam? By the way, I noticed you've been going out on only one date with numerous Welcome Huggers. I've been wondering if you'd like us to invite Fairlyn here for a long, fun weekend."

"I wanted to talk to you about Essie, Verity. She needs some attention from you girlfriends right now, but she's too shy to reach out and ask."

"Thank you, Sam, for bringing her to my attention. Is there anything specific, but not confidential, that you can share?"

"Her grandmother is failing – fast. I was wondering if any of you could pitch in and take her morning or evening shift so she doesn't lose her job."

I nodded and smiled. "I am rather glad we don't have an automatic dishwasher in this house. I've had more good conversations when someone's hands are wet than any other place in this home. Sam, I am truly grateful you trusted me with this information. Later tonight, I will talk with Fe and Annie, then with Brenda, the current President of our Welcome Huggers group."

We heard the door open, close, and dogs panting.

"Sam, you didn't answer my question regarding...."

"Yeah, I know I haven't. Just let it rest for now, Ve."

"Hey, I just want what is best – who is right for you. You know that, don't you, Sam?"

"Yes, Verity. I know your heart only wants me to have the girl that will delight me all the days of my life."

Sam put away the final pan, leaned down, and kissed me on the cheek. Hanging up the towel, and with a small, pleased grin on his face, he sauntered past Lark.

I raised my voice. "I need to see you two in the study in five minutes. I mean it, guys."

Upon my entrance, both men stood. I shooed them towards two comfortable chairs, then leaned up against the back of the desk, and put my backpack on the floor.

Looking back and forth between the two, I began. "So how long have you let the sores fester?" They frowned, but remained silent. I walked the couple of steps to where they were sitting and took a deep breath. I was about to reveal another secret or two. Leaning towards them, I held up a laminated card and said, "You might have heard or guessed. Look: I am a qualified paramedic. Both of you have at least one hot spot – sore, due to your prosthetics. Are you going to let me have a look, or are you going to the clinic or hospital? You cannot afford to let it become worse. You two have been looking after me and on your feet way too much. Please permit me to assist you as much as I possibly can."

As both men sat stoically silent, I knew I would have to share a bit more of my history with them.

"Fellas, I was my mother's assistant in the aftermath of fights with an ax, spear, or other weapons, and accidents of all sorts. I have seen maggots in sores, torn and bleeding wounds, and diseased flesh. You two are heroes. Please permit me the opportunity – the privilege – of helping to relieve your suffering."

Sam reached for his pant leg, took off his prosthetic foot, and placed it in my outstretched hand. I lightly ran my finger tip to check for a hint of roughness, then used a wipe to see if it hung up anywhere. Such a tiny, uneven spot. "For a month, I volunteered at a place where prostheses were created. I learned a lot, plus a few tips that you might find handy." I shared a few as I moved on to check his stump, which thankfully, was only a little inflamed. I pulled out two items and invited Sam to treat himself.

I had been taking quick peeks at Lark and realized he was not ready to have me see, let alone touch, his wounds. "I'll leave my backpack here. Sam, please help Lark in the same way I did you. I will be in the kitchen." My added words carried a threat. "Lark, we will carry you to the car if needed. You're already limping badly! Your sore or 'hot spot' must be treated properly – tonight."

Marilyn Stewart

With my hand on the door knob, I turned, looked at them, and hesitated. Giving a little nod, I quickly blurted, "My room is right above yours. Somehow I can hear you at night – though not your actual words. Guys, I know Boo helps by waking you from a nightmare. He cannot do massage, which might aid you to relax and go back to sleep. I maybe can help – like I do with the neck massages I have given the four of you. You two will need to be willing to let me try. I would use hot, moist towels, a heating pad, oil, and I'd only massage your back and neck. Let me know your decision. It would be a secret amongst us three."

I all but bolted out the door, my heart racing. It had been hard to share my awareness. I wondered if they'd accept my gift. I sat holding a cup of hot black tea and thought of many things. Would I have the courage to touch Lark? Would he have the guts to accept? Spring had just arrived – well, according to the calendar, anyway. I'd been in town for ten months. All too soon it would be summer. Although it was still months away, every so often I thought about the kissing booth at our Fair in the fall. Would I give it a miss or kiss as many guys as possible to get Lark out of my system before leaving town after the wounded warrior event. I loved Angel; however, I felt he was meant to live with a wounded warrior. His training, thanks to Boo and Sam, was going well. This knowledge suddenly settled me. On the other hand, I could not dwell on all the friends I had made in these three towns and how excruciating it would be to leave them. I would miss Peter – not so much Charity. Every so often, I saw the twins in the town of Unique. They were so cute – now running and saying complete sentences. They loved to play with their cousins, who were like extended family since they were together so much. I had days filled with sorrow and regret, but the deed was done, and I needed to move forward, even if it meant cutting all ties with my kinfolk. My mind drifted to who had recently asked about my middle initial or name. When and to whom had it begun to be so important?

I heard the study door open and saw Sam's hand gently place my backpack at the foot of the stairs. I tensed, then relaxed as both men said, "Thanks, Ve. Is the coffee hot?" I could take a hint to steer clear of any talk of wounds or my assistance.

Welcome Huggers # 2 – Verity

Annie and Fe raced down the stairs into the kitchen, laughing gleefully. Once they'd caught their breath, Annie blurted out, "How about a triple or quadruple date? You three interested?"

Lark said, "What are you talking about? Details, please. Are you sure you want us three along?"

"It will be so much fun! We all need a break, and we have always wanted to go on a date with our brother to see how he treats a lady. You know, learn how guys relate to girls. You are so transparent to us, Lark. We can take clues from you through a frown, raised eyebrow, or when your eyes get glittery and hard. Having Verity along will be special. Sam, you and a date would be an added fun bonus."

I realized the girls were assuming Lark and I would be together. I shut my mouth and briefly closed my eyes so I did not blurt out how insensitive they were to assume their desires were ours.

"Annie, Fe, you haven't told us yet what you have in mind," Lark went on. "Are you sure your sweethearts would want a possible future brother-in-law monitoring their actions? Maybe more to the point is, would you two want me to see you in action?"

Fe smiled sweetly at Lark. I knew it was a secret weapon Fe possessed where Lark was concerned. I didn't think Fe used it intentionally, but it was awesomely effective. I speculated briefly if sweetness might work for me, but I knew he'd realize my character was more mischievous – tart – than honeyed. Maybe I could try....

"We want you three to keep completely open the week after the three sets of parents get back from their cruise. No questions. We're working on the logistics," Fe exclaimed. "Oh, it will be a fabulous, fun time for sure. Just wait and see. JC and JJ are looking forward to it. Remember, keep an entire week free."

Lark stared at his sisters, then flatly announced, "When you give us more details, we three will decide."

Marilyn Stewart

Eighteen

The supper for eight had been a rousing success. Fe had printed up three questions and put them at each place setting. The first one was easy: state your first name or what you prefer to be called and a favorite activity. Since there were four males and four females and comments or questions were encouraged, it took a while to go around the table. Question number two had three options; you could choose to share a funny story; make up something and see if the others could guess whether it was true; or share something you'd like the others to know about you.

The last question was addressed after the table had been cleared, dishes done, and games had been played: would you like to share a concern, a joke, a special memory, or ask for prayer?

There had been numerous lingering kisses and thanks for a truly special evening. We girls each received a text from Fairlyn. She was cherishing the memory of a lingering hug with Sam.

The next day, as I locked the library door at eleven, my phone rang. Normally, Mercy would text or email.

I quickly answered. "Hi, Mercy. How can I help?"

She laughed. "Verity, you're getting to know me too well. Is Angel with you? Are you available for a couple of hours, and have you had lunch yet?"

"Angel is certainly with me. I am available until a half hour before the kids get out of school. This is an afternoon the kids read to Boo, Gem, and Angel. And no, I have not yet eaten. What's up?"

"Would you mind driving to my place since I live closer to the Ghost Town, where we will be heading? I'll fix us some sandwiches, and we can talk when you get here."

"Sounds okay, though a bit mysterious. See you soon."

I opened the back door of my car for Angel to hop in, saying, "We are going to see Gem and Mercy." I was positive Angel understood, for he gave one bark and wagged his tail. I kissed him on his nose, looked around, laughed, and said, "I never thought I'd talk to a dog as if he were a human friend. Angel, thanks for your unconditional love. You ease the ache in my heart."

Welcome Huggers # 2 – Verity

I pulled up at Mercy's, and almost immediately saw her and Gem waiting for us in the doorway. We smiled at each other, but neither of us offered a hug as we hurried our pets to the backyard. We played with them while talking about several needs of certain Welcome Huggers, then went inside and washed up. Before we had time to pull out our chairs, my phone rang. I mouthed 'sorry' to Mercy.

"Verity here."

"WHERE ARE YOU, girl? Are you okay?"

I yanked the phone away from my ear. "Lark? What is wrong? Of course, I am okay, and so is Angel. I am with Mercy this afternoon, and then we will go back to the library for the dogs to listen to the kids read to them. Are all of you okay?"

"I decided to come home for lunch, and you never arrived. I called the twins and Sam. No one knew where you were. It was as if you had disappeared. We have been worried."

"Why? I am not a child who needs to inform everyone of my whereabouts! Hold on for just a second." I took a deep breath. "Sorry. For years, I've never had anyone worry about my comings and goings. I apologize for stressing you all out. Why didn't you call me first, Babe? By the way, it is so sweet to know you cared enough to check. Thank you."

His volume dropped. "Glad you're safe. Keep in touch."

We giggled. I had noted Mercy's response to the word 'Babe,' so I briefly explained the campaign, which had worked. I admitted I was shocked at how easy the word had slipped out. Mercy smiled. "He sounded absolutely frantic, pushing the boundaries of exploding. See, I told you he is drawn to you. And you, telling him it was so sweet of him to care. It's amazing how you have him all wrapped up, but he won't let love triumph over fear. Has he even shared anything with you about his life or wounds?"

"No. It is so frustrating. His eyes tell me he wants to, but it is as if his mouth has a lock on it. Forget him. Why am I here?"

"If you don't mind, we'll head out to the Ghost Town and talk on the way. Come, Gem. Up, Angel." Before getting in the driver's seat, she attached a safety strap to each harness.

Marilyn Stewart

With the dogs settled in the back seat and us on the move, I spoke. "You've been chatting to the sheriff, haven't you, Cy? Or rather, he has been chatting to you and Unity."

"Yes, and he said you okayed his sharing. Someone in his office revealed you're not a qualified librarian, but hold a degree in counseling. We already knew you were a licensed paramedic. Sheriff Ben is checking who is sharing private information."

"Mercy, I am glad you know. If I can be of assistance on a call out, feel free to give me a bell – sorry, call. When I arrived, I was in desperate need of a complete change of pace. I had worked in a college library so had enough skills to get this library up and running – ready for a person with a degree to take over. You have no idea what seeing you and Katie sitting on my front porch that day did for me. The basket of goodies and total acceptance of me, a complete stranger, made me feel so very welcome. It was as if you gave me hugs of assurance that all would be well. Now, are you going to clue me in as to why we are headed to the Ghost Town?"

"If you don't mind, I think I would prefer your assessment of the individuals and the situation without any early input from me. Keep your eyes, ears, and senses on full alert status."

"Okay. Mercy, using words such as assessment, situations, senses, alert, and status has you sounding like Sam and Lark – probably due to your being married to a military hero."

"Thanks for your unquestioning support, Ve. It's like we have kindred spirits. It is lovely how we interact with many diverse people – such as the composite of the Welcome Huggers. While we welcome their company, only a few ever become true lifelong friends. There are so many levels to friendship. It is as if once in a while, God brings into our sphere a certain individual we connect with as if woven together by our many levels of similarities. I'm curious, Ve: what was your reasoning for qualifying in distinctly different fields?"

I shrugged my shoulders. "Oh, that's simple. I was planning on working overseas, part time with my parents. I knew the situation there and that both competences are in short supply. Enough about me. What about you? Why did you become proficient in various fields? I hear you are working on another."

Welcome Huggers # 2 – Verity

"As a young teenager, JC and JJ were taking me to the tarmac area beside our home. I think part of their reasoning began because they knew I missed my twin. They just sort of took over. Early on, they had me riding on the back of a motorcycle. I learned to move with the bike, see how to shift, and then of course, I was their lackey to clean it. I adore my older brothers. I was seventeen, having a lot of bad days, when they began bugging me to get out of my room and back to driving. You may have noticed, Ve, as I did about eight months ago, that the things I'm qualified in can be done by oneself. Being a big rig or bus driver, having my ham radio license, and becoming an EMT all keep me in control and at an emotional distance from people. Thanks to Gem and Unity, I'm emerging and growing. Yes, I'm studying to become a chaplain."

"Mercy, my friend, you definitely underestimate yourself."

Mercy started to object, but I silenced her.

"Hold on; let me finish my rationale. Way back when you were in the hospital the first time, I heard you shared Gem with others needing therapy from a pet. You might not have had all the words a chaplain would use, but you have a compassionate heart full of acceptance by which others are abundantly blessed."

Mercy sniffed twice. "Ve, my past still often haunts me. Actually, Unity and I both have frequent nightmares. I've been struggling lately, so I appreciate your words. Thanks. Here we are."

Mercy parked the car, then murmured, "Ve, I feel the need to offer up a short prayer before we proceed."

We bowed our heads, and after a few moments of silence, Mercy began, *"Dear Heavenly Father who weaves people, skills, and events together with care and love, help us. We need listening ears, open hearts, divine input, and right attitudes to serve these wounded in body and soul. P.S. God, please keep us all safe. Thank you, Jesus. Amen."*

I looked around at the people gathering and softly said, "Angel, heel. Sit. Stay. Good boy."

One fellow belligerently shouted, "You don't want your dog near us. You think we're not good enough; is that it?"

"No. No," I hurriedly replied. "It's not that. I don't want Angel to bother anyone, or go where he shouldn't."

Mercy intervened. "Turn him loose, Verity. Every so often call his name, then the word, 'Come.' It will be good training."

Glaring at me, an old guy spat, then snarled, "What are you doing here? We only want Mercy – and Gem, of course."

"Don't be like that, George. She is a friend of Unity's and mine, Lark, Annie, Sam, Zeke, and a lot of other people. Her parents were missionaries, but they and her sister were killed by a drunk driver. Today, she will be my assistant. Her name is Verity or Miss Ve. Most of you have seen her here before."

I kept my mouth closed and observed. They seemed to be a suspicious lot. The dogs appeared to calm and comfort them. Actually, if I read their body language correctly, they were being protective of both Angel and Gem. The people seemed on edge. Eyes were darting around the grounds, skillfully keeping track of everyone. Something was very wrong. The whole atmosphere had changed since my last visit.

I observed Angel sniffing a lot when near Bryce and Sheena, but interacting well, overall. I took note of the men both dogs avoided. When Mercy opened her medical kit, there was no pushing and shoving, but rather precise movement – as if there was a pecking order. At first, I thought it might have to do with age or sex, but then I realized they were making sure the ones most needing care were treated first.

After moving to stand next to Mercy, I checked out the contents of her medical kit. Mine was similar. A card table had been provided, so we didn't have to do a lot of bending. As I glimpsed the first wound – that of an ulcerated foot – I was taken back in time to a scene eerily similar. It was a primitive setting. Mum was the nurse, and I had been her assistant. An ax had slipped. Due to infection, it had taken weeks of treatment before the injured man's foot was saved. Each time we'd cared for the man, my main job had been to shoo away the flies. A sudden wave of home sickness unexpectedly rolled through me. I caught my breath, wiped my eyes, blew my nose, and put on gloves.

I knew the man thought I was crying over his wound, for he said, "It's better than it was, Miss Ve, thanks to our Miss Mercy, here." I smiled at him, nodded, then a fly landed. I instinctively reverted to my childhood upbringing as I plunked down next to the man seated on the ground. I grabbed my backpack and began automatically to shoo away the flies. Oblivious to my surroundings, I reached for his foot and unwound the dirty bandage. No one, least of all Mercy, commented on my actions. Only much later did I grasp what I had done and realized my 'cover' was blown.

Once we were back in the car, Mercy asked, "Care to share your assessment of what you saw, sensed, or concluded?"

"Okay, Mercy. I deduced mainly four things. First, there is a different 'air' or feel about the place. The original group are frightened and very angry. My guess? It is the three new guards. I'd not like to be around if their vicious dog got loose. I noticed Gem and Angel stayed far away from them.

"Next, I agree it is imperative that Wilton goes to the hospital. Maybe Unity, Lark, or Sam can convince or take him. I'm not sure if you caught it, but Jake and Tim were keeping a very close eye on two of the new men, who are definitely fixated on you, Cy. I don't think we should return – certainly not alone. The Ghost Town has become a dangerous place.

"Lastly, if you know the owner of that property, I suggest you make contact fast and have the DEA alerted. I've been gifted with impressive eye sight, am about five inches taller than you, and was in the right spot to see that they are growing stuff. Knowing movies had been made there, I'd expect to see potted trees, flowers, and shrubs. All of those identical green plants in the center are new. I'm sure our guys are unaware of them. I'd say those guards were never in the service, but rather, have come in from some gang or maybe even a crime syndicate."

"Oh, thank you, Verity. Neither Unity, Jeff, Sam, nor Lark have been there lately. I thought maybe I was just being paranoid."

"We've got time, Mercy. How about we drive to the hospital in Unique and let our pooches provide some therapy?"

"I guess you've noticed the SUV tailing us and don't want to head straight home. Can you see anything distinctive about it? Please call Sheriff Ben right now. I have a bad feeling."

"Right. I hope I haven't put you in danger. Maybe I didn't take Sam's warning serious enough." I dialed the sheriff's number.

"Sheriff Ben, Mercy and I are a little more than three miles out, heading towards Welcome. We have a vehicle tailing us. Dark gray, black, or blue – not really sure of the color – but it is a large SUV. There are three scary new guards at the Ghost Town. We aren't sure if some of the regulars are making sure we are okay or if we could be in trouble. Our plans are to go past your station, then head for the hospital in Unique to let the dogs bring comfort to some of the patients. I have you on speaker – Mercy can hear."

Sheriff Ben's voice rumbled, "You're an expert driver, Mercy. If they speed up, trust your instincts. I'll be listening."

"Good thing I know every bend of this road."

"They are moving up, fast," I gasped. "Maybe decided to give us a fright or a bit of a bump."

"We've a powerful engine in this…. Hang on, Ve."

"What's going on, girls? Are you all okay?"

He heard grunts, several ouches, a whine, the sucking in of air, then finally nervous giggling, followed by, "Woohoo, girls win! Impressive, mind-blowing driving, Mercy! Ah, sorry, Sheriff, there was a truck around a bend across both lanes. The people in the SUV tried to ram us. Mercy did the fanciest precision driving I've ever seen – better than any movie. We will have some bruises since we had to go off-road for a bit. Thankfully, all four of our restraints worked perfectly. Gem and Angel are also fine."

"Are you still being followed, Verity?"

"No, Sir, and we didn't hear any metal hitting metal. You might want to send a deputy three or so miles out of town in case the SUV is hung up in some shrubbery. It's not likely, although I reckon you'll see long skid marks. We're good."

"Glad everyone's okay. Someone will meet you at the hospital later. 'Bye."

"Mercy, if I am out of line asking, or you'd rather not share private stuff, tell me. But I am concerned about you. How are you doing emotionally? I'm wondering if you are grieving or struggling over your many losses and changes."

"Oh, Ve, thanks for asking. So many things altered my lifestyle – all within six months. We found the kids; Unity came home a wounded warrior; my arm was broken; I couldn't drive our tour bus. I still get backlash – good and bad – over disclosing my 'secret' at that church service. I had to face my kidnappers; got married; no more daily interacting with my loving, noisy, family; no longer qualified to attend the Welcome Huggers meetings; Katie, my best friend since first grade, left town. Don't get me wrong. I love Unity. Single to married is challenging enough, but so many upheavals has been hard. On the plus side, I've gotten to know you. I'd like to set a time for us to meet and talk in the next week or two."

"Love to get together. I also have something specific I want to discuss," I replied.

"Minutes ago, I reaffirmed myself as a fantastic driver. I bet soon we'll have from one to five men checking on us by phone or in person," Mercy said.

"Now, that is not a bet I'll take, Mercy. I've been thinking about our recent incident. Maybe it was a stupid, spur of the moment scare tactic – not due to my situation. They didn't want us to return. Someone got the idea of an accident. Girls' inattention while driving, coming around a corner, seeing a truck in the road, plowing into it, and them either barely hitting us or going on their way. What do you think, Cy?"

"I agree and will go one step further along that line of thought. They totally underestimated us 'girls.' They never dreamed we would be so alert, have such a hot car, and be able to out-drive them. As soon as we reach Unique, I'll make a call to the owner of the Ghost Town, and he can take it from there. Bad corner coming up. Keep an eye out for cross-traffic from that dirt road just beyond, Ve."

"I've been watching a dust cloud off to my right. I'm sure we are ahead of them."

"I almost didn't call you today, but had a gut feeling. Really glad you were with me, Verity."

"I am thankful you were not alone! There is going to be some serious repercussions from the men. I know Unity will probably try to hug the life out of you. Well, you know what I mean. I wonder how Lark will react. I imagine their fear will be masked as anger. I expect to get hollered at. Okay, here is an idea. If Lark gets all squinty-eyed, snarky, and starts to holler, I will walk up to him and say, 'thanks for caring' and kiss his cheek. What do you think? Good plan?"

"Oh, do, Ve. I'd love to see his face! I like you calling me Cy. It is good to laugh – relieve our tension. Reaction setting in. We need a cookie or something chocolatey and a sweet, hot drink to stop the shakes. After that, we will visit the patients."

"Excellent plan. We will be calm and serene when the guys show up. I'm thinking more like six or even seven possible fellows, such as your dad, Lark, Sam, Unity, JC, JJ, and Sheriff Ben. Then again, maybe the sheriff will keep the event absolutely quiet."

"Will you thoroughly check Gem and Angel? Make sure they are okay. I'll make that call while you go and get us a cuppa, as you say, and for my sweet, I'd like a brownie. Today, Ve, I'll need two sugar packets in my hot tea."

"Got it. See you in a few minutes. Oh, hang on a second, Cy. Why don't you call Unity, just to tell him where we are?"

*****

We visited with patients for an hour before begging off to head for the library. Despite interacting with people, I kept recalling the glimpse of a face at the Ghost Town and that man's reaction when my eyes met his. At first, the possible significance hadn't registered, but now, after having a bit of time and recollecting his features, I felt stunned by a possibility. I needed to call Peter.

When we turned our cell phones back on, we were surprised to see no calls from any of the guys. Looking towards Mercy's car, we saw Unity and Sam leave it and stride towards us. Neither were smiling. I looked at Sam and shrugged. Mercy ran to Unity, who wrapped her tightly in his arms, lifted her off her feet, and kissed her repeatedly while saying, "Sunshine, sweetheart, I love you." After putting her down, he tenderly asked, "You really okay, my love?"

I sucked in a deep breath from the intensity of desire flooding my being. I longed for such a mate who'd love me so much he'd not hide his feelings. I caught Sam staring at me.

Mercy grinned. "We'll probably have a few bruises due to effective seat belts, but we smoked them, didn't we, Ve?"

"You did, indeed. The fanciest bit of maneuvering I've ever seen. Really glad you have such amazing driving skills and a powerful engine in your vehicle. Maybe I can take some lessons from you, as well as upgrade my car or put in a bigger engine."

"The sheriff recorded your message and let me hear it," Unity muttered, then added, "The possibility of losing you, Sweetheart, scares me more than being in combat ever did. We're keeping the information confidential to see if and where it hits the gossip stream. I'm afraid to let you out of my sight, my love."

"Beloved, remember. We believe our times are in God's hands. Let's relax, trust Him, and enjoy each day fully."

I felt rebuked by Mercy's amazing faith.

Sam cut in. "Glad all is well with you two. We need to get to the library so as not to deprive the kids from growing their reading skills. Berwin is devouring the *Heroes for Young Readers* series by Renee Meloche. He loves airplanes. I placed a sticky note with his name on *Nate Saint* so he gets to read it today. Come, Verity. Up, Angel."

I giggled. "It sounded as if you were addressing two dogs, Sam. Ah, don't frown. I don't think this had to do with me so much as an attempt to scare us into not returning. My car is at Mercy's home, where anyone can access it. Thanks for saving that book for Berwin."

"I'm glad you're okay. I'll send out a mechanic to go over it thoroughly and have it brought home."

"Thanks, Sam. You going to tell Lark?"

"Probably not – unless you or Angel show some ill effects. Ve, back there, you briefly looked... almost distressed."

"It was Unity's undiluted loving actions towards Mercy. It made me long for a mate brave enough to show everyone he loves me."

Marilyn Stewart

I leaned back, closed my eyes, and gritted my teeth. I was already beginning to ache, and my list of things to do was long. Library, call Peter, supper, then finally, a long, hot shower and bed.

I got Peter's answering service saying he was out of town. What I wanted to ask was tricky, and I needed to see his face to gauge his reaction. My message was short. "Have to talk to you."

I was about to shut my phone off when a text arrived from Mercy. She had time tomorrow for lunch and a chat. Did I?

Nineteen

Now that Mercy and I were together, I wondered how exactly to begin. The topic would be a sensitive one.

"As you know, Mercy, I've now been a member of the Welcome Huggers for over ten months, thanks to you and Katie. During these last months, you and I have been privileged to be the recipients of confidential information. We have listened as hurting ladies have shared their stories."

"Ve, what is it?" Mercy probed to hurry me along.

I took a deep breath, watched her face and stated, "Mother's Day is in a few weeks. I wondered how you are coping."

Her eyes filled with tears as she blurted out, "I hate having to go to church on that day. It is so hard to smile and clap and be joyful. I know people expect me to forget I miscarried a baby because it resulted from rape. It was a horrible time, but Mother's Day brings it all back. Then there is my Mum and his grandmother and mother – all expecting flowers and celebrations."

"Exactly, Cy! As you know, I don't have that problem, but a different one. Peter's wife, Beryl, now mother to my twins, gets very insecure on Mother's Day. She does not want to see hide nor hair of me. Then there is Father's Day. My sweet half-brother always sends me a personal lovely card – from him – on both days, thanking me! I know he means well, but it.... So I was wondering about going out of town that weekend. What do you think?"

"It is certainly worth considering, Ve. I've been envisioning asking Unity if we could go somewhere. I don't want to make a big deal of it or have family feel hurt due to our absence."

"Cy, I realize this is the first Mother's Day celebration in which you are a wife. Has it made a difference in your level of sorrow? Sorry, none of my business, really."

"No, No. Verity, I appreciate your concern and willingness to address my emotional turmoil. No one wants to know or they are afraid to ask. You know I love my husband, but this is the one thing about me that he avoids. I get it. Part of it is the horror I suffered, but also – it was not his child. He can't change my past devastation or 'fix' it, so he would rather ignore than talk about it. I think it would do us good to cry in each other's arms and feel free to discuss our feelings. And to answer your question, it is weird, but true. Being married has made the ache worse. I often wonder who that child would have become."

Mercy sniffed and wiped her eyes, while I did likewise.

I broke the silence. "Last year, I skipped church, went to the graveyard, and cried for ages. I'm not going to church this year, either. People – too often Christians, as I am sure you've experienced – can be such harsh judges. I need your opinion on two things: first, regarding approaching ladies we know who have lost a child – regardless of whether it was from an abortion or through military service. I would never reveal a secret I have been privy to; however, I wonder about providing a chance to be with mothers who also never forget their 'missing' child. And secondly, whether or not having a picnic at a lake or park, say at ten, while people are still in church, might be a good idea. I keep wavering back and forth about being by myself or reaching out to hurting ladies. Any ideas you'd care to share would be helpful, Mercy."

"Jasmine, Daisy, and Becca have never hid their past, and last year, at that church service, I revealed my secret. Each of us has a different story. You, Verity, have a different situation. Like others, you, my friend, could be open for blackmail. I've been wondering if we should start a support group, but that raises all kinds of possible complications. I know you'd keep quiet, Ve, in deference to Peter and Beryl. But would it be wise for you to attend where pressure to share your grief would be strong, and if revealed, could be leaked?"

After tossing ideas back and forth, we decided I would talk to Brenda. She could decide whether or not to ask if anyone was interested in beginning a grief support group.

I pulled out my small calendar to check when our group's next meeting would be and noticed an interesting jotting. I smiled, chuckled, turned the calendar towards Mercy, and pointed.

"They'll be gone! How truly awesome! A miracle from God, for sure, that our mothers will be in the middle of their

Welcome Huggers # 2 – Verity

cruise! I want to dance and sing! Now I have ammunition that might entice Unity to go camping. Any idea of what you'd like to do, Ve?"

"Go sightseeing. Boyce Thompson Arboretum down by Superior, or Meteor Crater and the Petrified Forest in the Painted Desert aren't too far away. If I take an extra day or two, I could even visit Canyon De Chelly, or...."

"Will you tell your housemates, or just disappear?"

"I'd prefer to just vanish, Mercy, but it is only fair that I at least let Sam know my plans."

Mercy tilted her head, sighed, and then gently probed.

"Will you clarify the details to your housemates as to why that particular weekend? Would you welcome Fe and/or Annie to go with you? What would you do if Lark, or say, Sam decided you shouldn't be alone and wanted to go as well? Are you ready and willing to 'spill the truth' as to the increased ache in your heart that Mother's Day orchestrates?"

I stared at her, thinking it might be easier to wait until Mother's Day and just announce I was going for a long drive.

I stood up and touched Mercy's shoulder. "Thanks for the questions. I need to ponder them and be prepared. Our time has been productive. Guess we had better skedaddle."

"Thanks, girlfriend. I feel lighter – less stressed, with a plan."

It had been instructive to talk with Mercy. In my eagerness to help others, I had almost made a strategic error. At some point, I would have been questioned as to why I started and attended a grief group for mothers of deceased or missing children.

Maybe my first move should be to announce, at a Welcome Huggers meeting, that I hold a degree in counseling.

*****

A week later, we met again. Mercy and Unity were going camping. I had yet to tell my roommates. Mercy was checking with churches in our towns about an existing grief counseling group. It was so weird. During the week, both of us had speculated

152

Marilyn Stewart

about there being men skipping Father's Day due to the same type
of ache. We both reckoned they should be included in counseling.

Twenty

As a result of calling Brenda about Essie, Fairlyn had worked the early morning shift for two weeks. The morning I took over, Fairlyn came in early to make sure I got off to a good start – or that was what she claimed. I reckoned it was because Sam had brought me. It was rather fun waiting tables once again, as I had for two summers during my college days. I was being very careful and taking note of the arrival of every stranger. Amethyst, the other waitress, and I had a deal. She would serve all strangers. In return, I would help Amethyst with one of her tables, but the tip would be hers. It was entertaining to see who all showed up. Sheriff Ben came one morning, a deputy the next. Amethyst had two obvious and strong suitors in Keith and Mark, but I noticed Nathaniel slyly scrutinize her actions and responses. He was first in when we opened, always chose a table in a corner where Amethyst waitressed, varied his order, and kept a low profile. I was tempted to encourage him to stop 'biding his time' and invite her out. Lark had come three times and made sure to sit at one of my tables. He enjoyed having me at his beck and call. Sometimes Amethyst and I made the guys wait just a bit, while pampering others. People were taking notice and expressing shrewd comments. It was exhausting and hard on my feet, but just what I needed – lighthearted fun.

The Welcome Huggers and other substitutes all agreed: while we would accept all tips, the wages would go to Essie, as if she were the one working. Essie still worked either the lunch or evening shift each day. Ladies who didn't want to waitress took turns staying with her grandmother. We all knew Essie needed time away – a change and interaction with people.

During my second week working the breakfast shift, a stranger entered. Amethyst waited on him, while I avoided his table. His staring troubled me. He paid his bill, but instead of heading out the door, he deliberately took several steps and blocked my path. "Verity Rosa Tacker," he said, "you have been served." I immediately backed away from him and his paper while stating clearly, "That is not my name, and never has been." He held up a picture. "I was given this photo. It is you." I nodded. "I agree the picture is of me - looks to be about three years old. Who gave you my picture and the job of finding this Verity Rosa Tacker person?"

A couple of men near us got ready to stand. They appeared to be waiting to see if their help was needed before acting. In walked the sheriff, and one by one, they relaxed.

"Hi, Sheriff Ben. This guy thinks my name is Verity Rosa Tacker; you know it isn't. You need to talk to him before he leaves." I sped to the kitchen, fixed myself a sweetened cup of tea, and quickly downed it. By the time I returned to take care of my customers, Sheriff Ben and the man had left.

In all honesty, I'd never had so much fun or worried so little. It was due to my activities at the library, waitressing, making pottery, having a great home life, and sometimes, dating. I was practicing living in the moment and making good memories each day. I checked in by phone before heading out, and shared unusual happenings with Sam. The five of us, plus the two dogs, lived as if in a safe zone. Small squabbles occurred, but most often we discussed, listened, laughed, and teased, sometimes agreeing to disagree. The guys were lightening up and becoming more willing to share.

The four had taken to teasing me – a lot. I was due to have a fifth date in two weeks. Sam screened the men. Each date took place in full view of many people, and I checked in at least once during the outing. It had begun after my date with Jeff at the seminar, which both of us thoroughly enjoyed. Andrew asked me to go bowling. Rolin had preferred miniature golf. Tony wanted me by his side at a racquetball tournament. Mike and I went roller skating with a group of singles from his church. Martin was turned down since he wanted to take me flying. After all these months, tonight was my final big obligation to the library in the form of a fund raiser. My escort was to be Noah.

Now that Katie – the dating queen of our three towns – had arrived back home, and Lark was not opening up, I reckoned it was time to stop dating. There were lots of things to choose from each week from the Welcome Huggers calendar of events. From something said by both Mike and Tony, I had a sneaking suspicion Lark had orchestrated their asking me out.

I had just completed my second two weeks of waitressing. Even though I wore well-padded, high top walking shoes, my weak ankles were sore. Tonight, I'd be in heels for hours. I stretched out on my bed – feet up, shoes off – and sighed. Even though I was enjoying life, I absolutely had to take charge of my destiny.

What did I know that might solve the mystery of strange events in my life? Time to review all the facts. Where did Paul fit? I hadn't signed the papers and guessed he'd left town. Had what he'd shared been a lie? What else?

Recently at a grocery store, four men from the RV Park tried to hide the fact they were following me. I'd hurried my shopping and kept close to others, secretly afraid they'd box me in or....

I was worried Charity was somehow involved. Two weeks ago, I'd been invited to a picnic with both families. Charity's voice had been sweet whenever Jim or Peter were near, but her eyes were angry. Her hurtful digs showed me that I was not welcome. I unconsciously touched my upper left arm. Maybe it had been Charity who had left the message with my initials and R.I.P. at the grave site. I truly hoped she was not in back of my troubles. As I lay quietly, letting my thoughts flit freely, I was shocked to recall something from years ago. I sat up and swung my feet over the side of the bed, then quickly lay back down. My mind began hunting for clues to make sense out of vague words.

At breakfast, I had reminded Sam about the limo, in case it showed up tonight. Last night, I had seen it go past our place for the fourth time in a month. While I hadn't been able to get the license plate number, I had noticed a distinct mark on the grille – as if it had been in a slight fight. There couldn't be many limos in our towns.

There was something else tugging at the fringe of my brain and had been for days. Maybe if I relaxed and thought about other things, it would surface. I set the alarm, just in case I fell asleep.

Often, long after the guys had gone to bed, the three of us girls talked about our hopes and dreams. Spring and summer were the busiest times of year for the inhabitants of all three towns. Income made during the summer kept them from closing during the lean winter months. Annie and Fe shared how the flower shop was thriving – almost too well, now they were in relationships. Two weeks ago, JC and JJ began driving bus tours to the Grand Canyon, and soon they'd be traveling to distant landmarks. Fe and Annie, wishing to spend more time with their guys, were working on whether or not the shop could survive, let alone thrive, during the summer if they each took a turn to pay and go on a bus tour.

Over the past months, four Welcome Huggers had asked and stayed a weekend with us. Valerie, Amethyst, and Heather were great guests. Primrose was not. She kept trying to get into the guys' room. Twice she'd stated her full name, then asked me what mine was. Her visit unsettled our peace for days.

Annie, Fe, and I decided to pass on the Welcome Huggers cruise. We wanted to spend our hard-earned dollars elsewhere.

Last fall, the offspring in three families had bought tickets for their parents' dream vacations – a cruise to Alaska. Katie had returned home to help out in her mother's store. Mercy's kin were pitching in to release Hank and Mel. Unity would be helping his sisters at the hostel and B&B even more, while Eb and El were gone. Three weeks was a long time for the heads of three businesses to be gone. Everyone was determined to keep things running. Many Welcome Huggers, people in the RV Park, and some from town, pledged their support to help when and where needed. Katie was the point person with the list of people to call, if needed.

Pulling my thoughts back, I reflected. There were three things that needed to be addressed with vigor.

Had Paul told the truth or lied, and did he have anything to do with my assault?

Were the tiny twins at risk?

Was there possibly another member to our family?

It was imperative that I talk with Peter. He would also know if an insurance payment settlement were due any time soon. I wondered – could my woes have anything to do with identity theft, or inheritance ring groups, or was it someone closer to me?

Yesterday, Peter called, demanding I come to a family gathering at Charity and Jim's place – in seven days. I asked to meet with him before that, but he was adamant. "No. Busy. Later."

Time to rise and prepare for an extremely busy night.

Wishing to speak to Sam alone, I went downstairs early. As I descended, Lark came out of the study, saw me, and whistled. I blushed as he grinned and winked. I smiled, curtsied, and said, "Thank you, kind sir!" Having heard the whistle, Fe and Annie had popped out of their rooms to hoot and clap their approval.

Turning, I saw Sam and blurted out, "I have a gut feeling something is going to happen tonight. Maybe all will start to unravel and clear our vision to know who, when, why, etc. If I am wrong, then in the next day or two, I'd like to suggest a plan of action to get this resolved."

Sam nodded. "We won't be far from you, Ve. Detective Dan said the fellow who was smashing the trunk of your car just wanted to get warm. Your vehicle was the only nearby shelter. Our check of your entire car was a bust. The rose bush at your store is still a mystery. Only kids' fingerprints were found on the container."

"I had been wondering, Sam. Appreciate the update. Change of subject. What or how much does Noah know about me or my situation? Is he a lawyer, detective, or FBI?"

"Really, Verity? Why do you ask?"

I took a shot. "Well, Lark, how could you do such a thing as to pay both Mike and Tony to take me out? Did you end up paying for everything?"

Sam whistled. "You are so busted! I told you she'd catch on to what you did! Wow, you are good, Ve! You never let on."

Shooting Lark a dark look, Fe muttered, "Lark, how could you treat Verity in such an underhanded, shabby way?"

"Sam, be quiet. Girls, girls, don't be mad. I just wanted Ve to have some safe dates."

His sisters laughed. "I don't think so, brother. You didn't want any competition from the new, single, hot guys in town."

"Sam, neither you nor Lark answered my question about Noah. What can you tell me...." The doorbell sounded.

"Hm. Guess that's him now."

I opened the front door to find an eager Noah waiting on the stoop.

"You ready to head out, spend money for the library, dance, and maybe kiss me, Verity?" he said.

"I might just do all those things, Noah. I shall decide about each as the evening progresses."

"Works for me. See you all later at the party."

Our local radio station DJ was taking care to keep the background music at a level that enabled everyone to chat. He chose pertinent songs to introduce a business before reading their ad and thanking them for their support. Fe and Annie's flower shop was introduced with the song "Red Roses for a...," the hardware store, "If I Had a Hammer," and so forth.

I danced, mingled, wrote my assigned number and amount on numerous silent auction pieces. Although I was being outbid on every item, it was great to witness the amount being raised on behalf of our 'Paws2Read' Library.

The first thing to occur that was not on the program nor sanctioned by the library committee was actually a good thing. An auctioneer was found, and soon people were bidding on twenty items which had been brought in at the last minute. Fe bought a flute. Ken acquired a special cup and saucer for his Daffodil. AnnMarie obtained a signed painting by a local artist, and so it went. I was ready to bid on a huge cuddly teddy bear; however, as I began to raise my paddle, Noah decided to snatch a kiss. With my view blocked and attention diverted, I again lost out. Instead of smiling and laughing it off, I glared at him. "You knew I wanted that bear, Noah! That's the last kiss you'll ever get from me."

He walked off, laughing, while proclaiming, "I'll get you some punch to cool you down."

The party was almost over. My feet were killing me. Waitressing had taken its toll, and I'd not been smart to wear almost new heels to an event consisting largely of standing or dancing. I loved to people-watch, and thus caught two men, at different times, stopping for a quick chat with Lark. After each interaction, I'd deliberately caught his eye to share a perceptive little grin.

Noah returned with my drink. He seemed different – glum. Now, whenever I moved, he followed – standing way too close. I moved to chat with a group that included Sam, Tom, Rod, and Lark. The DJ tapped the mike and announced one last revelation. I felt positive this surprise reveal would be directed at me.

He began, "The mystery giveaway that started three months ago has so far been on the 15th of the month. This is a week early. Let's do a little recap. The first month, an anonymous donor gave fifteen hundred dollars to the family with the most kids in our three towns. It certainly blessed them, and what most do not know is that they passed on five hundred to another family. Last month's mystery giveaway was a gift to a veteran. The qualification was that it had to be a wounded warrior with two or more missing or partly missing limbs. They had to show up in person in order to take home $1000. It was a strange request and took quite a while before a veteran came to claim the money. The wounded warrior's comment had to do with so many others being more deserving. He, too, paid some of it forward.

Now, this giveaway has a twist. Our producers checked it out, and the money is for real. I've been told to make the following statements before reading from this paper. Please do not threaten or put pressure on anyone to reveal what they do not wish to be made general knowledge."

I was almost encircled by men and their ladies. Fear raced – seizing my brain, drying my mouth, and setting my heart hammering.

"Single female living in Welcome, Unique, or Hope. First name beginning with the letter V and middle initial of R. Last name must start with any letter between G and U. Proof needed will be a certified birth certificate or passport with her full three names. When verified, the sum of $2000.00 will be donated to the wounded warrior fund. This offer is good for thirty days."

With a shaking hand, I gently placed my untasted punch on a nearby high shelf. Reaching into my tiny purse, I shut off my cell phone. The mystery clues, money offered and who would benefit, was directed at me. Obviously, someone was willing to go to extensive measures to learn my middle name. Unconsciously, my right hand touched high on my left arm. Why should my middle name be so important? Through the material, I felt an old scar and dropped my hand. Long ago, Mum had told me an R could stand for Rainbow, Regal, Royal, or my own name. Mum had understood I needed something of my own – something secret which was not shared publicly in churches. A week before Mum had died she'd explained how she had convinced a judge to ensure my American passport only had an initial R as my middle name. Mum had shared a few other things as well...

I saw Noah look down at me, reach up and grasp my glass, then say, "Here, you haven't yet tasted your drink."

A buzz that had begun after the announcement filled the room. Under its cover, I softly queried, "Why do you want me to drink this? Did you put something in it?"

Noah glared at me, then Sam, shook his head, and stalked out of the building. I handed the drink to Sam. "Maybe this drink needs to be checked, oops, sorry. I'll hold it. Ask Fairlyn for this dance – I know you want to."

The DJ broke in. "While you are finding your partners for the final dance, we have an update. From the driver's license I'm holding, we might have a winner. It will need to be verified, however, since Violet Rowena Heron is living at the Willis RV Park, which lies outside the town of Welcome. Listen to this station for updates as to whether lawyers will be needed to sort it out. Now let's all enjoy the last dance of the evening."

Mercy moved in close to whisper, "Ve, Violet will be disqualified. She is not single. You are definitely the prime target."

I looked towards the double glass doors with one open, one closed, through which Noah had departed, only to see him returning. By the time Noah arrived, Lark already had me by the hand. Noah firmly stated, "This is my dance, Verity." He jerked me into his arms, then surprisingly whispered, "Sorry for the way I acted. Forgive me?" I gave a slight nod. On one level I was thinking what a great dancer he was while at the same time aware he was steering me ever closer to the open door. The dance was almost over. It seemed as if he was trying to distract me from his intentions by fancy footwork. Suddenly he slowed, pulled me close, said, "Sorry," then, "Verity what is your middle name?" I reacted instinctively. I yanked away from him, tripped over his foot and stumbled into the closed door. It hurt, but there was no way I would head out into the dark with Noah. Free of his arms, I anchored my feet while reviewing the self-defense moves Mercy had taught us. With my brain and hands ready for action, I demanded, "Why my middle name? Who is paying you?"

A deep voice floated in from the shadows. "Noah, you handled that rather clumsily."

I saw Lark was getting close, but still raised my normal speaking voice at least two notches. I wanted everyone to take notice and help me, if necessary. Half-formed thoughts became words that flew from my mouth. "Why are you hiding in the shadows? Please come inside. You must be the ones in the limo that keeps going by our place. Who are you? What did Noah handle clumsily? What do you want? Why are you harassing me? I'm sure the DJ will give you the mike so you can tell all of us."

By the time I ran out of words, Lark, Sam, and Unity had taken up protective positions nearby, along with Boo, Angel, and Gem. I began to tremble due to prolonged stress, not fear. It felt almost as if we were in a play of some kind. Lark whispered in my ear, "Relax my love, I am totally and forever yours." My brain seemed to be working on two levels – the men and Lark. The five guys didn't appear to be threatening me, but were intimidating in size and demeanor. Four of them had been at my birthday party. As for Lark, his timing couldn't have been worse for us to clear the air – as in follow up on his words with talk or kisses. Grr....

The DJ silently handed the oldest stranger the mike.

He sighed before saying, "This will nullify our claim; however, we might as well let the girl get on with her life. Yes, we have been in the limo trying to get a glimpse of you. Your mother, it seems, was my younger sister by seven years. She was a real sweetheart. You look just like her. I moved far away, lost touch, and had these fine sons. I never shared anything of my upbringing with them. Six or so months ago, a distant relative was doing our genealogy and came across your mother's death. About the same time, a lawyer and detective came, endeavoring to find you. There were several stipulations in a will. If the female heir was found, she had to have the first name of Verity; middle name beginning with the letter R, which would match a name in a sealed document. If she shared her middle name without any coercion, then all the relatives would get equal shares. If the unaware female heir would not freely divulge her middle name, all the money would be hers."

I butted in. "I'd guess Noah is the lawyer and the detective is Mr. Shepard at the Willis RV Park. It is getting late, and we are keeping all these special people from their rest. Sheriff Ben, plus a few others, will need to verify you are who you claim to be. Why the harassment? Why not just come and talk to me?"

"We've only driven by to see what you looked like – I wouldn't call that pestering you."

"Really? If you have told us the truth, the sheriff will contact you, and I will be willing to meet with you in the near future, with one stipulation: you must tell the sheriff the names of everyone you now have or had on your payroll to get me to give up my middle name. Please do not try to contact me except through Sheriff Ben."

Sheriff Ben walked outside with Lark, Angel, and me. When we reached Lark's vehicle, the sheriff said, "Verity, I think you have been planning to give Angel to Bryce and Sheena." At my nod, he shared an early bit of news. "Hours ago, the DEA raided our Ghost Town and arrested them, along with three others. They are all wanted felons who had relocated their drug and money laundering operation up here. They were never in the military. I'll assign Tom to check out your supposed uncle and cousins. They have an RV at the Willis place, but most weekends tend to fly in and out again. Well, we are progressing. Only need to find and clean out the identity bandits, and we should be back to being able to relax and enjoy our town and people."

"So maybe we have to look elsewhere for my stalkers?"

"I'd say so, Verity. We'll keep checking, though. Goodnight."

"Goodnight, Sheriff Ben, and thanks – for everything."

We were both quiet as Lark drove us home. I felt exhausted, having endured so many shocks with nothing getting resolved.

Lark's voice interrupted my thoughts. "Verity, honey, I should have kept my mouth shut tonight. I was a little premature. I am not taking back what I said. Please give me two weeks – I'll be free and ready to talk, explain, and share anything and everything with you at that time. Please trust me."

"I get upset with you from time to time, but I know I can always absolutely trust you, Lark. I've seen that you are polite, yet firm when a girlfriend tries to overstep your moral code. You, Sam, and Jeff are definitely in a class by yourselves. Well, there are a few other fellows in town as well, but.... Cat got your tongue, Lark?"

"You blew me away, Ve. So you ladies are watching and taking notes regarding character, huh?"

"Always, Lark, for you guys will be the fathers of the next generation, so it is a critical issue with us females."

"Verity, what traumatic thing happened years ago in relation to your name? I've observed that, whenever someone questions your middle name, your right hand automatically briefly rests on your upper left arm. All your tops or dresses have sleeves. Do they hide a scar? If it would help you heal by sharing with me, I would be willing for you to see my leg and other wounds."

"Wow. First, there is no price tag attached, as in, if I do this, then you have to do something in return. Of course, if you willingly want me to get a glimmer of what you've been hiding... I'm hesitant to tell anyone – even you. Your knowledge will color your future view of a family member. I'm sure neither Beryl nor Jim know."

"Looks as if we are the first ones home."

"Good. You know, it might be a relief to share my secret with you. You could give me insight on whether or not I should tell everyone my middle name. I'll start the kettle, run upstairs and change out of my fancy duds? These shoes are killing me."

"I'll change, play a bit of fetch with Angel, and meet you in the kitchen in ten minutes."

Marilyn Stewart

By the time I got to my room, I was wavering. Was it time to let go? Maybe that was my problem. With sudden clarity, I realized that in keeping our secret, I was trying to hang onto Mum. My thoughts drifted back to a week before their deaths. Mum had spent a lot of time with me – even sharing her dearest wish. One day, Mum said, "My dearest Verity. I pray you will walk all your days in the light of God's love. May you be filled with love for others, wisdom in your choice of mate, discernment in your choice of service, and your soul be at rest." Recalling her words gave me a sense of peace. Mum had been pronouncing a blessing on me.

Feeling reenergized, I hurried down the stairs with no thought that a dog who loved to greet me might snake between my legs. In an effort to halt my speed, my heel caught, ankle twisted, and I skidded down the last two stairs. Grabbing my ankle, I muttered, "Stupid, stupid, stupid girl!" My weak ankles, tired from waitressing and high heels for hours, a dog, and my desire to get back to Lark while he was still communicating had landed me here. Lark hurried towards me, carrying my backpack, which I usually kept by the door for emergency call outs. While tightly wrapping my ankle, I asked Lark to get some ice. As I hobbled into the kitchen, I was saying, "I'm so glad it was my left ankle...." when I came to a sudden halt. My eyes started to leak. Angel was gazing at the big bear I had missed buying due to Noah's kiss. I instinctively turned to Lark, threw my arms around him, kissed him thoroughly, gingerly stepped back, and admitted, "Thanks; I needed that."

"Wow! Smoking hot, addicting lips, my dear. I'm your man for any more such gifts. If I were a piece of chocolate candy, I would now be a melted blob at your feet."

I stared at him in awe – he spoke! I felt my skin redden, but laughed happily and declared, "That's so good to know." I quickly turned a bit, so Lark would have full view of my arm, and jerked up my sleeve. His bright, twinkling green eyes left mine and abruptly changed into dark, smoldering fury. He sucked in a breath, pressed his lips together, stooped down and gently kissed a rough old burn in the shape of an R.

Car doors slammed. Lark pulled down my sleeve, stalked over, and I saw his hand shake as he poured himself a cold cup of coffee. I could feel the anger radiating from him. I sat down, put my foot up on a chair on the other side of the table, added the ice, and then grabbed the stuffed animal. His sisters were coming. I hugged the bear as a distraction and possible conversation piece.

The twins came bursting in, full of news. "We hope you don't mind, Ve, but we told someone it would be okay to stay overnight. We know the spare bed is now in your room, so we should have called, but it was one of those spur of the moment things. She'll be here within fifteen minutes."

"Okay – fine with me. I washed the sheets today. Would you two please make up her bed? Is it Heather?"

"No. It is Hope, Mercy's sister. Is this a problem?"

Both girls abruptly realized they might have interrupted something going on between Lark and me.

"Are you two okay?" Fe timidly inquired.

I nodded. "Everything is just fine. Shall we make hot chocolate for everyone? Do we need goodies?"

Annie and Fe hurried off to change clothes, make a bed, and – I knew – talk about us.

"Lark, I've lived with this scar for a long time. The short version is that I was seven. Charity wanted to know my middle name. She repeatedly asked, but I wouldn't tell her, so she heated a wire coat hanger...."

It had been such a crazy night, I figured one more thing wouldn't matter. "Lark, when you hear your sisters coming, would you pucker up and kiss me so they will not worry about us?"

"Your wish is my command, Princess. Delighted to comply." He helped me stand. "Ready?" Our lips touched just before the girls came into view. At the squeals of delight from the twins, we unhurriedly pulled away. Lark kissed me on the tip of my nose, winked, and made a big display as if reluctant to let me go. For a few seconds, I felt cherished. As he reached out to help me sit down, the twins saw my bandaged foot. Lark explained. They sympathized while getting the refreshments ready.

Marilyn Stewart

Lark realized he'd stepped over the line a few times lately. His word had been given, so unfortunately, no more kissing his dream girl – for a little while.

No one knew quite what to do when Hope arrived, for Eric James, or EJ as he was called, was with her. He announced that he wished to talk to the men. Hope needed to have the girls' sympathetic ears. Oh, and one more thing: Unity and Mercy should be arriving at any minute.

Sam started a new pot of coffee so the four men could have the strong stuff and leave the hot chocolate for the ladies. Once the men were in the study and we were all settled at the table, there was a short, awkward silence.

Hope finally began. "At home, we have family interventions when something needs to be addressed. I couldn't do this at home, Mercy, but I had to do it. I've felt guilty for so long. This is the most loving, safe, and accepting place I could envision. Mercy, I could make a lot of excuses; however, the simple truth is, I have been envious, jealous, and spiteful towards you. I laughed when I saw Casey covered in green and heard her explanation at the Welcome Huggers meeting. On the way home, I quit laughing. A couple of days later, EJ's words cut me to my core and made me face my sin of harboring evil towards you. I've belittled and said hurtful words about you due to my jealousy. You are a fantastic EMT. Our towns are fortunate to have your skills. For many years, I have made your life miserable. I am so ashamed and truly sorry. You, Mercy Delight Willis Unique, are a treasure. I'm so thankful you are my sister. I am very sorry to have been so resentful and caustic. I know I have been intolerable. Please, can you forgive me? Can we spend time and do some things together?"

"Oh, Hope, I forgive you totally! I have so needed you, my sister. I will be thrilled to spend time with you. Honestly, I'd love to have you as a presence in my life. When you get home, check your calendar and call me – soon. Okay? I love you."

"Oh, Sis, I don't deserve it, but thank you. I love you, too."

Tears flowed, followed by a round of hugs. Laughter prevailed. The fellows were alerted that all was well. Everyone gathered in the living room and proceeded to hash over some of the interesting events of the evening.

At a crack of thunder, five of us sprang up. Sam moved his chair, and Boo bolted to hide under the table. This time, no one was tipped over. Angel quickly joined Boo. Hope and EJ got a glimpse of a dog struggling with his own war-related issues.

Hope chose not to spend the night. I was relieved. It was still a secret that some nights the guys needed my soothing hands.

I was so very tempted to share with Sam my disquiet, but finally talked myself out of revealing a guess. It wasn't even a valid hunch, so… I would wait until I talked to Peter next week.

Marilyn Stewart

Twenty-One

I arrived at Jim and Charity's home a few minutes later than Peter had requested. As I rang the doorbell, I contemplated. It had been a long, slow week, but I was thankful to finally be walking without limping. Lark had retreated into his usual silence.

I heard Charity shouting at Jim to answer the door and put my happy smile on. I genuinely liked and respected my brother-in-law. No sooner had I entered, than all five children came running up. Peter and Beryl's twins grabbed my legs and lifted their faces to mine. I leaned down and kissed each child on the top of their head. Knowing kids spout strange thoughts, I wasn't at first overly concerned by my nephew's words.

"You don't look like a witch, Auntie Ve."

I saw Jim shoot a quizzical look at his eldest son.

"What do you mean? Like a picture in a book?"

"No, Auntie Ve. Mummy said, 'I wish that witch Verity had never been born. She stole my brother's and Daddy's hearts away from me.' So how did you get to be a witch? How did you steal someone's heart? Will you please give it back to Mummy?"

I saw Jim freeze and felt as if a spear had pierced my heart. The enormity of hatred evident through a child's mimicked words brought silence to the entire group. I knew I was not the only hurting person here.

"Charity, you must never have opened the wrapped present from Dad which I passed on to you at the memorial service. It was addressed to you in his handwriting."

"The first thing I did when I came home was to throw your lousy present in the trash."

"What a pity. Dad spent an enormous amount of time making your gift. He had been planning to spend several days with you over your birthday. Ask your husband. Jim was in on the preparations for Dad's surprise visit with you."

"So, Auntie Ve, are you a witch? I like you. Maybe you are a really nice or a good witch?"

"No, James Taylor, I am not a witch. I am your mother's half-sister. So sorry. I can't stay. Obviously, I'm not wanted. I'll leave."

169

I hurried out of the house, stumbling as I fled due to tears blurring my vision. I was not far from my car when I bumped into someone. Mumbling "Sorry," I sniffed, side-stepped and tried to move forward. Sharp words were about to leave my lips when a familiar voice ground out, "Verity, my love, what is wrong? Who hurt you?"

I gasped, then began to sob. Lark pulled me gently against his chest. I only permitted him to see a brief rain storm before pulling back. I sniffed several times while hunting for a tissue to dry my eyes and wipe my nose.

Head still down, I mumbled, "Why are you here, Lark?"

"Peter invited me to come meet your family. Doesn't look to me as if they treat you very well."

"Our family relationships are tricky, at best, Lark."

"Your brother-in-law is standing on the porch looking ambivalent. I think he wants to talk to you, but is not sure if he would be welcome."

"Motion for him to come, Lark, but please stay close."

I heard Jim's footsteps approaching.

"Hello, you must be Lark. I am Jim. Peter said he'd invited you here today to meet our two families."

Lark didn't mince his words. "So, who shredded Verity's heart this time?"

"Ah, yes, that is probably an accurate description. I am grieved – sorry – shocked regarding what I just heard. Our son, James Taylor, obviously overheard my wife talking to someone – probably Peter's wife, Beryl, and just now repeated the information verbatim. I had no idea of the deep-seated enmity my wife has harbored unjustly against your mother and you, Verity. By the way, I retrieved the parcel from the trash where Charity had thrown it. I had forgotten about it. The box hasn't been opened. I will keep it hidden until she earns the right to have it. Peter and I will make sure our wives, and maybe we, along with them, get counseling."

"Thanks, Jim. It will be a start. You might ask Charity if she ever left something for me at our folks' graves."

Just then, Peter ran up, out of breath.

170

Marilyn Stewart

"So sorry to be late! I see you've met Lark, Jim. What are you all doing outside? Oh, Ve, what now?"

Jim answered Peter. "James Taylor asked her if she was a witch. He'd overheard our wives talking and exactly replicated Charity's tone of voice. I couldn't believe I've totally missed the extent of her emotional hatred towards Verity."

"Verity, love, let's go far away from here."

I took a long look at Lark, due to his tone of voice. His eyes held no hint of warmth. His hand was tightly clenched and he stood rigid, as if barely controlling his anger. As he looked into my eyes, his green eyes softened, but the roguish spark was missing. I swung my gaze to Jim and Peter. Their faces looked ashamed and distressed. I reached out and gently touched both faces. Sighing, I wearily quoted, '...forgive us our trespasses as we (or in like manner as I) forgive those who trespass against me.' Such a tough mandate, but necessary for healing and letting go of bitterness."

It appeared as if Lark and Peter were in a staring contest. Peter blinked first. He quietly said, "I was wrong to insist on your word of honor, Lark. You are free of our agreement and have my blessing."

Lark hesitated, nodded, and then replied, "I do mean to follow through on what I told you, Peter."

Peter nodded and slightly smiled. Turning to me, he handed me an envelope. "Ve, the claim is settled regarding our folks' deaths. I'll share the particulars with the others now. Call me later."

"Peter, I have to talk to you – it is of critical importance."

"Tomorrow. Breakfast at Welcome to Dine. Seven a.m. Okay?"

I nodded and took Lark's arm. "Is your van here?"

"No, love, someone dropped me off. I planned to hitch a ride home with you."

"Okay, let's go. I am feeling awfully wobbly. I need to sit for a bit."

"I'm sorry I can't give you a break and drive your car, Verity. I haven't yet the right touch with the artificial foot. Remember, I had an extra accelerator pedal installed to the left of the brake in my van. I don't know if I told you, but there is a toggle switch to activate so anyone can drive."

171

Welcome Huggers # 2 – Verity

I barely heard what he was telling me. "Thanks for sharing. I need to sit and be quiet for a few minutes until I stop shaking."

"Before we get in the car, how about sharing a hug, darling girl? A really long, comforting hug. I think I need one as much as you do, Love. I am so angry on your behalf."

I looked into his storm-filled eyes and groaned. "Oh, Lark, do not pick up an offense on my account. Believe me, Larkspur, that would not make me one little bit happy. Thanks for the hug. I am feeling better. Want to go do something strenuous?"

"What have you got in mind, Darlin'?" His rakish tone was back, along with a hint of a suggestion.

I looked at him for a few seconds, obviously puzzled, then bloomed bright red. I gulped. "I was thinking bowling, racquetball, a good, long hike, line dancing, ice skating, maybe a run? I'm not real good yet at a lot of those, but I'm getting better. I bowled an all-time high of one hundred and four with your sisters and some of the Welcome Huggers last week."

He chuckled. "Now you are being a bit chatty, Verity."

"I am perplexed as to what Peter meant as we left, but it looked as if you both settled something. Care to share? Why did Peter invite you today, or did you ask to come?"

"Well, it was a little bit of both, I guess. We met by accident – at least on my part – at a breakfast and talk for men. He was at my table. Have you mentioned me to Peter?"

"Hmm. I don't think I ever have, but he was at my birthday party, and he does have ears. Sometimes it seems as if almost everyone in these three towns are telepathic. I doubt cell phones are as advanced as the speed of the gossips here. So, you wanted to meet my relatives? Why?"

I figured, why not push a little? I didn't want to wait the two weeks he'd requested. He was so closed-mouth about everything. It was driving me crazy.

Lark gravely stated, "I'm an honorable and patient man."

"What in the world is that supposed to mean? Those words tell me absolutely nothing, Lark. They are a cop-out – a total failure to actively communicate." I broke my outburst to ask, "Do you want me to stop or drop you off anywhere besides home?"

Marilyn Stewart

"Would you mind stopping at the hardware store?"

"Hm. Not sure why I am supposed to mind stopping, but yes, I will stop at the nut and bolt store for you."

As I pulled into a parking spot and turned off the engine, Lark spoke. "Verity, Love, would you care to talk about what happened back there? Is Charity always the opposite of her name? Why are you looking at me as if you've not seen me before?"

"Are you really Lark? Wanting to communicate with me? Oh, wait, stupid me. I am to convey to you, not you...." I sighed. "What about you? What did you think? What are you feeling? Oh, yeah, and what was it with you and Peter?"

"If I agree to share with you, will you do the same with me? Both agree to be totally honest?"

"What?" I screeched. I was outraged! "When have I not been totally open and honest with you, Lark?"

"Right. Sorry. That was a dumb thing to say. 'Verity' means truth and you exemplify honesty. I'll strive to communicate better on all levels, soon. Please give me two weeks."

"What I don't understand is your silence. You could give me a clue! I look at your face and eyes, but you've become a tightly-closed book. Why? Why won't you share with me without thinking a while as to what you won't reveal?"

"You just aren't ready yet, my sweet Verity."

"Hogwash! I find that extremely hard to believe. How can you say such a thing, let alone honestly think it!"

"You are dealing with many things. Loss; grief; change, uncertainty; family relationships; fear of unknown people and your past. They are all weighing you down, plus for several weeks you have been troubled by something new that occurred."

"So you determined all by yourself, without talking to me, that I wasn't ready – for what, a relationship? Didn't it ever occur to you that you could have helped me deal with all of it better than leaving me alone and guessing? I've been wondering if it is the slim possibility of the twins becoming my responsibility that accounts for your emotional distance."

"Verity! How could you think such a thing? You saw my movie clips and how children were an integral part."

"Reality to Lark! Four of you made those movies. How was I to know your input was the dominant one? I saw you as the cameraman, not the producer. Besides, there is a whole lot of difference between a cute movie and noisy kids living with you 24/7."

"What would you know about kids, anyway?"

For a couple of seconds, I was silent. His comment had stung like a nettle. Sucking in some much-needed air, I finally retorted, "I didn't get to this age without doing a lot of babysitting, plus kids in the tribe were always around – even lived in our home at times. How much time have you spent with kids – not movie-related? Would you even ever want to be a father?"

I couldn't believe I'd actually blurted out those words. A strange look crossed his face, but due to his silence and my embarrassment, I quickly rambled on.

"I have no idea what kind of a woman you are looking to spend your days with, but I need a guy who will be open and willing to share his whole life with me. Not one who leaves me guessing all the time. So much for being open and honest. It certainly didn't last very long."

"I am truly sorry I said that about kids. I didn't mean to hurt you. Later, Ve. Remember what I asked of you." With that, Lark exited the car and headed for the store.

I was furious with myself. Why had I not reined in my tongue when I knew I was tired and emotionally devastated? It hurt even to think of moving away from this incredibly fun, supportive home, the Welcome Huggers and the many people I had come to know. No more glimpses of the little twins growing up with their cousins, and the mixed reactions I always fought. I sniffed. I had waited months and didn't think I had a whole week, let alone two, of waiting left in me. *"Oh, God. You'd think by now I would have learned to wait for your timing. You've given me enough practice. Waiting to get home from boarding school – so many times. Waiting to see and live with my family - here. Waiting to deliver.... Waiting to be near family again. I hate to wait. Seems as if I am always getting left or torn from ones I love. I am so tired of it."*

Marilyn Stewart

In an effort to change my thinking, I pulled out the envelope Peter had given to me. I saw my name and the name of the solicitors. If I were back with the tribe, all of us would wail and cry together. But here I sat – alone and unwilling to know what price tag a court had put on Dad, Mum, and Ruby's lives.

Twenty-Two

I was still holding the yet-to-be-opened envelope when Lark got back in the car. It was a silent ride home.

It was strange – almost eerie – having the whole house to myself. The guys had a meeting and the twins, dates. I repeatedly threw the ball for Angel, we worked on his tricks, then I gave him a thorough brushing. Wandering through the house, I contemplated tomorrow.

Sitting on my bed, I picked up the envelope and whacked it against my hand a couple of times. It was still sealed. I stood up, then sat back down. I grabbed my devotional book and decided to read only what the verse was for tomorrow. *Psalm 118:24 "This is the day the Lord has made; let us rejoice and be glad in it."* Underneath was written 'an older version states,' *"...I will rejoice and..."* I sat there frowning. Either it was going to be a really good day or I would have to decide to 'rejoice,' even though I might not want to. I shook my head – that was tomorrow.

I put the envelope back in my purse and settled down to organize my 'tomorrow.' I set my alarm for 5:30. I would have my devotions, then open this envelope so I could talk about its ramifications later with Peter. A shower, play a bit with Angel, fix breakfast for my roommates, and I'd be ready to leave by 6:45 for my 7 a.m. breakfast appointment. Later, I would make an appointment to talk to Katie's dad, Matt, who was the owner of the bank in Unique.

Now that I had that settled, I went downstairs and cranked up the volume on the CD player. I danced around the table while slowly fixing a sandwich and a cup of hot chocolate. Eventually, I turned off the music to soak up the quietness as I pondered my life and situation. I was tired of looking over my shoulder with sorrow, regret, and tears. It was time to pray, prepare, and proceed. I put on the CD "The Lord is Good" by the Collingsworth family, and left the door open while I sat on the veranda to enjoy my dessert and tea.

Marilyn Stewart

I double-checked. Everything was locked up tight. I headed for my bedroom and suddenly realized how very spoilt I'd become due to interacting with four people on a daily basis. Whereas I used to be content all by myself for hours – almost days, I found myself – lonely. There was a book I'd been wanting to read, but instead I just wanted to cry. I was so tired of pretending all was well. It seemed as if my entire life had been a struggle – to fit in and be loved. Charity had never accepted me. I had lived briefly with three different families, in a boarding school, but only rarely, from age nine on, with my family. Right now, I was only thinking about my losses. Finally, just as I was really getting to know and enjoy living with my folks, they were torn away. I was miserable. What was wrong with me? This was a great place to live. So, all right, I loved that Lark's eyes could be so soft and loving one minute, and the next, like green glacier ice. I was fooling myself. I flat-out had to stop dreaming of a life with him. It was imperative I wrap my head firmly around the reality of the necessity of making the move to a new place and leaving without a backward look.

I told myself, 'I will not cry; I will not cry.' Normally, Angel slept on the floor next to my bed, but my weeping disturbed him. He persisted in trying to comfort me with many licks. With the decision made to leave, I hugged Angel, wiped my eyes, and fell into a deep, dreamless sleep.

In the morning, I followed my plan. Reading the dollar amount hurt, but my tears disappeared down the shower drain. Just as four people entered the kitchen, my cell rang. It was 6:30.

"Hi Peter; I'll see you at seven," I joyfully said.

"Sorry, Verity. I am on my way to the airport – work-related. We can talk when I get back in a week."

I exploded. "No! I will not wait that long. It has been weeks since I asked for a bit of your time. You can answer me – now! Yes or no is all I need right now, Peter. Just tell me – Yes or no!"

"Okay, Ve. Yes or no it is."

"Do you – we – have an older half-brother?"

"What?"

I was almost screaming by now. "Yes or no, Peter."

"Ve, how? Where did you get that idea?"

177

Welcome Huggers # 2 – Verity

I spat out. "Peter, it is a simple question: yes or no?"

At his prolonged silence, I turned off my cell, took a deep breath and walked out to the back porch. Looking up, I said, *"Lord, am I still supposed to rejoice and be glad? I will try - okay."*

After my behavior, I was reluctant to go back inside, but eventually I did. I silently fixed tea and toast, smeared on vegemite (which Sam calls black tar), and plunked down on the empty chair.

Sam placed his fork on his empty plate and looked at me. "Ve, what is this about? When did you...?"

"Remember the visit Mercy and I had to the Ghost Town several weeks back and the resulting actions?"

Sam nodded. Realizing I wasn't quite ready to go on, and the other three were clueless, he filled them in on that past event.

With three dumbfounded faces staring at me, I hesitantly proceeded. "Well, that day, I saw a face – ever so briefly. It wasn't until I was in bed, replaying my day that a possible implication hit me. In the few seconds we exchanged eye contact, his features revealed – shock, regret, followed by what appeared to be hatred. You see, when I saw his profile, I'd instantly thought – Dad? Peter? But then he turned towards me. He was older than Peter, but way younger than Dad. I have been trying for weeks to get Peter alone so I could see his face when I asked him about this guy. Yesterday, Charity said something about me having 'stolen her brother's and Daddy's heart.' I thought she was just referring to Peter, but then I got to wondering if she knew something I didn't. Maybe we had an older half-brother."

Fe blurted out. "Well, what did Peter say?"

I shook my head. "In the end, he didn't say a word!"

Sam got up. "I'll notify Sheriff Ben. Please write down your folks' names, birthdays, if you know your dad's previous wife's name and date of death, etc., Ve. What are you doing today?"

"I'm headed to the bank, then going grocery shopping. How about we have a barbecue tonight? Steaks, potatoes, corn, etc. Let me know soon how many extras will be at supper. You know something? I am grateful – as in, really thankful, for you

Marilyn Stewart

four awesome roommates." As we all headed out, I received four silent, prolonged hugs that left me feeling exceedingly loved.

Twenty-Three

At two in the morning, Sam and I arrived home from an emergency call out. The house lights were all on. For a few seconds we forgot the grimness we'd left in concern for what might have taken place here. Racing up the porch stairs, I threw open the door and yelled, "Is everyone okay?"

Lark responded, "We're fine, Love. Just been sitting here talking, waiting up for you two to get back."

By the time he finished speaking, I was already in the kitchen with my hand on my heart, checking for myself.

Seeing our tense faces, Fe poured me a cup of hot chocolate. Annie handed Sam a hot cup of coffee, and Lark added several goodies to an almost empty plate. Having seen our stress and attire as we entered, Lark inquired, "Need to share a hug?" I nestled against his chest, tears cascading down my face.

Fe, Annie, and then Katie, who was staying with us for a second time, each gave Sam a long hug.

Katie burst out, "You five really love each other. I mean, you are tightly connected and care on all levels. You pay attention to the needs of each other without talking. I am beginning to understand what Mercy means. She has told me repeatedly that I need to pay attention to the people around me. Thank you for having me here again. I've been caught up in physical attributes and being scared I wouldn't measure up. It was a bad call out, huh Sam?"

"Worst one in a while. Boo and Angel found two kids we didn't know existed. They'd been thrown out of the bed of a truck. One has broken bones, but the other has head injuries as well. Their parents are in stable condition. Two teens in another car are in critical condition, and two people died."

"Anyone we know, Sam?"

Sam and I looked down as we nodded. It was only now that I realized our clothes were streaked with blood. I choked out, "Essie and her grandmother. The others were not from around here." I pleaded, "Please can we talk about something else? I can't get their images out of my mind."

Annie assessed me and said, "Lark, we'll look after her. A hot soak and a good massage should help."

I saw Katie eyeing Sam, and then she opened her mouth. "You need a hot shower and a massage. You know, like Verity gave you both last night; well, not the shower, she didn't."

I froze. Sam's voice was icy as he said, "How do you know that, Katie?"

"Sam, she got up at 3 a.m. and tiptoed out. I thought maybe she was sleep-walking. Mercy did sometimes when she was troubled. I heard a noise, trailed her, and peeked in your bedroom. After all, I am a part-time reporter, but, guys, I won't tell."

"What are you saying, Katie?" queried Fe and Annie.

Lark stood, frowned at his sisters, then, with a hand on my shoulder, announced, "Annie, Fe, Verity's room is above ours. Months ago she offered her assistance. She puts hot towels on our backs before giving us neck and back massages. She hums, sometimes a bit off-key, but it relaxes us so we can get a couple hours' sleep. Nothing inappropriate has taken place. It has been our secret. The mornings we aren't at breakfast are usually because we've had a rough night. Sometimes we go for a run."

"That's why you didn't want the spare bed switched into your room! Did Fairlyn find out?"

I glanced at Fe and nodded. Sam sucked in a breath before asking, "The second night she was here, uh, she massaged my back, didn't she? I was almost out, but felt a slight difference."

I smiled and nodded. "We saw you twitch, Sam, and held our breaths. Good night all. I truly love each of you."

In the morning, Katie called Sheriff Ben to find out if Essie had any kinfolk. He told Katie the Welcome Huggers could go over and clean the house – except for the study. Deputy Sophia would do that, while he continued searching for answers.

Katie organized everyone, then called her Dad. Since he was the owner of the bank she knew Essie used, Katie asked him to call Sheriff Ben about Essie's banking affairs.

Within several hours, the small house had been thoroughly cleaned. They'd washed the sheets, remade the beds, thrown out everything in the refrigerator, and given it a thorough scrubbing. Many of the girlfriends had gone by the time Sheriff Ben arrived.

Sam had spent the morning repairing the back steps of Essie's porch. He'd just finished painting them when Sheriff Ben drove up. He got out of his vehicle, only to duck back in when he saw Boo racing towards him. The large dog had patches of light blue paint dripping off his body and scattering like rain onto the grass. Sam bellowed, "Boo, halt!" Boo looked back, then chose to slide to a stop. At Sam's firm, "Come," Boo stood, waved his tail high in the air, and slowly moved back to where Sam stood with a hose. Katie found some shampoo. Fairlyn laughed, took the bottle and walked over, soaped up her hands, and began to help wash the paint out of Boo's coat. Sam and Fairlyn silently worked together. Their hands touched, lingered a second, and Sam quietly asked, "Would you go out on a proper date with me?"

Fairlyn nodded and softly asked, "Where?"

Sam named the most expensive place he could think of and had not yet visited.

Fairlyn's face lit up. "When?"

"Friday night?"

"Love to," was her response.

A throat being cleared nearby caught their attention. They looked first at the nearby sheriff, then over at the porch where the girlfriends were busy snapping pictures and giggling.

Sheriff Ben requested Sam move over to the police vehicle for a private conversation.

"Sam, we were able to locate their wills. I have read them, but not the personal letters that were with them. There are two: one for you, and another for Verity, dated last month. They had no relatives. The house and contents are all yours."

"Mine? No way! Are you positive?"

"Yes, Sam. It is all yours. Are you okay, Son?"

"I guess so. No. I'm not. That was a tough call out. They were lovely ladies. I can't believe they are really gone."

My letter from Essie was brief. She wrote of their gratitude that I introduced Sam into their lives and for getting people to help

Marilyn Stewart

out at work. They had donated money to the city in my name to help pay for fuel and supplies to aid us volunteers.

We, his housemates, and the Welcome Huggers, along with many townspeople, assisted Sam with the costs and details for a double funeral.

Twenty-Four

Days passed. Peter had yet to contact me; I had an idea why. Everything seemed to be moving along, except my love life. Birds were chirping, dogs needed exercise, and work awaited.

Annie happily proclaimed, "The guys left already. Time for girl talk. No guys to raise their eyebrows and butt in!"

We talked and laughed our way through breakfast, until I shocked not only myself, but also the sisters, with my sudden statement. "It is almost time for me to move on. I've nearly accomplished what I was sent here to do."

Annie changed the subject with, "Did you know Jake and Lark might be headed out in a day or two to Hollywood?"

"No, I didn't. See, that's the problem with some of the guys around here. It is a need-to-know only among the guys – not extending to the girls. We are not to be ignored or set aside for their convenience. Relationships are hard enough without being clued in to pertinent information.

"Oh, please, don't mind me. I'm just venting. Must be the lack of sleep, or my family turmoil that is making me cranky. What Lark does or doesn't is not my concern."

Fe muttered, "We do understand your frustration. We're upset with him, too. We'd like to bop him upside the head if it would do any good. He won't talk to us about you. He's always been soft of heart. Maybe he needs to make sure it is true love and not just to try and fix things for you."

I clarified a little. "Now that everyone knows I am qualified both as a paramedic and counselor and not a librarian, I'll be moving on. I was hired to get the library up and running until the town could get funding to pay a full time librarian. Serah is now ready to take over, so it is time for me to leave."

Fe wailed, "Verity, that doesn't mean you have to leave Welcome! There are other jobs, and what about your pottery classes and fill-in work? You sort of promised you'd stay through the Wounded Warrior Weekend. What about learning if you have another half-brother and sorting Charity out and your maybe-cousins? Peter and you need to resolve things."

"I love being here with all of you. If I stay much longer, leaving will tear me apart. My relatives' issues will resolve themselves, in time. It isn't as if they want to know me. Well, the youngest, Colin, might. I saw the way he watched me."

"Where will you go, Verity? Please keep in touch with Annie and me. It was so much fun helping while the parents were on the cruise. It is lovely to have Katie back, but something is troubling her deeply. We love you, Ve!" Fe hugged me then, and Annie joined in for a group hug.

The three sets of parents had returned from their exciting cruise. JC and JJ had separately contacted Lark at the library celebration, and the next week, met with him individually in secret. Last night, Fe, Annie, and Lark had been at the Willis home for a big family celebration of the twins' engagements.

"Annie, Fe, you both have enough to think about without me clogging your thoughts. Let me once again admire your rings. They are brilliant. So unique to each of you."

They were not to be side-tracked. "Please stay, Verity. We were really and truly hoping for a triple wedding, but it looks as if that dream is now shattered. Never mind. We still want you to be our one and only attendant."

My heart ached. "Oh, Fe, Annie, I love you two more than members of my own family and will sorely miss you. I think I'll take off for a month and return well before the fair and the wounded warrior events. Your double wedding is after that, so you won't have any last minute worries that I won't make it."

"But we will worry about you. The rapist and who knows who else is still out there roaming around. And what about that maybe-brother? They probably know what your car looks like. What if someone intends you harm, and no one is there to help you?"

I tried to smile. "Ah, girls, don't cry. That's a lot of 'what if's.' Look at your beautiful rings! Your guys obviously knew your middle names to have used the stones along with diamonds in such intrinsic settings. No more tears. In time, both Angel and I will find our place – the one God has for us."

Hearing a deep voice announce, "So, my dear, you're going to run!" made us jump.

I retorted, "No more than you, Lark!"

"Anything or anyone who might be able to convince you to stay?" I couldn't believe he'd ask such a stupid question. If he didn't know by now, I was certainly not going to enlighten him.

I stood up, stamped my good right foot hard and muttered, "Men!" As I plodded my way up the stairs, I kept muttering, "Clueless man!"

It made me feel a little better. Not much, but it helped a little to vent my frustration regarding one Larkspur Jade Lane.

Marilyn Stewart

Twenty-Five

I knew I was going to leave town sooner than I'd hinted to Annie and Fe. Hope of Lark loving me more than like a brother had dimmed. It was the flowers I'd gotten during the days he was gone that had kept me hoping. I worked feverishly, getting the last of the clay used, pots completed, fired, and on display at the gallery. Even though the space was paid up for three months, it was now clean and ready for someone else. Most of my dreams for our Paws2Read Library had been implemented. Now Serah could delete or add new items of her choosing. I was pretty much ready to leave town, and wished to do so without any fuss or notice.

Yesterday, I called Franklin, a financial analyst Matt had recommended, to thank him for his sound advice. I'd added that I would be out of touch for a while, but he could contact me through Mr. Greenland (Matt), the owner of the bank in Unique. Only Matt had my new cell phone number.

After years of being poor and living almost from paycheck to paycheck, I was reluctant to touch the money. I feared I'd become like a child in a candy store – greedy to share and buy indiscriminately. One item I did need, badly, was a new car.

I now had in my possession eight hundred dollars in travelers' checks, and six hundred in cash. For this last week, my bike had stayed on my vehicle. I took it off to ride and put it back on, so as not to tip anyone to my plans. I had to leave – just *had* to.

Yesterday, most of the townspeople had been at the Willis place, celebrating July 4th. All day, I stayed very visible, but distant, from Lark. I'd served, cleaned up, run errands, and as darkness settled, departed. I could see the fireworks from my bedroom window as I hurriedly raced in and out, packing my car. I'd almost left then, but decided to leave after breakfast so as not to raise a fuss. Of course, today, everyone sat and talked and talked, in no hurry to move from the kitchen. I felt like squirming, but forced myself to act as if I, too, were in no hurry. I asked Sam and Lark what cars they'd recommend, as I was thinking of upgrading my wheels. What did they think of the Subaru Outback, Ford Escape, and Honda CRV? Should I think large engine, 4WD, or would a small, economical car be more practical?

187

Finally, with the dishes done and dogs exercised, we all headed in different directions.

I slowly drove down the lane, leaving Welcome Home for what could be the last time. I was sure no one suspected. Memories flooded my thoughts of the Welcome Huggers and others in these special towns. Maybe someday I would return.

A while back, I had promised to return for the twins' wedding. Now, I didn't know if I could stand to see Lark at all, let alone him walking down an aisle with a sister on each arm. Since I had given my word, I reckoned I had to return, though briefly.

As I drove, my thoughts ran through a checklist. Key to the library handed over to Serah. Key, a box of books, and a short letter left in my room. Two notes in my purse, ready to go in the mail tonight to Peter and Charity. My car had been tuned last week and fueled yesterday. Angel and most of his stuff was on board.

I scooted through Unique, carefully checking not to exceed the speed limit. I almost started crying thinking of Mercy, a 'Unique' by marriage. I was finally becoming excited to hit the open road. It had been a long time since I'd traveled any distance. I'd stayed home on Mother's Day due to my still-painful ankle. Only two miles and I'd be through Hope. Then I'd feel I'd escaped. Checking my rear vision mirror, I saw a patrol car's lights flashing, moving fast. I pulled over, hoping it would continue on its way. No such luck. I gritted my teeth and quietly muttered, "They didn't even have the courtesy to turn off their flashing lights."

"Hi, Verity."

"Sheriff Ben."

"Do you know why I pulled you over?"

"Not a clue."

"Did you think you could leave town without saying a single goodbye?"

"Because it isn't a goodbye. It's a sad 'bye."

"Will you be back for the twins' double wedding?"

"No comment."

Marilyn Stewart

"Now, Verity, you gave your word to Fe and Annie. You said you would return in plenty of time for our fair and Wounded Warrior Weekend – well before their weddings."

"You going to give me a ticket, Sheriff Ben?"

"I'm thinking seriously of doing just that and putting on there the date you have to show up in my office or face a huge fine and a suspension of your driver's license."

"I would think a lawyer could beat a rap like that, very easily citing intimidation tactics."

"You coming back, Verity? We'd try to talk some sense into Lark, but he told me 'yesterday was two weeks.' That mean something to you girl?"

"I wouldn't want him on those terms, Sheriff. He has to…. Sheriff Ben, I'll see you when I see you."

"Okay, Verity. Drive carefully. I'll hunt you down if you aren't back in thirty days. By the way, we have all but one thing cleared regarding your uncle and cousins. Looks like they are legit. Still don't know about a brother. I'll be in touch."

I couldn't resist asking, "Sheriff, have they even asked to see, or like, you know, meet or get to know me?"

I saw by the way he looked away for a second, that the answer was no. He shook his head.

"I'm sorry, Verity. Really sorry. They are the losers. You are a delightful and special young lady. You know I am a crusty, short-on-words guy, but one who speaks the truth."

My eyes smiled up at him through a mist of tears. I couldn't resist challenging him. "Sheriff Ben, you might take a leaf out of Unity's book of words for Mercy. We've heard them enough times. Go try them on Sheriff Ann, and then try a couple of hot smooches. I double-dare you!" He backed up fast, and I drove off, laughing. Glancing back, I saw he was leaning up against the front of his cruiser, watching my departing car and talking on his cell.

I reckoned he was not calling Sheriff Ann, but Lark.

A mile past the town of Hope, I stopped at Fabulous Deli. It was the last restroom for a while and a good place to get a take-away sandwich, cookie, soda, and chips. I put a cooler with apples and healthy snacks in the boot (or as you Yanks say, 'trunk'). Two gallons of water were also snugly in place. I felt the increasing

189

urge to hurry. It was sixty miles to the interstate. I'd soon be able to put my foot down and roll. Only when I got to I-40 would I feel totally free.

Hurrying through the deli door, laden with a small sack, I raised my head and looked towards my car. Surprise made me halt mid-stride, causing the couple following to bump into me. Leaning up against my car with his feet crossed was Lark. Oh, my, but he looked tempting. What to do? What to do? I knew if I once looked into his beautiful green eyes, I'd just grab him, kiss him, and never be willing to let him go. I took tiny, swift glances, trying to read his body language. I was clueless as to why he was here and what he might want. I moved slowly towards him, trying to make up my mind as to what to say, and came to the conclusion that I'd wait for him to speak. However long it took.... No. I'd wait two minutes, then get in the car and drive away without speaking. With my decision made, I lifted my chin, stared into his smiling green eyes, and walked swiftly to him. I stopped just out of reach. His sparkling green eyes were enticing, but I was strong and determined not to be easily swayed.

We heard a motorcycle thundering nearby, but never glanced towards it. With the turn of a key, the noisy bike was silenced; however, Lark had deliberately raised his voice. All nearby heard him say, "Ah, come on Sweetheart, give me a kiss."

Off to my left, I was shocked to hear, "That's right, Sweetheart, why don't you give him a kiss like the one I shared with you a couple of years back. I've been tracking you for quite a while, or having my sister do it when I was unavailable."

I turned to look at the fellow. Fear raced through me, but I was angry and tired of being a victim. "So you have a sister living close by. The sheriff will be interested. What have you to do with me? I don't believe we have ever kissed."

"Well, you wouldn't remember, would you, since you were out cold. Hey, back off! I'm talking to the lady here, and she...."

When Lark heard the fellow admit to what he thought was a vicious crime against his beloved, he took action – military style. The guy now lay on the ground, out cold. Lark knew questions would follow, but that was okay with him, for his Verity was unharmed.

While Lark retrieved cable ties from a kit in his vehicle, Angel stood guard, and I called the sheriff. Lark took pleasure in fastening together the guy's hands, then his feet. I was amused at the efficiency Lark displayed – definitely military efficient.

I suddenly wanted to stomp, shriek in frustration, or hit something. Now, Sheriff Ben had a reason to keep me in town. No way. My brain triggered an idea. I had time if I left now. I clicked the remote to unlock the door and raced around to slide into the driver's seat. I couldn't believe it – Lark was blocking the door and grinning at me! Wow, but he could move fast when he so desired.

"Please, Lark, please let me leave town before the sheriff arrives. I promised I would come back. For my sanity, I have to leave. I might even kick your good leg if you don't move."

"Too late, Sweetheart, the sheriff is nearly here, and Bubba is about to wake up. What are you doing?"

I had grabbed a small notebook out of my large carry-all and began to write, fast.

Just then, the sheriff drove up and got out of his car.

"I see you caught her, Lark, and it looks as if you constrained our wanted man as well. Good man. Verity, I reckon you'll now be staying in town for a while."

"Nope. Nada. Not happening. Here is my written, signed, and dated statement regarding what I heard and saw. I plan to be on my way as soon as I replenish my food, which got trampled. You can't hold me."

I didn't like the huge grin the sheriff was wearing as he announced, "Oh, yes, I can, Verity. I can detain you for leaving or trying to leave the scene of a crime before you have been authorized to depart. You can glare at me all you please, girl, but you are staying. Lark, once our technician swabs your knuckles, take her in and get her something to eat."

I wanted to scream with disappointment! I'd come so close. I bitterly spat out, "This is almost as bad as Jonah in the belly of the large fish for three days. He couldn't escape his situation, and neither can I."

Lark had the gall to laugh. "So by that statement, you are insinuating that you, like Jonah, are running from God."

By now, I was feeling really snarky. "Sometimes, Lark, you are entirely too perceptive, and at other times, absolutely clueless. I am exhausted. Too much trauma the last couple of years and stress the last six months. I want to hike in quiet woods, check out ruins, or visit a National Park. I need to get away from people!"

I'd almost said, 'from you.'

I could hardly believe it when he said, "Would you mind if I went with you? We could go for several days or a week and just wander. We would get two rooms each night and enjoy getting to know each other better – away from everyone and everything."

For a second, I melted. "Oh, Lark, do you think the sheriff would let us go?" Just as quickly, I sternly stated, "If you don't plan on opening up and sharing with me, then I'd rather you not be anywhere near me. If you choose to come, you need to be willing to talk and talk, and bring your trumpet."

My eye caught on a person about thirty feet past Lark's shoulder. Oh, no. Why did I have to see those two people together? Regardless of the consequences, I turned and took off running towards the sheriff, who was about to get into his police car. He saw me, stopped, and slammed the patrol car door closed. "What now, Verity? I told Lark you both could leave."

I muttered, "My timing stinks today. I don't believe it! I'm sure the man in your squad car is a shill, a plant. He is not Bubba. He is too tall and didn't smell like oranges. Did you check his arm? Sheriff, look over my shoulder at the people sitting at the picnic table. Look at his profile. Who does he remind you of?

"Peggy, sitting next to him, was his girlfriend after me, and Ruth is one of the newer Welcome Huggers. Doesn't she work in your office? I put down in my notes this fellow mentioned a sister was keeping track of me. I think he knows the sister, but is not her brother. Maybe Ruth is his girlfriend. I feel absolutely sick. I wonder if he is my rapist." As the words left my lips, I could hardly keep myself from throwing up. I began to shiver.

Marilyn Stewart

Sheriff Ben ordered that Lark and I not acknowledge we'd seen the group. We were to stop and eat, go home, and wait for him. He was calling in reinforcements.

Lark put his arms around me. I thought he was trying to distract my thoughts, but then he whispered, "Peek over at who just now sat down with the people at the picnic table." I sneaked a quick look at the area indicated and sighed. Lark lowered his head, taking the opportunity to share a sizzling kiss. I decided to make sure he knew his kiss was extremely welcome. It went on and on until I couldn't breathe and realized people were whistling and clapping. With my eyes fixed on Lark, I teased, "What about the kissing booth being too public a place in which to share a kiss?"

"Times and people change, Precious. Every time I've ever looked at you, I've wanted to kiss you and never let you go."

"Wow!" I whispered. "He can talk, and he likes me!"

"Ah, Sweetheart, he not only likes you, he loves you, wants to marry you, and told Peter so months ago. Peter extracted a promise that I found extremely hard to keep, especially living in the same house. This just now was not a proposal, but information regarding what I hope is in store for us. Unfortunately, my darling, we have some unfinished business to iron out. Let's get something to eat in Hope, where Angel is permitted to be with us. We can plan a road trip, then go home, Ve, my love, and wait for Sheriff Ben."

We ate, talked, and kissed before heading to our residence.

From the second Lark and I exited our cars, Annie and Fe started dancing around us. A girlfriend had sent them a very recent photo, which caused them to rush home. They were laughing, smiling, and talking about a triple wedding. Angel danced, barked, and dashed around. I smiled, peeked at Lark, and was reassured by his radiant face and brilliant smile. I only blinked twice before he had me in his arms. He kissed away my tears, then with obvious intent, slowly lowered his mouth to unashamedly demonstrate his love for me to his sisters. I could hardly grasp the change in this man's demeanor. The sound of hands clapping made me feel deprived of a significant tender moment in our budding romance. Where had all these people come from? They were stealing precious minutes I longed to joyfully savor.

Despite the influx, we stayed holding each other close, so Lark had not far to lean to whisper in my ear. "Not engaged. Special place for that when we can get away. Okay?" I knew I was beaming as I gave him a quick kiss, a nod, and turned so Lark was standing behind me. He chuckled, and I blushed at his understanding of my reasoning at shielding him.

Sam made his way through the girlfriends to tell us he'd just now locked all the bedrooms as well as the door to the house. He was endeavoring to get people to clear out when Sheriff Ben arrived and everything changed.

With a couple of blips of his siren, the sheriff had their attention. "We have a bit of an emergency, which we hope to reveal to all of you in the next couple of days. Please permit us to do our jobs and keep you safe by getting in your cars and leaving, so we can secure this area. Several vehicles are waiting to enter. Please go home or out to eat – anywhere as long as it is away from here. We will arrest anyone who violates this command."

Sam said quietly to the four of us, "Get into the house right now and go into the study."

Lark and I locked our cars and grabbed each other's hands. Boo and Angel obeyed Sam's motions and entered the house. Side by side, the dogs ran, sniffing room by room on the first floor before heading up the stairs. I smiled at how Angel mimicked Boo.

Sheriff Ben entered, saying, "That was an effective way to get everyone to leave without making a fuss. I don't have much time to explain. Those were our identity thieves at Fabulous Deli. The DEA raid at the Ghost Town scared them. They were preparing to leave our area. We are missing one – a possible shooter, or so we have been led to believe."

"So I guess Paul and Brenda are brother and sister, and Paul made up almost all of what he told us."

"Right on all accounts, Verity. Well, almost. Paul and Brenda are half-brother and -sister. She is six years older as well as the ring leader in the inheritance/identity theft ring."

"You mean our Brenda?" Annie gasped. "The president of our Welcome Huggers girlfriends group? You know, when she took over, I wondered why we suddenly were asked to fill out a page of personal documentation when we never had before."

"Yes, Annie. She had information regarding all your names, birth places, medical issues, family, etc. Verity, you became a target when you wouldn't give up your middle name and medical history. She, according to Paul, became fixated on you. She'd also learned of your inheritance. Verity, we don't think the man Lark flattened is your rapist, but we will definitely check his DNA. He said he'd overheard Paul say you were unconscious when he found you, and so, to bug Lark, he added the rest. Now, we might have a shooter nearby; therefore, I'll have Sam inside and another deputy stationed outside all night. I'll keep in touch. Oh, and Verity, I'm relieved you are back home – for good. 'Bye now."

The identity thieves were people we had known and liked. I had almost given Angel to Bryce and Sheena, who were drug distributors. Changes often happened rapidly – take Lark and me, for example. I'd decided to flee, and now there was the distinct possibility of a triple wedding in the fall.

Lark chuckled. "Today, we definitely saw God's hand at work. Sheriff Ben pulled Verity over to chat. She decided to stop at the deli. Both of those events allowed me to catch up. A fellow on a BSA motorcycle rode up. He ended up on the ground, with Verity calling the sheriff. Remember complaining to me, Ve, that Jonah couldn't get out of the belly of the fish and you couldn't get out of town? Before the sheriff left, you spotted certain people at a picnic table. I see the amazing split-second timing of God."

I nodded. "Driving home, I realized I've been running and trying to do everything in my own strength. Yes, I prayed for God's help, but then worried and worked to get things to turn out the way I wanted and in my time frame. I appreciate your reminding us that God really is in control, for which I am very thankful. I know we have many things to discuss. I'd like to ask each of you, my dearest of friends, to help me make a hard decision. Do you think I should reveal my middle name to everyone?"

"You want our gut-honest truth, don't you, Ve?"

I nodded at Sam, stood, looked at Lark, almost touched my arm, but refrained when I saw him twitch his head. Instead, I said, "My secret has been very costly." I plopped down on the couch and snuggled close to Lark. He put his arm around me and pulled me even closer. What a day. I was content, relaxed, and ready to listen to their input. I'd welcome their perspective.

Boo and Angel had been sniffing around a very large trunk by the window (a recent yard sale acquisition), but all of us had been focused on other things. The dogs weren't showing any stress; rather, they were acting as if someone had dropped bacon or a treat near there.

Sam began, "Oh, Ve, I forgot to tell you. A medium-sized trunk arrived today for you. I signed for it and put it in your bedroom. Here's the key." Upon hearing a thud, the dogs began to bark, and Sam and Lark jumped up. Sam ordered, "Ladies, leave this room immediately!"

We girls flew out of the room and into the hall. I peeked back in to see a gun drawn. Sam and Lark were standing at each end of the trunk getting ready to lift the lid. I only realized how tense I was when I felt the key dig into the palm of my hand. We heard a brief scuffle, then silence. Finally, Lark opened the door to tell us the room was secure and we could return.

Boo and Angel stood just out of reach of a man sitting bound, but not gagged, on the floor. At our entrance, the fellow lifted his head and snarled at me. "Verity, you have absolutely destroyed my life!"

I called Boo and Angel over, kissed their heads, and said, "Good boys. On guard." The dogs once again became focused and ready to pounce on the intruder. Looking intently at the fellow, I finally replied, "No, Sir. You made a choice that has ruined your own life. By the way, who ordered the hit on me?"

"I want a lawyer."

"It might go easier on you if you give us or the sheriff the information. Was it Wanda?"

"How did you know that? You psychic? I could have clipped you a couple of times except for your military boyfriends."

"So their habit of walking next to the road saved me."

"You read my mind again. So you must know I would never shoot a wounded warrior."

Marilyn Stewart

"Good to know," I responded before stating, "Sam, would you tell Sheriff Ben I don't remember ever having seen this man. Girls, let's go upstairs and open my trunk."

With all the angst in my life, I had completely forgotten the strange letter that came a week ago. As we climbed the stairs, I remembered two things Mum had shown me in the last week of her life.

Wow! What a day! I smiled at God's perfect timing and laughed with delight. I asked Fe and Annie to wait in the hall until called. It took me less than five minutes to be ready. As they entered, I slowly twirled. Their gasps, hand-clapping, and laughter complemented mine. We were like sisters sharing a joyous event.

Hearing someone approaching, Fe bolted the door, and we began to whisper. I eased out of Mum's wedding dress and carefully tucked it back in its wrappings. The dress fit my new shape as if perfectly created by a tailor.

"I hear you all in there. Ve, are you okay? I'd like a kiss, Sweetheart, and the sheriff wants you all to come downstairs. Any plans for supper tonight, or should I order two large pizzas? One pepperoni and one ham and pineapple along with a salad?"

We popped out of my bedroom, and each of us gave him a kiss. Lark had climbed the stairs! While Fe and Annie thought it was a first, Lark and I remembered an earlier time he had climbed them in order to share a comforting hug.

Fe laughed with delight. "So love does conquer all. Well done, Lark." She skipped a few steps. "I feel like dancing!"

Lark wrapped an arm around my waist, grinned, and asked if he was going to get to see what had arrived in the trunk.

We giggled and laughed while shooting knowing happy glances at each other. I kissed his cheek. "All in good time, my love, all in good time. Pizza sounds great, along with your choices."

Sheriff Ben and staff had been super busy. They wanted us to know our information was secure, and that eventually, everything would be shredded. The identity thieves only utilized stolen data months after they left a town. This was the shooter they had been looking for, and he was ratting everyone out as fast as his tongue could flap. Sheriff Ben beamed as he added, "Guards are no longer needed, and Verity is permitted to come and go as she pleases."

Lark's eyes sparkled. He sported a huge grin as he shared, "She is staying, Sheriff Ben."

Later, Fe, ever the sensitive, caring person, had looked at Sam with a winsome a smile and proclaimed, "Sam, please don't worry about moving out just because Verity no longer needs your protecting presence. You have become very dear to us. We are adopting you as our brother." With a swift change of tactics, Fe added, "Come on! Let's celebrate!"

Since Lark hadn't yet ordered pizza for supper, we decided to go out to eat. The sisters' phones became busy dialing JJ and JC. Sam revealed he was on duty until eight, so to count him out. I looked at my phone. There was still no communication from Peter. I somberly deleted two Welcome Huggers, Brenda and Ruth. I decided to call Peter later and hoped he'd pick up.

It had been a very traumatic, and yes, rather dramatic, day. There were six of us having a grand time eating, talking, and laughing, when out of the blue, emotional overload struck. For a second, there, I thought the force of the massive wave hitting my brain had been so strong it had knocked out the power. I'd been oblivious to the summer thunder and lightning storm raging until that crack and boom. Funnily enough, it was the loud noise, followed by the acute silence and then hard rain and hail that seemed to reset my stress level back down to normal.

Sometimes I got ideas for life lessons from nature. I had been trying everything to 'get away' – white noise, as it were. I recalled several scriptures regarding 'stillness or quiet,' and now we were getting much-needed, refreshing rain. I could equate it all to my recent days. *What a day You orchestrated for me – in spite of my crying, whinging and running. It is a reminder for me to trust You, God – in all things – to wait for your timing and not be afraid. That 'maybe-brother' item and Peter's silence I lay in Your hands, Father. Thank you, Jesus. Amen.*" Lights crackled, then flashed on.

Lark gripped my hand and murmured, "Seconds ago, I thought you were going to cry. Are you okay now, Sweetheart?"

Marilyn Stewart

I nodded, and with one finger, touched his mouth – purely instinctively. He kissed my finger and winked at me. I was rapidly brought back to where we were. His sisters had obviously caught the action and promptly hooted!

"Verity, what have you done to our rarely open, undemonstrative, mostly impassive brother?"

I chuckled. "Care to share, Lark? What happened?"

He smirked, scratched his head, and admitted, "Darned if I know. This blushing beauty walked into the Ghost Town and left with my heart. I told Peter, and he made me promise to leave her alone until after she'd been here for at least a year. At the time, I never dreamt how hard it would become, living in the same home. I was 'besotted,' but forced to choose my words and actions very carefully."

Twenty-Six

In the morning, as I turned the corner to come down the stairs, I saw Lark staring up at me with a funny look on his face. I stopped on the last step. He wrapped his arms around me and hesitatingly asked, "Yesterday wasn't a dream, was it, Sweetheart?"

I grasped him tightly around the waist, lowered my head slightly, and whispered, "It better not have been." Kissing thoroughly and long was what both of us needed. "You reassured now, my love?" I queried. I felt him relax and heard him admit, "Ve, I was so afraid it had all been just a lovely, elusive dream."

While both of us wished to sit down and talk in depth, life kept interfering for the next several days. I spent a lot of time answering questions. The DEA wanted to know what I had seen and heard at the Ghost Town. Regardless of how innocent I was, they were sure I knew something – maybe trivial, but vital. The FBI's questions were all about the identity thieves. Was I sure I hadn't realized Brenda and Paul were related? Early on, Brenda had been my lawyer – more of a notary, I explained. What had happened? Nothing; I just hadn't needed a lawyer's assistance. I wondered how many times I had to tell them I did not know anything. I was beginning to think I needed a lawyer – not that I now had one – and Peter was still avoiding my calls.

Jeff, the owner of our local newspaper, requested interviews and photos. He wanted to feature 'our' story. How the five of us got together and interacted daily, and tips for others thinking to do likewise. He asked astute questions about Lark and Sam being wounded warriors and living in a house with three females.

Jeff promised to keep certain information revealed off the record. I realized many questions weren't for his readers, but himself. Katie had recently told him about spending two weekends at Welcome Home, and how it had helped her. While Katie and he weren't yet dating, he hoped they soon would be. Although Sam and Lark already knew, Fe, Annie, and I were now let into his world of injuries. While we were shocked and saddened, he quickly realized we didn't treat him any differently. He thanked us over and over, in various ways. We invited Jeff to stop in, often.

It was ten days from the day I'd 'run away' that Lark and I left a note on the kitchen table and slipped off. Our phones were off, so regardless of what came up, we'd deal with it later. Lark had chosen a serene, secluded area, where elk and forest creatures were known to roam. He had actually gotten down on one knee to say, "I love you, Verity R Tracker. Will you marry me? Be my helpmate and wife of my dreams for all of our days?"

I grinned and nodded all during his speech, then blurted, "YES! Yes, please, Lark. I'll be delighted to be linked forever with you."

"Verity, this ring signals our devotion to each other and intentions to be wed. I hope you like it. I was going to give you our mother's or grandmother's ring, but my sisters will get those two. I wanted your ring to be designed by me – as you were for me."

I waved my hand back and forth to let the ring catch the sun's rays. "Lark, it is stunningly beautiful and so different. Sweetheart, I absolutely love the colors, and the setting is unequaled." Angel checked out the rectangle of watermelon tourmaline surrounded by jade and diamonds, then insisted on playing fetch.

I laughed, eyes leaking with happiness. Lark was talking and sharing *everything*. He'd wanted to propose where we'd met, but the DEA still had the area cordoned off. He'd been quiet when I'd brought up his being a father because he'd been surprised by the intensity of his longings. He'd reckoned the possibility of being a father to my future children was slim, and that had hurt.

We held each other tightly, kissing and hugging. I reluctantly pulled back, admitting we had some long months ahead of us before.... Lark asked, "How about we go to Holbrook, get a license, and get married? We can always get remarried with my sisters." Looking at my face, he pretended to pout, then laughed. "Darling Verity, you, my dear, are worth waiting for, Love." Lark admitted to being filled with relief and excitement since I'd welcomed his love. We walked hand-in-hand along a dirt footpath to a creek. I was loving it, but this was a man accustomed to action. I could tell he was aching to do something – at least to alert his family. At my smile, he reached for his phone to send a text to Fe, Annie, and Sam, requesting they meet us at Welcome to Dine for lunch. We had news.

Often these days, Fe, Annie, and Lark were heard harmonizing with a song on the radio. Life was fantastic.

One day, Sheriff Ben, who'd had a respite from visiting us, came to our home. He'd heard JC and JJ needed to check out a medium-sized bus for their parents in a distant city and desired to have Fe and Annie go with them. He suggested that Lark and I go as well and leave town early tomorrow. I needed a break from people asking questions. Months back, Annie and Fe had asked us to keep a week open for this very reason. Our week away was only now happening two months later than planned.

Pulling me aside, Sheriff Ben said my uncle and cousins were who they claimed to be and had clean records. He suggested I set up a meeting at the bank this afternoon – while they were here. I agreed – it was long past time to clear the air.

*****

I sat quietly glancing from face to face, seeking a bit of, I guess, love or interest in my well-being. Nothing. Noah checked my birth certificate next to the one from the just-unsealed envelope. The bank owner, Matt, and his partner, verified the match. My relatives didn't care about my middle name, or me – just that I sign over a couple million to them. Maybe it was petty, but I had them all sign a legal document stating they would never threaten or ask for money from me ever again. I did ask them to consider setting up a memorial fund or scholarship in Mother's name.

After they hurried away, with nary a glance at me or a thank you, I put my head down on the table. I was hurt, angry, and struggling not to retaliate by stopping the check. Why should I be generous to my greedy relatives? As I prayed for peace in my own soul, I abruptly wondered what their lives were like. Had anyone ever shown them kindness? After all, it was only money, and I still

Marilyn Stewart

had more than enough, plus I had a great number of friends, and I knew Jesus loved them as well as me. Wiping away my tears, I smiled and left humming the tune, *"There's Within My Heart a Melody...." I knew resentment might kick back up from time to time, but I would try to remember how abundantly blessed I am.

At supper, Sam offered to look after Angel while we were away. I shook my head. "Thanks, but no way, Sam. Angel has decided Lark and I will be his guardians. He goes, and will sleep in the guys' room during our time away."

I caught the small, relieved sigh from Lark and the nod that passed between the men. Later, Sam passed me in the hall and whispered, "Good call, Ve. I am pleased with your decision."

Twenty-Seven

The days away were amazing, fun, and definitely a time of learning and growing for all of us. Each day, we'd go sightseeing – either in twos, or as a group. With six people to dote on him, Angel got a little spoiled. Four of us got a tiny sample of life as experienced on the road by JC, JJ, and yes, Mercy, at times.

Lark had fun videoing bits of every day. From time to time, one of us managed to wrestle the camera from him. Of course, we were all taking still shots of everything and everyone. I was thankful the days of waiting (as well as paying) for film to be developed were a thing of the past.

Before falling asleep each night, we girls chattered for an hour or two, going over our day or weightier problems. Being so close to our fiancés for so many hours each day was great, and yet difficult. Our wedding date was still almost three months away. Fe couldn't decide what to do about Welcome Home, as none of us desired to live there after marriage. She threw out names as to who might be a good manager, or whether she should sell the property. Annie brought up the flower shop. Maybe it was time to think about hiring help, so in future, they could go on road trips with their husbands.

I mentioned my angst regarding the tiny twins and how to deal with strained family relations. I kept quiet about my issues concerning a rapist still being on the loose, as well as the fact that I was now very, very rich. After several nights of discussion, we decided to share our feelings and thoughts with our guys.

The pastor had given us homework to begin before we started marital counseling. A few of the easy questions had us all interacting together. The first lively discussion with the six of us centered on where we wished to live after we were married. Mostly, though, we only discussed a question as a couple. We girls didn't know if the guys talked about the questions later, but at bed time, we three certainly nattered on and on about them.

At breakfast on the third morning out, a question was posed that had the guys choking and sputtering. During our nightly chat, we talked about a zillion different things, including a certain subject. This morning, the men were sitting across the table from their fiancés. They'd taken a mouthful of food when Annie said, "We heard something on TV and decided to ask you guys if it is true. Do guys think of much, other than sex?"

There was a lot of silence, giggling, and food going into mouths, but no words.

Once more, Annie broke the silence. With an impish grin at JJ, she admitted, "We got to talking last night and figured someone needed to answer the question."

JJ held her look. "We're wired that way, Doll. You, Sweetheart, are pushing my hot buttons. You tempt me, Annie, with your smile, laugh, and swishy, knee-length dresses."

Annie turned red, gulped, and stuffed food into her mouth so she wouldn't say what she was thinking.

JC looked at Fe. A smile lit up his face and his eyes sparkled with mirth, but all he said was, "Ditto."

Fe blushed, nodded, and gave him a cheeky grin.

Now all of us focused on Lark. He was trying to hold a poker face. I looked into his green eyes and shivered slightly at the heat in them. Suddenly, they began to twinkle and he drawled, "Sometimes it is hard to think of anything else when you are near me, Babe."

I coughed, looked down, laughed, and said, "How about those Diamondbacks...."

Talking returned to what was on tap for the day; however, each of us knew question number ten was now wide open for honest and open discussion.

Sam called to ask when we planned to arrive home. He wanted to welcome us back with a full-on barbecue supper.

The girlfriends had gotten to him. Upon arriving, most of the Welcome Huggers were waiting to give us girls an early surprise shower – after we'd all eaten and the guys had departed.

Days were busy and weekends full of dates, decisions, and lots of wedding planning. Annie and I realized neither of us had anything at all except our clothes – nothing to set up an apartment or home. Upon hearing us talking over the things we would need,

Fe made a decision. She'd leave Welcome Home fully furnished and start her new life with everything fresh, the same as us.

Lark began spending time at the Willis place. Each time he returned home, he seemed more confident and accepting of himself. Several times, we talked about sneaking over to see what was going on or bribing one of the office workers to at least take a picture.

One evening, Sam and Lark retired early to the study. Fe, Annie, and I sat at the kitchen table sharing girl-talk freely, now we were alone. I inquired whether they had asked JC and JJ what kind of a wedding they'd like. We all broke out laughing, then both Fe and Annie said together, "Short, flowery, and no goof-ups."

"Have you asked Lark that question?" came from Fe.

I blushed and disclosed he'd just said one word, "soon." We giggled, then all nodded in agreement.

Annie piped up, "We want the same basic wedding, but we'd like each of us to be distinctive. Fe and I don't plan to get the same type of wedding dress. We're glad to have seen yours, so we won't get one similar. Also, we don't want the men to wear identical-colored clothes."

Fe confided, "Annie hopes JJ will wear a dark gray tuxedo and a red rose in his lapel. I'd like JC to wear a light gray tuxedo with a lavender rose." She then queried, "What color lapel rose should Lark wear, Verity?"

"Orange or yellow-orange," popped out of my mouth. Fe and Annie sighed. "We all chose potently significant colors!"

We all agreed to movies by Jake, stills by Unity, and the ushers to seat everyone would be Sam and Jeff. We had various ideas as to how red, orange, and lavender rose petals could be strewn. I laughingly suggested we train Angel and Boo to shake a basket as they trotted down the aisle. The twins cautiously aired the thought of either the tiny twins or that Jim and Charity's children help us out. We shelved the idea for further thought.

I blurted out, "Have you three talked about singing a love song at our wedding? It would be a cherished memory."

Annie and Fe looked at me and shook their heads, then in unison asked, "Is there a song you were thinking of, Ve?"

Marilyn Stewart

"Uh, Wind Beneath My Wings, Be My Love, or something. Have you decided yet on your dresses?"

"We were wondering if you would like to go with us. We've narrowed our choices at three shops. Since we are going to be each other's bridesmaids and none of us have mothers living, Annie and I thought we'd like just the three of us to know what our dresses look like."

I felt incredibly included. "I'd love to go with you, absolutely! Thanks. Uh, would you want to ask Mrs. Willis, your future mother-in-love, to be in on this? She is such a lovely lady. You are going to be so lucky to be blessed with her and Hank."

Fe thoughtfully admitted, "It's an idea to think about."

Annie slid in a comment. "So what do you plan to ask Lark to wear at our wedding, Verity?"

I didn't even need to think. "His military uniform."

Fe and Annie laughed as they said together, "Well, that's better than saying 'nothing'!"

We were still laughing lightheartedly when we heard a noise, then realized it was Lark.

"We still might put a bell on you and Sam. How long have you been listening to our conversation, Lark?"

He leaned down, kissed me, and said, "Long enough to know what my sweetheart wants me to wear. Now, how about rings? Engraved inside? Do you ladies know there is a new artisan in Hope? He does outstanding work. All three of your engagement rings were created there."

I had to talk to Lark, soon. It was eating me up, wondering whether he'd want to wear his wedding ring on his prosthetic or right hand. I once again brushed it aside and decided maybe it was time to share my secret with my housemates. I brought out one item Mum had shown me during the last week of her life. It had come in the trunk. I laid two almost identical birth certificates on the table. Both of them, mine. One had Verity R Tracker, and the other one held the key to what Noah, the lawyer for my uncle, had needed. My middle name was made up of bits from four names. My great-grandmother's, grandmother's, mother's, and even a bit of my own name at the very end. I told them I had decided to say it publicly when saying my wedding vows.

207

Welcome Huggers # 2 – Verity

Sam answered his phone. He laughed, agreed it was a pleasant surprise for once, and he'd tell us right away.

"One of the ladies in the office overheard a couple talking about your rose bush, Verity. It turns out it was left by a thankful couple. Little Charlie is now doing well in school thanks to the reading to dogs program at the library. His folks let him leave the plant in appreciation. The scrap of paper the kid signed must have blown away."

"Thanks, Sam," I said and added, "Now all we need to find out is who left the two initialed boxes, and whether I have another half-brother, older than Peter."

Sam nodded. "Still working on those, Ve. We haven't forgotten."

Marilyn Stewart

Twenty-Eight

Faint noises beneath my room alerted me once more to action. Tugging on jeans and sweatshirt, I grabbed my backpack and hurried, barefoot, down the stairs. Angel padded next to me.

I softly knocked, opened the door a smidgen, reached my hand around to flip up the light switch, and placed the backpack inside the door. It sounded as if tonight there was no time for hot, let alone moist, hot towels.

I grabbed two clean towels off a nearby shelf. Both men were already lying on their stomachs. By now I'd perfected my system of attack. I placed a towel, then a large heating pad on each back and pulled up the blanket to heat them fast. I whispered, "Who is worst tonight?" As usual each man said the other's name. Scrutinizing them closely, I could tell: tonight it was Sam.

Early on, I insisted that the person I was massaging had to recap his nightmare out loud. Sam slowly began to mumble into his pillow. I removed the layers and dripped some warm oil on his back, then proceeded. With the massage over, I tucked him back up and looked over at Lark. He was fast asleep. Sam whimpered, "Terrible cramps in my legs, Ve. Can you help?"

Making sure he stayed covered and one leg had a hot towel, I squeezed a tube of balm, then proceeded. Within a few minutes of finishing his second leg, I could tell the cramps were gone. I made sure both heating pads were unplugged. My work was done.

Looking back, I saw Boo once more stretched out between the guys' beds – all were sound asleep.

As I crawled back into my own bed, I thought about all those with PTSD and no one to help them. Seeing Sam's stump hurt my soul. I decided to reach out to Mercy via a text message requesting a get together.

*****

Mercy and I decided to go to the park and walk our pooches while addressing my questions.

"I know you might tend to think this to be too private a matter to share, but I'd really appreciate your feedback, Mercy."

"I'm here to listen and help in any way I can, Ve."

Welcome Huggers # 2 – Verity

"Is there anything you can or care to share about being married to someone with issues, such as yourself, or PTSD, as you've said afflicts Unity?"

Mercy sighed. "Being married to Unity.... Curious, I have never thought of him as Isaac, let alone Isaac Orion Unique. Huh. I know I am going off subject, but I just had a 'light bulb' moment. Isaac means laughter. Orion is a star. Unique means unequaled. Oh, my.... Sorry, Ve. Back to what we have learned. Shall I list some?"

"It would be helpful. Thanks, Cy."

"Keep a food journal of your night meals to spot triggers. We've found if Unity has cheese at an evening meal, he seems more likely to have nightmares.

"Have your dog lay beside your bed, not on it. Gem has learned to bark, rather than get near or between us.

"Buy a king-sized bed. Some nights, we put a super-sized pillow between us so Unity doesn't get whacked. It pains me to say, but I still wake up fighting when I sense a presence nearby.

"Do not surprise him – speak loudly. Unity has learned not to touch me until he knows for sure that I am fully awake.

"We leave a small night light on in our bedroom and the door slightly ajar. These are for my benefit – so I don't feel trapped.

"Each day, get plenty of some form of exercise."

After her last statement, I noticed the shade of pink Mercy's face had turned and grinned with understanding.

"Thanks, friend, for being candid. I will bear in mind your words, especially for after I am married. For now, a journal might be a good starting point for both Sam and Lark."

"I knew you'd pick up on the meaning of 'exercise,' Ve. It is so much fun to have a bit of girl-talk. If you learn something that works for you, once you are married, I'd appreciate hearing about it. Everyone with PTSD has different triggers. One Vietnam vet we know flips out if there is white rice on a table."

"Thanks, Cy. I, too, will be open to learning more."

Mercy beamed. "I am so excited to be getting Fe, Annie, and you as sisters! Verity, Unity and I have talked it over, and as far as we are concerned, you will be just as much related to us as Fe and Annie when they marry my twin brothers. We are going to have so much fun! Just thinking about it makes me smile and want to dance or prance with joy."

"I'd love to have you for a sister, but you don't need to stretch friendship that far just for me, Mercy."

"Hey, girlfriend, it will be a boon for me also. It has been a relief to have you swapping weeks for emergency call outs. Unity and I want Lark and you to feel connected to our family. I just got to thinking, Verity. What an absolute hoot! Hope, Sharilyn, Fairlyn, Annie, Fe, Katie, you, and I would make eight of us past or present girlfriends who might soon all be related! Oh, fun days for sure."

"So, Mercy, you, too, are thinking Unity's sister, Fairlyn, and his cousin, Katie, might end up with Sam and Jeff? Maybe we will need to think about starting a New Wives club."

"Ve, I've been thinking about that very idea. We could meet once or twice a year, or more often, due to common interests or hobbies. This way, not just new wives, but all wives would, I hope, feel welcome."

"Thanks for sharing, Mercy. For the next two months, I will enjoy the Welcome Huggers group. Soon enough, I, too, will no longer qualify. Woohoo! Happy days."

Twenty-Nine

Sam and Lark discussed various ways in which to properly thank Verity. Her massages and missing sleep to care for them during numerous nightmarish hours needed appropriate thanks.

They had eliminated the common-place things, such as candy and flowers. They reckoned gifts could be a little tricky. While they appreciated Fe's and Annie's input in their lives, they didn't want to cause dissention. Still, Verity needed a special gift. As Verity would say, it had to be "spot on."

Lark decided to approach JJ and JC regarding their gifts for their brides to be. He had a proposal to discuss....

Bike riding was very popular in their three towns. Since it could be used as a firebreak, or an emergency access road, the cyclists had been permitted to bulldoze a wide swath adjacent to the existing road linking all three towns. There were bike clubs ranging from serious to chatty. Of course, the Welcome Huggers had their own group of hot shots who were into racing and competition. Four of the speedsters were Katie, Sharilyn, Carolyn, and sometimes Annie. Fe, Heather, Fairlyn, myself, and whoever else desired to ride with us were into chatting, while enjoying the scenery. Our bikes were okay to ride back and forth to work, but that was about it. The large baskets in front were most often loaded with supplies for our shops.

Even though we were only three stores apart, I sent the sisters a text to find out when they were leaving for the day. We liked to ride home together.

A half hour later, we exited our places of business, made sure the doors were locked, and headed for our bikes. We were in the midst of discussing the evening ahead when Fe let out a groan.

"Would you look at that! No way! We can't all have flat tires on the same night."

Annie questioned the statistical feasibility. "Don't suppose someone might be pulling a joke on us?"

Marilyn Stewart

I yanked loose the bicycle pump and got busy airing up the tire, then checked to see if it would hold. After bouncing it several times, I grinned and handed the pump to the twins to see if that was all that was required for theirs, also.

As we went to mount our bikes, Annie grumbled, "Now, who would do such a thing?"

"We would," came the answer.

Our three heads swung towards the response. Four men were grinning at us. They were standing next to three new, impressive bicycles and color-coded helmets. JJ's hand rested on a red-hot racing bike. JC wheeled a top of the line lavender-colored cycle over to Fe. Lark and Sam beckoned me to come over and check out a yellow-orange beauty. As Fe and Annie looked closer, they saw their birth name flowers interwoven with their nicknames. JC and JJ told them their sister, Lily, had done the art work. This was an early bride's gift from their spouses-to-be.

Of the three bikes, I knew mine was the most expensive. One evening several weeks ago, after reading an article, the five of us had discussed bikes.

Sam and Lark leaned close to me. "There is no way we can express how much we appreciate your help. Please accept this from both of us."

I hugged Sam, kissed his cheek, and did the same for Lark. He boldly announced, "Oh, no, Sweetheart, I get a proper buss!"

"Thanks for the great wheels, fellas. How about you guys riding the old bikes home for us?"

"JC looked at Fe and admitted, "For you, anything, Love," and reached for the handle bars of the weary, old bike.

Lark's words stopped him. "How about we take the old bikes home in JJ's truck, and you two stay for supper?"

Thirty

At nearly eight one evening, Lark and I received text messages from Mel and Hank. We were invited to lunch at the Willis home the next day. Figuring it had something to do with a surprise for the twins, we kept the invitation quiet.

Hank and Melody Willis welcomed us with smiles and hugs. Talk began with sharing information about our lives. Hank queried Lark as to what it would take to make a movie demo. He was thinking of three, say, fifteen- to twenty-minute maximum, DVDs on how to drive, set up, dump, etc., a recreational vehicle. The reason for three instructional videos was due to the fact that the differences between backing a trailer, 5th wheel, or a motor home varied greatly. Hank suddenly stopped talking, looked at Mel, and sheepishly said, "Sorry, Melody, love. I had this brainstorm and got carried away. Honestly, you two, when we invited you here, that was the farthest thing from our minds."

"He's right, you know. I've not heard a peep about a video before now. Neither did we invite you here regarding either set of twins. Lark, we are delighted by your sisters and their obvious love for our sons. No, we wanted to ask you both a favor."

Lark and I saw how choked up Mrs. Willis had become. Looking back and forth between Hank and Mel, we waited anxiously to hear what was desired of us.

Hank stated, "What Song of My Heart and I want to say is, when you are all married, we would love it if you both would consider being as much our kids as Fe and Annie will be. Melody would love to be called Mom, Mum, Mel, Mrs. W, or whatever you choose." We were blown away. Totally overwhelmed. Tears shone in Lark's green orbs, while they poured down my face. I tried to choke out a response, but all that came out was a squeak.

Lark handed me a tissue, kissed my cheek, and then huskily stated, "As you can see, we have been blindsided by your love. Thanks, Mum - and Dad-to-be, you have bestowed on us a huge blessing. We will try to be good kids, eh, Verity?" I noticed he'd used my lingo.

Marilyn Stewart

I nodded, gulped, sniffed, stood, went to Hank and kissed his cheek, then headed for Melody. I saw the shooing hand movement Mel gave the guys before wrapping her arms around me. She encouraged me to cry as long as needed. After a prolonged hug, I pulled back, looked Mel in the eyes, shook my head, then laughed. "I'm going to tell you a secret, Mum-to-be. More than one of us Welcome Hugger girls have said we'd be tempted to marry JC or JJ just to get you and Hank for in-laws. I've thought a time or two how lucky Fe and Annie were going to be. Lark, through his sisters, would be sort of related, but I would still be left out. I know both sets of our parents would have deeply appreciated your open hearts and arms to all of us. Thank you."

Time sped up, or so it seemed, as the busy summer unfolded. We had to fit counseling with the pastor into our schedules. It was easier for Lark and me, as we were usually in town.

Fe and Annie and I teased our fellas about the upcoming kissing booth. Mercy and Marigold were already married, Brenda was in jail, and we, being engaged, made six fewer girlfriends to raise money for the wounded warrior fund. The men stated there were still more than enough single women to be in the booth without us. They even offered to count how many single girlfriends there were and go encourage them to participate in the kissing booth. We'd laughed, and in return, offered to count up the available single men and encourage them to kiss and kiss and kiss.

Helping with the events of our towns' fair kept us busy. One of the girlfriends who loved words made a new sign for the kissing booth: BSS=K, and in brackets underneath, To Buss; Snog; Smooch = To Kiss.) As a tease, and to raise money, Unity and Mercy, JC and Fe, JJ and Annie, and Lark and I took turns standing near the kissing booth. We'd put in a twenty and kiss, buss, snog, smooch, and laugh. Soon, Daffodil and Ken, Marigold and Ron, then Hank and Melody and other long-married couples joined in the fun and took a turn. It was the highlight of the fair, for it had encouraged many to buss, smooch, snog, and kiss in public, all for a good cause, of course. I was hoping Sheriff Ben... but no.

215

I thought back briefly to all the angst I had put myself through, wondering and planning to kiss not just one fellow repeatedly, but many. I was so happy. I was afraid it couldn't or wouldn't last.

I was so pleased that when Lark needed his prosthetic hand and lower leg and foot refitted, he invited me to go with him.

I recalled the time the six of us had spent together driving and sightseeing. It had changed us. Lark openly sharing his struggles the first night with JC and JJ had set the bar for honest interaction. Angel's aid in reducing Lark's nightmares gave JC and JJ insight into like situations that Gem had to be performing for Mercy and Unity. I remembered how, when we'd all met up the second morning, the atmosphere had changed from tense to calm. Seeing our men relaxed, interacting, and accepting each other had brought lightheartedness and renewed joy on our journey.

One lazy day, Lark asked Sam to look after Angel for a bit. He had a surprise to share with me. All was quiet at the Willis tarmac area. He had been driving his vehicle with the switch over to the left. He pulled up, stopped, looked at me, and said, "Will you trust me?" At my nod, he flipped the switch so that he would be driving using his prosthetic foot. We zipped expertly in and out around cones, then proceeded to do it in reverse. I only briefly looked at the course before turning to watch his face. I was so glad his sisters and I had not pursued the idea of bribing an office worker. This was the secret he'd been working on to build his confidence. He slowed, drove over to a spot in the shade, parked the car, shut off the engine, and turned his face towards me. I saw in his bright eyes and smile the contentment he felt. Happiness radiated from my beloved Lark. I leaned sideways, gave him a quick kiss, and pronounced, "Awesome driving, Sweetheart!"

Lark sucked in a breath, then began sharing.

"I know I was really grumpy and anti-social when we met. I'd had enough of do-gooders, trite words, and pity. I was making an art of words to push people away. While I desperately wanted a loving home for both of my sisters, I'd given up on ever having a wife and family myself. I was fast turning into a lonely, apathetic person. I was giving Annie grief in so many ways. I didn't verbally or physically abuse her, but often gave her the silent treatment. I was in denial. Looking back, I am ashamed of myself and shocked I still had any friends left at all. I'm sure you remember our first meeting. I cringe every time I think of what I put you through, my dear. Sometimes we military guys can get a trifle crude in our teasing and enjoy seeing a girl blush."

"I was so dreadfully embarrassed."

"I know, I know. Yet, in a way, Love, good has come out of that confrontation. You know, Mercy, Hope – even the sheriff – keep some pads in their emergency medical kits now."

"I didn't know you knew that, Lark. We used several on the night Essie.... They certainly helped two patients that night."

"One night, early on at the Ghost Town, we could've used three, so I shared the information with Sam and Unity."

"So, my Love, do you now carry napkins, or as women here call them 'sanitary pads,' in your emergency kit? I bet you didn't go and buy them."

"You've got me there. The sheriff had one of the office girls buy some supplies. As you told me that day, they are a tool to be used. They are sanitary, absorbent, and could save a life. Did you come up with the idea, or...."

"No, my mother did. A few times, we cut them in half to use on two persons at once. I've often wondered if the military might not be wise to use something like them in combat situations. For all I know, maybe they do."

"Verity, you bless and enrich my life in so many ways: your total acceptance, smile, laugh, attitude, and joy, not to mention your love and kisses. What I'm trying to say, Sweetheart, is I'm not finding the right words to explain to you why or how much I love you. Thank you for choosing to love me. Why me, Precious?"

"I don't understand how it works, Lark. The first time I looked into your eyes, it was as if I saw your true nature. Strange how I could interact with many men, yet be riveted – captured – only by you. I reckon it is a God thing."

We leaned towards each other to share a kiss, only to be startled by a rap on the roof of the van. We burst out laughing

Welcome Huggers # 2 – Verity

when we heard Hank's voice. "Okay, kids, this is not a.... Oh, hi, there, Lark and Verity!" he said as Lark rolled down his window.

I sprang out of the car and ran around to give 'Dad-to-be' a hug while blurting out that we'd just had to share a smooch in celebration over Lark's ability to drive using his prosthetic foot. Hank looked at us for a second with a 'tell me another story' then suddenly said, "I think I'll find my Melody for our own celebration," and hurried away.

Lark gave a bark of laughter, and glancing at me, grinned. "Sweetheart, you are such a girl – you were embarrassed at getting caught. Your upbringing is showing."

I nodded, then exclaimed, "But you are such a guy – being caught was good for your ego! Oh, Lark, I want their kind of marriage."

He nodded as he started the car while softly admitting, "Me, too, Love, me too."

Marilyn Stewart

Thirty-One

Sam, Annie, and Fe had left for work, knowing Lark and I had scheduled this particular morning to stay home and talk. Last night, we had agreed to swap papers listing information each of us would like to discuss.

We slid the papers across the table to each other and simultaneously flipped them over.

I let out a squeak. "This is it, Lark? Only three things?"

On the other hand, he looked as if he'd been hit by a truck. "Wow, Honey. It's going to take me a week just to read this, let alone understand and talk about it to your satisfaction."

I grinned at him. "Well, Sweetheart, we have all day." He shook his head and muttered something under his breath.

I got up, came around the table, sat next to him, and touched the first item.

The doorbell rang. It was if he'd been let out of prison, the way he shot out of his chair and down the hall.

I could hear repeated voices murmuring, then silence. I admit to being curious, so I peeked around the kitchen door. There were three men headed towards me. I turned back and picked up the two papers on the table and placed them in a drawer.

Lark came in first and tucked an arm around my waist. Peter was next, and finally, the man I'd ever so briefly seen at the Ghost Town.

Peter walked up to me, kissed my cheek, then grabbed my sleeve and flipped it up. "Now do you believe I am telling you the truth? Years ago, I ran into the house due to Verity's screams. Charity still had the heated coat hanger in her hand. You have been lied to, Joel. Dad loved you. He'd been searching for you. Did he find you before…?"

I sagged down onto a chair. "Who are you? Would you mind introducing him to us, Peter?"

"So sorry, Ve. This is another half-brother of ours – by Dad's first marriage, which ended in divorce. His ex-wife got Joel. He is five years older than I. This last furlough, Dad was determined to find him and reconnect."

219

Welcome Huggers # 2 – Verity

"Unbelievable! Dad was married three times? Joel, why did you look at me as if you hated me? Was it because you were on a job and was afraid I might blow your cover?"

When all three men looked at me in surprise, I huffed, "Why do you think I didn't push to 'find' you? I figured maybe you were Peter's doppelganger in the DEA. I'm not stupid."

Peter and Joel sat down. I motioned to the coffee pot and they nodded their heads. I got up, poured them each a cup, then announced, "I have one or two more questions, then I will shut up. Joel, did you leave the cardboard with R.I.P.V. at the gravesite, and later a note tied to a rock and a small box here for me to find?"

The next two hours seemed to pass in a flash, as Lark and I were admitted into Peter and Joel's confidence. They did a lot of undercover work. Joel had met several times with Charity over the last two years, and admitted to doing her bidding regarding the three items I'd mentioned. He'd truly believed me to be a monster.

As we were winding up our time together, Joel brought out his birth certificate and a notarized document with a picture. But what clinched it was an old photo of when he was about ten... standing next to Dad. When I saw them together, I immediately blurted out, "Peter, we need to redistribute the money we got as a result of the folks' accident. Joel needs his share!"

Peter laughed, slapped his leg, pointed at Joel, and said, "See, I told you! Didn't I tell you she'd say that before we left?" Glancing back at me, Peter admitted to having learned of Joel's whereabouts over two years ago from a lawyer. Joel had been included in the payout. Peter finally glanced at Lark, who'd stayed silent. Lark stood then, and glared at them. Without mincing words, he expressed to my two half-brothers how utterly despicably they'd treated me.

"You two shouldn't be in law enforcement. Joel harassed Verity!"

As they went to leave, Peter hugged me tightly and apologized. Joel slowly reached for my hands and shamefacedly asked if there was any way I could forgive him. Upon my smile and forgiveness, he grinned, looked at Lark, and asked, "Would you mind releasing my sister long enough for us to share a hug?"

Marilyn Stewart

As soon as they'd left, I turned to Lark. "Now, please, Lark, I need a long hug and some kisses from you." He hesitated for a second, and at my inquiring look, muttered, "You now have two able-bodied brothers to love and take care of you."

I didn't know why, but I was instantly furious with him and felt like slapping him upside the head. Suddenly, it dawned on me, and I felt like crying, so I did.

I flung my arms around him and blubbered, "Larkspur Jade Lane, you make me ache with sorrow. I know you suddenly felt deficient, but you have got to know I love you! You are my rock! You stood up to my brothers for me! No, you aren't perfect, but hear me loud and clear: no one is! And what they have hidden eats at their souls. I respect you for your courage to move forward every day. You cherish and love me, Sweetheart. Now how about some kisses, my love?"

It was a bit of time before we got back to our lists, and not before I made him promise not to ever back away, or think that he needed to 'give me up' ever again. I was thankful he'd promised because of what I was about to share.

One of the things both of us had written down was where did we want to live? Well, that tied in and hinged on what I needed him to know – exactly how very rich I had suddenly become.

I pulled out of the drawer the two pieces of paper, along with another one I'd placed in there earlier, and once again sat down across from him. I wanted to see his face.

"What's this, Babe? Another long list?"

I grinned. "Flip it over."

He squinted. "Where is the period? Two commas?"

His jaw dropped. "So that's why you made me promise!"

I chuckled. "Yeah, all those zeroes have been a total shock to me, also. Lark, just think of all the good we can do together. Scholarships, prosthetics, and maybe housing for wounded warriors; charities; dogs for vets; helping our towns (anonymously); building a home. We both need new cars. And now, we can afford to buy our own home! I'd rather keep the amount a secret, if that is okay with you. It will take a lot of careful thinking and planning. I don't want us to throw money here and there, indiscriminately."

Lark shook his head. "This is some kind of tremendous responsibility, Sweetheart. I think we should pray for wisdom."

We immediately bowed our heads, and Lark prayed.

Marilyn Stewart

Thirty-Two

It seemed to suddenly dawn on the five of us that there were only three weeks left in which we would be together as a family unit. Instead of ignoring the pain parting would cause, we attacked the situation head-on. Two nights each week, everyone would make an effort to be home. Just in case those nights never happened, all of us would try and gather for an hour each night. We'd celebrate by sharing stories, lessons learned, suggestions, and working together: cleaning, sorting, and tossing.

Fe decided to advertise for a manager – preferably an older widow. No one would be moving in to Welcome Home until it had been cleaned and repainted inside and out. Jasmine, Valerie, Katie, and Heather were scheduled to become the first renters.

Every time Sam entered the house he'd been gifted, he was haunted by memories; so for now, it would be a rental.

Fe, Annie, and I secreted our wedding dresses at a secure location. Only Mrs. W would be privy to our getting dressed. A limo would take us to the church, and later, it would all three couples to the reception to be held under a tent at the tarmac area.

Late afternoon, the day before the wedding, Sam and Lark got ready to depart. They were meeting up with JC, JJ, Unity, and Jeff. We girls tearfully joined Sam and Lark in a group hug. Lark pulled me close to share a lingering kiss before setting me aside with an impudent wink. As the guys went to go out the door, I gave a little cough, then said, "Lark, Sweetheart, I'm sleeping in your bed tonight." The shocked look on four faces dispelled any lingering sadness. Fe and Annie let out a squeak of disbelief before saying, "After all our waiting? You wouldn't do that, would you, Verity?"

With a chuckle and a gleam in my eyes, I retorted, "Oh, yeah, I am for sure sleeping in his bed tonight."

Sam figured it out first and smirked. "So who is going to be sleeping downstairs in my bed, Verity?"

"Now that would be giving away a secret, Sam."

Lark let out a deep breath and grumbled, "You had me dreaming for a second there, Precious."

223

Welcome Huggers # 2 – Verity

"Good! See you tomorrow, husband-to-be," I proclaimed.

"Verity, quit teasing him." Sam tugged on Lark's sleeve as he said, "Come on, Lark, not one more kiss. Let's go."

Soon after their departure, Mercy, Katie, Fairlyn, Heather, and other girlfriends arrived, hauling their sleeping bags. Amethyst and others would arrive after their shifts were done. Katie had organized the evening to include massages, facials, pedicures, games, goodies, a devotional, and time for sharing and laughter.

It was only after our wedding that Fe, Annie, and I learned what the fellows had done on their last afternoon and evening as single men. While we girls had nattered and pampered ourselves, the six men began by running one of the loops. They proceeded on to the Willis home, where they played a two-out-of-three to fifteen racquetball tournament, followed by a barbecue supper, and ended with a Bible study and prayer time. We were overwhelmed to learn the men had prayed for us, as well as the wives yet to come for Sam and Jeff.

Marilyn Stewart

Epilogue

Even though the wedding was not until ten o'clock, the church was packed by nine-thirty. The grooms were quiet and talkative in spurts. As Unity took pictures, he told them how lucky they were not to be the sole focus of attention. It was finally time for Lark to go out to the limo to meet his sisters, and JJ and JC to take their places up front.

The white runner was quickly strewn with red and lavender petals, tossed by people sitting on the aisle seats. After Lark took his place up front, Boo began his slow stately walk, gently swinging a large basket brimming with orange and yellow petals. Two tiny twins raced up to him. Due to incessant tugs from little hands, Boo lowered his head until the container was within their reach. The kids began grasping handfuls of petals. Chuckling gleefully, they flung petals everywhere until the basket was empty. (This had not been planned, but came through great on the video.)

Many ladies found themselves wishing they'd be recipients of such obvious love as that which beamed from the grooms.

Joel had asked if he could share walking me down the aisle. I kept my eyes focused on Lark's face. Just looking into his twinkling, hot green eyes had me blushing. I was thinking only of Lark and this moment in time, until I heard...

"Auntie Ve doesn't look like a witch. She looks like an angel. Is she an angel, Mummy?"

"Yes, sweetie. I truly believe she is an angel."

I stopped short. Peter reached for his hankie. As I wiped my eyes, I felt pressure on the front of my dress. Looking down, I saw faithful Angel had come to meet me. I remembered the laughter Fe, Annie, and I had shared when this dog had left a turd next to the sheriff's chair. I actually checked to see if he'd left one beside a pew. My tears immediately dried and I smiled. We moved forward.

Peter, Joel, and I stopped. The guys looked at Lark. "You love her – always." At Lark's loud answer of "Yes, I will," they placed my hand in his. The tiny twins came up, grabbed Angel, and pulled him back to sit on the floor with Boo and them.

Before the pastor could begin, I heard a note from the piano. Fe, Annie and Lark, looking only at us, their sweethearts, began the ceremony singing "Be My Love...."

After three prolonged kisses, we radiantly happy newlyweds faced the congregation. The pastor introduced each husband and wife to the audience, but no one moved. They'd been instructed to wait for a surprise.

Three instruments were brought. A trumpet was handed to Lark, a guitar to JJ, and a flute, which Fe had bought for him at the auction, was given to JC. A nod from Trevor at the piano had the men ripping out a tune that instantly had everyone standing. It was the beginning of the Hallelujah Chorus. They played six Hallelujahs then stopped as abruptly as they'd begun. The three men grinned with delight and obvious relief. In the brief silence following was heard, "Auntie Ve, can we go play now?" To the audience's amusement and acute embarrassment of the new wives, a fervent "I wish!" was said by each new husband.

Annie, Chrysanthemum Coral Lane Willis, smiled cheekily at JJ, Joshua Jasper Willis, when he whispered, "All right. Let's get this reception over with!" then slid a possessive arm around her waist and pulled her close.

Fe, Delphinium Opal Lane Willis, and JC, Joseph Caleb Willis, shared grins of pure delight.

I, Ve, Verity Rozelyneve Tracker Lane, locked eyes with the roguish green-eyed Lark, Larkspur Jade Lane, who mouthed, "finally." I choked, blushed, smirked, and nodded in agreement.

At the reception, before friends began sharing various tales, the pastor spoke briefly. "Before these couples leave today, they'd like everyone to join them in singing the Hallelujah Chorus. Sheet music will be provided. It is good to begin a celebration with Hallelujah or praise to God. He was, is now, and forever will be. These couples hope this song of praise will resonate and lift up our thoughts and hearts daily to The Holy God who loves us."

With six people to toast (or roast), came lots of tales. We girls thought only the men would have stories told on them;

Marilyn Stewart

however, we had not considered the many Welcome Huggers present.

As the chorus ended, a mad dash of girlfriends ensued, positioning themselves to catch one of the three bouquets.

Fe, Annie, and I spaced ourselves four feet apart. On the count of three, flowers flew as if guided by missiles. We, the new brides, laughed, did high-fives, then hugged – tightly.

Jeff, Derek, and Sam could not hide their hopeful, happy grins, for the bouquets had been caught by Katie, Heather, and Fairlyn.

The End

Welcome Huggers # 2 – Verity

Next in the series: Welcome Huggers # 3 – Katie

*Be My Love, written by: Sammy Cahn for Mario Lanza

*He Keeps Me Singing, written by: Luther Burgess Bridgers

*Hallelujah Chorus, written by: George Frideric Handel (some people stand; others don't; if you are curious, Google the reasons why for each.)

Recommended reading:

Tending the Warrior Soul by Louis Harrison; Xulon Press

Renee Meloche has written twenty 'Hero books' for kids; YWAM (Youth With a Mission)

Marilyn Stewart

Guardian Marilyn with Texas, her rescue Pom

Marilyn Stewart has come a long way. Growing up in the outback of Australia amongst a primitive tribe of Aborigines, dogs were for hunting and warmth – not pampered pets. Rarely speaking English, it was a shock at twelve to be relocated to Canada. Going from barefoot and hunting for her snacks to snow and dorm life was a challenge. At seventeen, she found herself uprooted once again to return to the land she'd left at age two – the USA. Marilyn has lived in three countries, foster care, boarding school, Seattle, San Francisco, and now resides with her husband and Pomeranian in Mesa, Arizona. She loves doing crafts, traveling, viewing nature, reading, and writing.

Books by Marilyn Stewart:

Non-fiction:
Footprints & Fragrance in the Outback
Child of the Outback

Bible study:
Created to Celebrate

Novels:
Welcome Huggers # 1 – Mercy
Welcome Huggers # 2 – Verity

childoftheoutback1@gmail.com